After reading Modern History at Oxford, Tim Jarvis spent his career in the corporate world. Finally free from the shackles of full-time employment, he now has time to expand his literary aspirations beyond blogging about film and writing the occasional short story.

The Woman in the Wings is his first novel.

For Susan

My dearest partner of greatness.

Tim Jarvis

The Woman in the Wings

All good wishes.

Tim Jarvis.

Austin Macauley Publishers™
London • Cambridge • New York • Sharjah

This is a work of fiction. Names, characters, businesses, places, events, locales, and incidents are either the products of the author's imagination or used in a fictitious manner. Any resemblance to actual persons, living or dead, or actual events is purely coincidental.

A CIP catalogue record for this title is available from the British Library.

ISBN 9781035828470 (Paperback)
ISBN 9781035828487 (Hardback)
ISBN 9781035828500 (ePub e-book)
ISBN 9781035828494 (Audiobook)

www.austinmacauley.com

First Published 2024
Austin Macauley Publishers Ltd®
1 Canada Square
Canary Wharf
London
E14 5AA

I'd like to acknowledge a lifetime of support and advice from family and friends, together with invaluable feedback on various drafts of this book generously provided by members of a local writing group.

Table of Contents

Chapter 1
The Meeting

'All the actors kept strictly to the script, as a heavy penalty awaited anyone who departed from the authorised version. No one knew when the Auditors would be in, and if they ever heard any dialogue the Guild had not approved then that meant trouble.'

The Musician's Destiny

On the last night of the production, with the stage full of light and noise, Toby found himself alone in the dark and silence of the wings: anything could happen here and there would be no witnesses. As stage manager he was responsible for running the show but had lost his place in the script when two of the actors decided to celebrate their final appearance with an extended session of ad libs. Searching frantically through the pages of the prompt copy, Toby had no idea how long they planned to continue with this unscheduled improvisation, and he began to wonder if they ever intended to return to the script.

Like everyone involved with the Old Chapel Theatre, Toby knew the story of the White Lady, allegedly a sitting tenant from the venue's previous incarnation as a place of worship, who haunted the backstage area. Many of those who had been alone in the building late at night would even swear the story was true, although only a friend of a friend had actually seen her. However, such lurid stories were currently far from Toby's mind as he continued with his desperate search.

Focussed on his quest, Toby failed to hear the door behind him open, and only the soft click of the latch, as it closed again, attracted his attention. He turned his head as a pale slim creature with long blonde hair emerged out of the darkness. She wore a flowing white robe decorated with elaborate runic devices, in her right hand she carried a heavy wand of polished birch, and her impressive wings shimmered as they caught the shafts of green, yellow, and purple light from the racks of stage lanterns suspended high above.

After a moment of silence, the being spoke. ‘Greetings mortal.’

Toby had worked with the being all week and knew her well. ‘Evening, ma’am. You’re right on time—as usual.’

The decision to stage *Cinderella* as a Christmas production had been controversial. The actors were only amateurs, but a significant majority believed a pantomime would not stretch their collective talents. More importantly, such a choice might dent their artistic credibility with the local drama community. However, a stirring speech from their young director had finally won them over.

Full of delusions of grandeur after several years of university drama, the enthusiastic director had promised to re-invent the stock characters for a twenty-first-century audience and produce a play rather than a pantomime. Hence Kate portrayed the Fairy Godmother as a character drawn from the pages of a fantasy novel. She was a powerful actor and always stayed in character for the duration of the performance, and Toby humoured her in this as he could rely on her not to miss an entrance.

Nonetheless, despite Kate’s punctuality, Toby always carried out what he called a pre-flight inspection before she made an entrance. ‘Are you ready to run through our checklist?’

‘Of course. Wings? Yes. Ring of Power? Yes. Magic wand? Yes again.’

Toby sensed what was going to happen even as Kate’s hand slipped on the polished wood of the shaft, and he jumped up and caught the wand before it hit the floor. ‘You need to be careful. If this was loaded, you might turn someone into a frog.’

As he returned her wand, Kate regarded him with disdain. ‘Of course it’s loaded. If it wasn’t, Cinderella wouldn’t get her wedding dress for the finale.’

Toby decided to play along. ‘Any magic to spare?’

‘Only if you stand up properly and ask me nicely.’

Toby tried to smooth out the creases in his dusty T-shirt and did his best to flatten his fair hair that had become somewhat dishevelled as a consequence of his frustration with the impromptu activity on stage. ‘Please?’

‘That’s good enough for me. Concentrate on something, and I’ll see what I can do.’

Toby did his best to clear his mind and focus on a specific thought. However, he found it difficult to forget the pleasant dream he had enjoyed last night about the pretty chorus member who had stopped to talk to him during the dress rehearsal. Since their conversation, she had displayed an ongoing interest in his responsibilities as stage manager that he found both unexpected and flattering. He was enough of a realist not to expect anything much from these encounters, but wondered if they might at least continue their discussions at the cast party.

Surrounded by the overlapping pools of coloured light encircling her, Kate focussed her attention on Toby. He shivered as the air around him appeared to grow cooler, and he felt as if her gaze reached right into him. This sensation seemed to go on forever although, in reality, the moment could not have lasted for more than a few seconds.

Then, while humming a strange melody that bore no relation to any harmonic series Toby could recognise, Kate stretched out her wand, tapped him gently on the chest, and drew a pentangle in the air. A sudden smile on her face broke the mood. 'There you go. But don't forget, as the old song says, you can't get what you want until you know what you want.'

'Thank you. I didn't feel a thing.'

'You're not supposed to. I use premium-quality spells, and all my magic comes with a one-year warranty. In the event of any unfortunate side effects, I offer an immediate no-quibble refund.'

A round of applause from the audience interrupted their conversation. The Ugly Sisters, dressed as characters from a popular television soap opera, had clearly reached the end of their scene that tonight's improvisation had extended far beyond its usual duration.

Kate turned towards the stage. 'That sounds like my cue. Excuse me, but I have to fly.'

She floated into the wings, ready for her entrance. Once Kate was in position, Toby, relieved the actors had finally returned to the script, sat down again at the stage manager's desk and switched on his headset to speak to the lighting team in the control box at the rear of the auditorium.

In evolutionary terms, the lighting team was slightly more advanced than the stage crew, the lowest form of theatre life, in that its members had to deal with dangerous forces like electricity. They knew their technical skills were invaluable, and Michael, a slight individual with receding hair and pebble-thick glasses who led the team, exploited this power to the utmost. He was rude to anybody and everybody, safe in the knowledge that without his team, the actors would have to perform in complete darkness.

Michael always tried to distract Toby at key moments in the performance, and as Toby counted down to the cue, he ignored a stream of comments about the little surprise Michael's team had prepared to make this final performance a night to remember. 'Stand by for the effects and follow-spot for Kate's entrance. On my backwards, count of three, two, one—and go.'

A loud explosion close to the wings produced a brilliant flash of green and purple light, followed by a thick cloud of white smoke through which Kate made her entrance. Toby had known what would happen, but tonight the explosion had been far louder, the flash much brighter, and the cloud of smoke much bigger than during the previous performances. This, he assumed, was the little surprise from Michael and his team.

On stage, Prince Charming began to sing a love duet with Cinderella while her Fairy Godmother, illuminated by the powerful beam of a follow-spot, gazed admiringly at the happy couple. Usually, this musical interlude gave Toby a few minutes of peace before the frantic activity of the final scene change, but the thick cloud of smoke now drifting inexorably towards him made this impossible, and he struggled to stifle a cough. He tried waving his arms to clear the air around him, but this achieved nothing, and the smoke only began to disperse when he picked up his folder and used it as a fan.

Toby danced around the crowded backstage area waving the folder furiously as he did so, and was making real progress in clearing the air when, almost hidden in the smoke and shadows and standing further upstage, he caught sight of a figure. The stage crew generally stayed away from the wings until required for a scene change, and Toby felt embarrassed someone had witnessed his lunatic gyrations.

As he placed his folder back on the desk, a voice spoke, 'Don't mind me. I'm only here to watch the play.' It was a female voice. The smoke continued to drift away, and the voice spoke again, 'Can I stay? I promise I won't get in the way.'

As Kate moved around the stage, the beam of light from her follow-spot shone briefly into the wings, and Toby now saw his visitor for the first time; her shoulder-length dark hair and black clothes made her almost invisible in the backstage gloom. He had never seen her before and wondered who she might be. Despite this, he very much hoped she would stay, as something about the way she looked at him made him want to talk to her about far more than his stage management responsibilities. 'Of course you can stay. Though there's not much left to see.'

'What's happening at the moment?'

'The hero and heroine are together at last. All they have to do now is tie up the loose ends. Then there's a big wedding, lots of curtain calls, and the pair of them live happily ever after.'

'So that's what happens when you get married. I've often wondered.'

'I've been here all week, and it's happened every time. Despite the unexpected pyrotechnics, I think we can assume the same will happen tonight.'

'And what about when the play's over?'

'It's time for the cast party. The actors all tell each other how wonderful they were. Then they tell everyone else what they really think.'

Toby hoped his visitor could not tell what he was really thinking. With less than a page of dialogue before the scene ended, the stage crew would soon arrive to change the set for the final scene, and the entire cast would not be far behind. These combined hordes would bring this unexpected but very welcome encounter to an abrupt end.

When Toby met an attractive woman for the first time, he always suffered invisible agonies while he worked out what to say. He found unplanned conversation in such circumstances a high-wire act with no safety net, and over the years he had suffered many broken bones. However, for some reason his visitor seemed genuinely interested in him, so he knew he had to seize the opportunity the moment offered.

He therefore ignored the familiar inner turmoil and did his best to adopt a laid-back tone as he asked the obvious question. 'Are you waiting for anybody?'

'No one in particular. I'm here with some people with friends in the cast, and they came backstage to see them in the interval. I left it too late to get back to my seat, so I ended up watching the second act from here.'

'Then perhaps you'd like to stay for the party as well. Despite what I said, it could be fun.'

'Do you all get invited? I mean not only the actors.'

'Indeed we do, although the stage crew prefer to go to the pub.'

'What about you?'

'I'll be heading off to the party, but only once I've cleared up a bit around here.' He made a vague gesture taking in the chaos of the backstage area, where a massive papier-mâché pumpkin, an impressive golden throne, and a large props table on which sat a solitary glass slipper filled most of the available space.

'I'd love to come...'

'Great.'

'...but I don't know how I'd get there.'

'I can give you directions—or you could follow me.'

'Actually, I got a lift here tonight as I'm only visiting and don't know the area.'

'You could come with me if you like.'

'That's very kind—if you wouldn't mind taking me back to my aunt's house afterwards as well.'

'No problem at all. I'd be honoured to be your chauffeur.'

'Thank you. Once the show's over, I'll speak to my lift and let her know what I'm doing.'

'Don't worry, there's no rush. I'll be around for the rest of the evening and beyond—my work here won't be done until long after the final curtain.'

Another round of applause from the audience reminded Toby that their brief moment of solitude was about to end. 'Can you excuse me for a few minutes? Duty calls, and I have a big scene change to manage.'

For the most part, an audience has little idea of the drama played out behind the scenes in any stage production. In the majority of shows, there is one point when the odds of a major catastrophe shorten with remarkable speed—and this was the scene change Toby now had to manage. As Cinderella, Prince Charming, and the Fairy Godmother made their exit from Baron Hardup's kitchen, the members of the stage crew emerged from their lair, swarmed ungracefully over the stage and, in a flurry of activity, began to transform the space into an opulent ballroom ready for the finale.

The stage remained in semi-darkness to allow the stage crew to remove furniture and props while the actors took up their positions for the new scene. During this frantic activity there was a real chance of catastrophe as the two Ugly Sisters, both now dressed in extravagant crinolines, made their entrance through a narrow doorway, while a large kitchen table and a complete set of chairs sped through from the other direction. Fortunately, the moment passed without incident, the curtain rose again and the new scene began.

With the actors all safely on the stage, Toby turned to speak to his visitor again, but she was nowhere to be seen. He assumed she had moved out of the way to avoid the chaos. The sound of the door behind him closing made him think she had returned but he was to be disappointed. Josh was a good friend, but at this point he was not the person Toby wanted to see. Josh played Buttons and, taking a cue from the name of his character, the wardrobe team had covered his yellow frock coat with dozens of purple and green buttons so he looked even more like a half-remembered pop star from a classic music video than usual. As Josh moved towards the stage, he bowed low to Toby.

For the previous performances Toby had attempted some form of half-hearted bow in return, but tonight he had a more important matter on his mind. 'Josh, a few minutes ago there was a woman backstage that I'd not seen before. Did you see where she went?'

'I haven't seen anybody. Everyone else is on stage or ready in the other wings for their curtain call. Who was she?'

'I don't know. We only talked for a few minutes, and then it was time for the big scene change. She accepted my invite to the party—and then she disappeared.'

Josh sniggered. 'That has to be a record—even for you.'

'That's not funny. She definitely said she'd come.'

'Don't worry. I'm sure she's still around here somewhere. If not, you're bound to catch up with her again once the show's over.' A loud cheer from the stage, as Cinderella and Prince Charming returned in their wedding outfits, caused Josh to move into the wings. 'You'll have to excuse me: that's my cue.'

He strode onto the stage, and Toby settled down to follow the final pages of dialogue in the prompt copy. He kept breaking off to look around, but he need not have bothered; there was no one else backstage, and he had the whole area to himself once more.

As soon as the actors had taken the last of their curtain calls, Toby checked the auditorium, foyer, and bar but found no sign of his unexpected visitor anywhere in the building. Once the actors had changed out of their costumes, they assembled in the bar before setting off for the party, and Toby and the stage crew soon had the theatre to themselves.

All the members of the stage crew always worked at top speed, and they would dismantle the set and reduce it to its constituent elements in a matter of hours. Some of them lived only for the practical aspects of their work, regarding actors merely as a necessary evil to be tolerated between scene changes. Toby set to work packing the props into boxes for return to storage, while the stage crew removed the large flats and painted backcloths flown in for each scene.

Pausing for a moment to watch the frantic activity all around him, Toby once again marvelled at the ephemeral nature of the production, that something so complex which had taken so long to rehearse could be over so quickly. A stream of fluid landing on his head from the gantry high above brought his reverie to an abrupt end.

Toby hoped the liquid was only water, and as he rubbed his hair with a grubby handkerchief, a voice drifted down from the darkness of the flies. 'You can't afford to stand around doing nothing, young Toby. You're wasting valuable drinking time.' The voice belonged to the leader of the stage crew, a large individual known to all as Hairy Dave, whose party piece involved him scratching his knees with his hands while standing completely upright. He had a legendary capacity for beer and had earned his position as leader of the stage crew after a long evening in a bar during which he drank everyone else under the table. 'We're heading off for a few beers once we've got this lot put away. Do you fancy coming along?'

Toby had once been out drinking with the stage crew on a Friday night after work. The evening had been long, his hangover had lasted for the entire weekend, and once he had recovered, had promised himself never to repeat the experience. 'No thanks. As soon as I'm done here, I'm off to the cast party. I'm due to meet someone there.'

'Are you deserting us? I hope you're not getting ideas above your station and consorting with the enemy.'

'Don't worry, she wasn't in the cast. She was someone new I met backstage earlier on tonight.' He hoped he had struck the right note of nonchalance.

'Glad to hear you're not letting the side down. Make sure we all get invites to the wedding.'

'For God's sake, I only spoke to her for a few minutes.'

'Then you'd better get a move on. You don't want to keep the lady waiting.'

Once he had packed up the last of the props, Toby made his excuses to the stage crew and went upstairs into an empty dressing room to change for the party. As he opened the door and switched on the light, his reflection greeted him from the large mirror on the opposite wall: his jeans bore the scars of a week of dirty work, his T-shirt was now even grimier, and his fair hair, still damp from Hairy Dave's water, stood up in stiff spikes. The slogan on his T-shirt read *Things Fall Apart*, and this suggestion of universal entropy had always amused him, but currently the words also provided a succinct summary of his dishevelled state. When he turned on the shower, he discovered the actors had used up all the hot water, so after steeling himself to brave the icy deluge for a moment, he changed into clean clothes and set off for the party.

Outside, a light drizzle misted the air, and as Toby drove through the chilly streets he went over the details of his brief conversation with his unexpected visitor in his mind: she said she would come to the party, but then she disappeared before they could finalise their travel arrangements. Had someone invited her as well? If so, who could it have been? The only other person backstage at that point had been Josh, but he had seen no sign of her.

Suddenly, Toby realised what he should have done: he ought at least to have found out his visitor's name, and unless she had another way to get to the party, he had probably missed his chance ever to see her again. Not for the first time, he wondered how he managed to function reasonably effectively on a day-to-day basis when his brain operated in a time zone approximately two hours behind the rest of his body.

Chapter 2
The Party

'When the Guild had banned all types of music, it had been unprepared for the unrest this had caused across its entire territory. People knew wizards utilised music as an integral part of their power, but music still meant a great deal to a large part of the population who were not willing to live without it.'

The Musician's Destiny

There comes a time in the life of most men when, no matter how young at heart they feel, they no longer recognise the music playing at a party and wish someone would turn down the volume. When it came to the question of his age, George freely acknowledged he had reached his early fifties, and although he had long since conceded to himself that at some point he might be required to transition to his mid-fifties, he planned to remain at that age until he needed to update the initial digit.

George had not been involved with the production of *Cinderella*, but as founder and director of an annual outdoor Shakespearean production in the picturesque nearby village of East Upbury, all local actors treated him with the respect and deference due to someone who might cast them in one of his productions. Thus George always received invitations to cast parties, and he generally enjoyed such occasions although tonight, as the evening progressed and the music grew louder, he had been forced to stage a strategic retreat.

He now found himself alone in the quiet refuge offered by the kitchen, a large airy room with heritage paint on the cupboard doors and work surfaces of solid oak. The invitation had been for both George and his wife, an accomplished amateur actor, but Peggy had already been booked for a belated Christmas celebration with the East Upbury History Society. Consequently, George had come alone and had brought with him a late pass, a six-pack of beer, and a bottle of a tolerably decent red he had concealed in one of the cupboards.

Having refilled his glass and returned the bottle to the safety of the cupboard, George jumped as he heard the door behind him open. However, he relaxed when he recognised Toby, who smiled a greeting. 'Evening, George. I'm surprised to see you here. I didn't think our show would be your cup of tea.'

'I'm afraid it wasn't. Your director's concept sounded brilliant, but I decided to pass on the opportunity to witness your production for myself as it's not really my sort of play. Nonetheless, I couldn't resist an invite to the party as a chance to catch up with some old friends. However, that "music" in the other room forced me to take refuge in here. It's more your era than mine, but surely even someone of your age can't actually like it.'

'I've only just arrived so I can't really say.' Toby paused for a moment as he felt a little awkward about what he needed to ask. 'George, earlier on at the theatre I met a woman I'd not seen before. I wondered if she might have travelled here with one of the actors.'

'The other room is full of stunning women, none of whom I've ever seen before, so feel free to take your pick. Who is the lady you seek?'

'I don't actually know her name.'

'Then is there a reason for this quest—beyond your entirely understandable desire to complete a formal introduction?'

'Not really. She said she'd come to the party, and I wanted to see her again so we could continue our conversation.' A lame response, but under the circumstances he could offer nothing better.

Despite Toby's reservations, his words satisfied George, who made a proprietorial gesture around the large kitchen taking in both the assortment of bottles brought by the cast and the remains of the extensive buffet provided by the director's parents before vacating their house for the night. 'If she's here, then she's bound to want a drink or something to eat. This is where the refreshments, liquid or otherwise, are. So why not wait here? And, while you're here, why not have a drink yourself? You look like you could do with one.'

'I will, thanks. It's been a long day. A long week.'

George retrieved his bottle from the cupboard. 'You know, in my experience it's best not to appear too keen when you meet someone for the first time. The night is still young, so you should play hard to get and wait for her to come to you.' He poured a drink for Toby, topped up his own glass, and then returned the bottle to the cupboard. 'I brought this myself, and it's rather good. Cheers.'

'Cheers.'

George had not come to the party with any agenda but could not overlook the opportunity presented by this unexpected encounter with Toby. 'What do you plan to do with yourself now the pantomime is over?'

'I'll probably take things easy for a while, and I definitely need to catch up on some sleep. Why?'

'Over the past few summers, I have directed a number of Shakespearean productions in my village. You may, perchance, have caught one of our shows.'

He paused, and Toby, aware he needed to respond but unsure what to say, nodded his assent.

Toby had clearly given the right signal as George immediately resumed his speech. 'They have always been a sell-out, but some local philistines thought last year's production of *The Tempest*, imaginatively set on a crashed spaceship in a galaxy far, far away, was a bridge too far.'

He paused again, and this time Toby knew he could not rely on a diplomatic silence. Josh had played Ferdinand and had tried to dissuade him from seeing the production, but Toby had bought a ticket anyway. He decided his safest course would be one of subtle equivocation. 'I found your concept absolutely fascinating.'

George chose to acknowledge his response as a compliment. 'As a cultured man whose opinions I respect, I thank you for your kind words. Unfortunately, you currently hold a minority view. There are histrionic fundamentalists everywhere, and locally, they're in the ascendant. This year a faction on the village Culture Committee, known informally as the Ministry of Love, mounted a coup while they discussed the plans for our next production.'

George paused to take a consolatory sip of wine as he recalled the painful details of the meeting. 'They baulked at my proposal for *Much Ado About Nothing* set in the aftermath of the Gulf War as "too radical", and we then had the usual inconclusive discussion about what else we could produce. Finally, some bright spark suggested that, with the centenary of the end of the Great War looming, we should choose a play to commemorate our local heritage at the time.'

He took a further sip to fortify himself as he approached the climax of his story. 'Then the chairman, a pernicious worm of a newcomer who's burrowed his way deep into far too many facets of village life, denounced Shakespeare as elitist, forced a vote on the issue, and won it with his casting vote. As the committee controls the purse strings, I had no option other than to accept their decision. For good measure, they've also ousted me as director and brought in an outsider, a university friend of one of our illustrious chairman's most fervent groupies, as a replacement. However, in view of my hitherto unblemished record, they've graciously allowed me to assume the role of executive producer. In other words, I do all the hard work, and Maggie, our new director, gets the credit.'

To Toby, this sounded intriguing, but more in terms of the choice of play than the unexpected spotlight George had shone on to the murky world of village politics. 'What less radical show will you be performing this year?'

'The committee has, in its infinite wisdom, opted for a new play called *Yonder Deep Green Field* written by a woman in our village. It's about a group of local men who join up together and are killed at the Somme. The action takes place in the village, and the focus is on the women and families left behind, so it offers far more distaff parts than any play by the Bard. I wasn't impressed when they made their decision, but now I've read the script it's pretty good—provided strict naturalism floats your boat.'

Toby offered what he hoped was a supportive smile that also contained an appropriate element of sympathy for the cavalier behaviour of the committee.

George carried on regardless. 'Our new director has signed up to the script "as is", God help her. As it's a play about local history, she won't be able to cause any upsets. Thus the committee has given her carte blanche on how she produces it—and it's up to yours truly to deliver it.' He turned to Toby with a hopeful look on his face. 'Our auditions are in early April, and knowing your interests, I wondered if you'd be interested in stage managing it.'

George had been referring to Toby's involvement with the production of *Cinderella*, but Toby had already been struck by the subject matter of the play. The history of the First World War had fascinated him since he had first studied it at school, and he had already decided he could not miss an opportunity to be involved with a play set during his favourite historical period.

As a relative newcomer to the area, Toby knew little about local history. However, before he could ask George any more about the play, the door swung open and Josh burst into the room. 'Quick! Out of my way. I'm on an errand of mercy.'

Oblivious to any distractions until he had secured his objective, George ignored the new arrival, so it fell to Toby to react. 'What's the matter?'

'It's Kate. She's finally arrived, and she needs an immediate restorative.'

'What took her so long? She's usually one of the first to arrive—and always the last to leave.'

'Geography's not her strong point, so we agreed she'd follow me here. Unfortunately, she lost me at a roundabout and then latched on to someone else in a similarly coloured car. When she finally realised what she'd done, she called me in a panic from the middle of nowhere, and I've been giving her directions over the phone for the last half hour. She's finally arrived, but as you can imagine, she's in a bit of a state.' He picked up a glass, poured a generous measure of gin into it, and then opened the fridge in search of tonic water.

As George watched Josh top up the glass with a large quantity of tonic before adding some ice cubes from the adjacent freezer, he broadened the scope of his pitch. 'When you arrived on your mercy mission Ferdinand, I was telling Toby about our summer production, so now you're here I can tell you as well. I wonder if you'd be interested in auditioning for it.' George covered his dreadful memory for names by addressing his actors by the name of the characters they played in his productions, and continued to do this long after the production itself had finished.

Josh had narrowly escaped a painful injury after tripping over a light sabre during the final performance of *The Tempest*, and with the memory of this still fresh, he gave a non-committal reply. 'What have you chosen for this year?'

George turned up the charm: he knew the play would be difficult to cast, and he wanted Josh to be in it. 'We've decided to break with tradition and perform a new play about the history of our village—with no flying saucers anywhere to be seen. Moreover, I have surrendered the burden of directorship to another: for this production my role is merely that of executive producer.'

Josh relaxed. 'Okay, I'm sort of interested, but tell me more.'

Toby, amused by the way George had already rewritten the story of the coup and keen to work with Josh again, tried to offer George some support. 'And George has asked me to stage manage it.'

'Even that doesn't put me off.' Josh paused and looked at their expectant faces. 'Fine. I'll come to the audition.'

George beamed at him. Then a new thought struck him; as he read the script, he realised Maggie would probably struggle to find enough male actors of the right age to cast in the main roles, although he knew several local people who would be keen to stage manage the production. Now it fell to Toby to feel the full force of his charm.

‘You know, Toby, it’s a shame we’ve never managed to persuade you to tread the boards or, to be strictly accurate in this case, the sward. We need three young male leads for our play. I hope after tonight we can pencil in Ferdinand for one of them, but beyond this, we’ll be struggling. I wonder if you’d be interested in auditioning as well?’

Toby knew from experience that George would not take a simple “no” for an answer, and he therefore needed to make his position clear and unambiguous. ‘Absolutely not. One hundred per cent no. Not me. Never. The only part I play is strictly backstage.’

Even in the face of this onslaught, George remained loath to give up. ‘I wonder then if you know anyone else who might be interested.’

Toby thought for a moment. ‘There is someone: a friend from work came to see *Cinderella* tonight, but I don’t know if Adam would actually want to be in a play. I don’t even know if he has any experience of acting.’

‘Can you ask him? The Ministry of Love has informed me that our new director excels at working with novices, so it would be good to provide her with another opportunity to demonstrate her skills.’

Toby had no idea what Adam would say, but relieved at his own narrow escape, he decided to be optimistic. ‘I’ll ask him next week. I’ll work out an angle and see if I can get him hooked.’

‘Excellent! One more thing: there’s a local girl who’s keen to help backstage, although she has no experience at all. Her name’s Hetty, she’s extremely forceful, and I didn’t have the heart to say no. Actually, she wouldn’t let me say no.’ He shuddered as he remembered the encounter the previous week: Hetty had arrived at his house one evening without warning and informed George she would be helping backstage with the production. George had been unable to persuade her to leave until he had agreed to her proposition, and he hoped he could pass the problem on to Toby. ‘I thought she could be your deputy or something.’

His voice faded into uncertainty, but the arrival of Kate prevented Toby from discovering any more about his forceful new deputy. ‘I’m feeling completely abandoned, so I thought I’d better help myself before I die of thirst.’

George enveloped Kate in a massive hug and kissed her on both cheeks. 'Miranda, how lovely to see you again.'

'George, it's lovely to see you too, but you're so behind the times: tonight, I'm Toby's fairy godmother.' She gave Toby a brilliant smile. 'I hope my little enchantment worked.'

Toby shrugged. 'I'm afraid it seems to have fizzled out.'

'Don't worry, I used a long-lasting spell, so it's not had time to get properly started yet.'

Josh turned to Toby. 'Have you tracked down your mysterious woman yet?'

'Not so far. But I just heard the front door again, so I'd better check out who's arrived. I guess I should also take a look in the other room.' Toby finished his drink, put his glass down on the work surface, and left the kitchen.

After a moment of silence, Kate found it impossible to contain her curiosity any longer. 'Who's he looking for?'

'He doesn't know. He met a woman backstage at the theatre earlier on but didn't find out her name. He invited her to the party, she said she'd come, and then she disappeared.'

'Poor old Toby.'

'One foot in reality and the other well and truly in a world of fantasy. Some things will never change.'

George followed their conversation with interest but wanted to return to the casting of the village production. 'Now Miranda, while you're here let me tell you about our summer production. We'll be performing a play set in our village at the time of the Great War, and you'd be perfect as Maud, the older daughter of the family in the big house. We're casting in April, so I hope you'll come along to the audition.'

Kate smiled as George outlined the story of the play and described the character of Maud. The role sounded a good one, and she knew that being involved in the production would give her the opportunity to ensure the unfinished business with Toby came to its proper conclusion.

Chapter 3
The Flat

'The inns that Duncan's Company visited in the more remote provinces were neither large nor prosperous, with the accommodation on offer always dirty, uncomfortable, and infected with fleas. Nonetheless, after the exertions of a long journey, the stresses of a live performance, and an evening spent in the bar the members of the Company always slept soundly.'

The Musician's Destiny

The light on his face made Toby begin the long crawl back to consciousness, and he opened his eyes to find the pale sun of a winter morning shining through the thin bedroom curtains. He had returned late from the party, and once he collapsed into bed, the long days of the past week finally caught up with him. Now, as he readied himself to face the day, he thought again about the previous evening, especially his unexpected encounter backstage at the theatre and the anticlimax of the party. In reality, the party had been no different to others he had attended in the past, but the absence of his visitor from the theatre meant he had been in no mood to enjoy the occasion and, in the end, had left relatively early.

If anyone asked Toby if he was seeing anyone, he liked to describe himself as being between relationships, although the current "between" phase had lasted significantly longer than any relationship he had so far enjoyed. When it came to the matter of women, he still felt little better than an awkward teenager. However, now he had passed the psychologically important mid-point of his twenties, the pale face looking back at him from under the thatch of hair in the shaving mirror each morning told a different story, and he often wondered how much longer it would be before anything interesting happened in his life.

As Toby gazed up at the ceiling, a series of unanswered questions hung in the air above him. Who was the mysterious woman? What was she doing at the theatre? And, most importantly, why did she disappear after she accepted his invitation to the party? After several minutes of fruitless speculation, he realised for him to have any chance of finding answers, his brain required the stimulation that only a large dose of caffeine could provide.

He therefore climbed out of bed, stumbled along the narrow corridor into the kitchen, and switched on the coffee machine. While the coffee brewed, he flicked through the small pile of unopened post that had accumulated during the previous week, but apart from an amusing postcard from his older sister to wish him luck with the play, it consisted of the usual mix of circulars, junk mail, and a utility bill.

The smell of the brewing coffee soon filled the small kitchen. Toby opened the fridge to retrieve the milk, but as he picked up the carton, he realised its contents had separated, with the solid mass at the bottom well on the way towards reinventing itself as soft cheese. This prompted him to check the rest of the fridge for any other food items posing a potential health hazard. A quick scan of the interior confirmed if he wanted to eat, he needed to go shopping: the fridge contained three cans of beer, half a bottle of white wine and an unopened carton of orange juice. However, in terms of food, he could only see some butter, a lump of indifferent Cheddar, and two eggs probably long past their sell-by date.

Toby drank his coffee black, but the welcome caffeine did not help him resolve any of his unanswered questions, let alone decide on his priorities for what remained of the day. He wondered if he could afford to spend some time working on the novel he had started to write last year. His commitment to the play plus a string of large projects at work had prevented him from even looking at his draft for weeks, and he had fallen far behind the schedule he had set himself to finish it. However, his stomach told him it needed feeding, so he knew food had to be his first priority. After he had eaten a healthy and nutritious meal, he would be in a much better state to make a fresh start on his writing, and then later on he would tidy his flat and make his usual preparations for the start of the new working week.

On his return from the shops, Toby carried the two large bags of shopping up the steep flights of stairs to his top-floor flat. The developer had managed to fit five blocks of flats onto a patch of brownfield land and had also converted the old mill that had once dominated the whole site. The mill itself had escaped demolition only because it was listed, and Toby's tiny flat, wedged in under its roof, had a unique and idiosyncratic layout. Despite this, in Toby's eyes the building had the inestimable advantage of being properly historic. This meant he could overlook the numerous flights of stairs to gain access, the low positions of the windows, and the unusual layout of the rooms, and after a week of painful bruises, he had learnt to avoid hitting his head on the sloping ceilings too often.

After enjoying an extremely late brunch, Toby went into what he called his library to write down a good idea that had occurred to him while in the supermarket. His best ideas often arrived at inopportune moments, and he knew from experience that if he did not immediately record this new idea for posterity, it would depart just as quickly. The letting agent had optimistically described the large cupboard with a small window as a second bedroom, but after Toby had crammed three bookcases into the tiny space he felt justified in describing it as his library. The room also contained a small wooden desk, and once Toby had made himself comfortable on the ancient office chair, he extracted a thick pile of white paper from the bottom drawer and picked up his favourite pen. He was no technophobe, but by trial and error had found a pen and paper to be by far the best way to capture his initial thoughts: the hard work began when he had to decipher his pages of scrawled text and innumerable crossings out to produce the first typed draft.

Toby had always loved fantasy novels. From his early teenage years, once he had given up waiting for his invitation to Wizarding School and had stopped talking to the family cat in the hope she might answer back or even change shape, he had pinned his hopes on securing a place at the Unseen University. However, he did not live on a disc travelling through space on the back of a giant turtle, so he knew the likelihood of this occurring was somewhat remote. Nonetheless, his interest in fantasy had continued, and early last summer, after five months of extended procrastination, he had begun work on the first book in what he planned would become a multi-volume epic fantasy saga of his own. Once these became global best-sellers, he intended to sell the film rights and exploit the associated merchandising and spin-off opportunities to make his fortune.

He had always assumed first novels were essentially autobiographical, and this made him wonder where fantasy writers found their inspiration. He lived in an all too mundane present with no obvious sign of magic visible anywhere, so he knew it would be a challenge for him to find that vital first spark of creativity to fire his imagination. In his quest for inspiration, he also ransacked his historical memory, which had been bolstered by a three-year study of the subject at university, and finally settled on a period that might work as a setting. After innumerable false starts and far too many blind alleys which forced him to retrace his steps, he finally worked out a story he wanted to tell.

Then, as Toby began to develop his characters and the outlines of his plot, he discovered inspiration all around him. For the past three years, he had worked as a proposal writer for an IT services company, and through the strange prism of his imagination, he began to see his employer as the most recent incarnation of an ancient organisation engaged in an endless struggle against wizards. The creation of such a monstrous behemoth pleased him, and he decided his antagonist should work as a newly commissioned wizard hunter. However, as a lifelong liberal, his real sympathies lay with the wizards, so he made his hero an itinerant musician who subsequently discovers he has magical powers.

Toby was a small cog in a large machine producing bids for large service contracts on a regular basis. Thus, it did not take a massive leap of creativity on his part to see how the Guild, the portmanteau name he had allocated to his creation, might have different teams competing in their hunt for any unauthorised use of magic. The Guild had named this ongoing campaign *"The War on Wizarding"* and had adopted the slogan "*Market Forces to Defeat Dark Forces*" as its mission statement.

After a few tentative steps as he began to explore his world, Toby had now drafted seven chapters of a novel which rejoiced in the working title of *The Musician's Destiny*. Once he had written a further seventeen chapters and found a publisher, he would be well on the way to becoming a best-selling author.

He had only intended to make a quick note of his idea, that his hero meets a woman who disappears before he can find out her name. However, this then made him wonder how they could meet up again. After he had sketched out a potentially workable scenario to address this, he tried to develop their relationship further. Unfortunately, this proved a far more difficult challenge, and by the time he had finished, the sky outside had darkened. When he re-read the pile of scrawled manuscript pages spread across his desk, he convinced himself they worked reasonably well as a first draft, so he typed up a clean copy and added the printed pages to the folder containing the current versions of the earlier chapters.

Later on, while returning a few stray books to their rightful homes in his library, he picked up a paperback history of the First World War he had owned since school and remembered his conversation with George about the East

Upbury summer production: after a night's sleep, the idea of stage managing a new play set during this period seemed an even more attractive proposition. He would do his best to persuade Adam to come to the audition, and then it would be up to George and Maggie to cast him if he performed well.

The next morning, as Toby walked towards the anonymous glass and concrete block where his company had its office, he once again marvelled that someone paid him real money for the time he spent there. He had started work three years ago on a temporary basis to support a team bidding for a massive government project, the company had won the business, and shortly afterwards he had been offered a full-time contract. He now spent long days converting innumerable, hastily assembled texts of dubious literacy into coherent, consistent, and polished prose for incorporation into the regular bids submitted by his company.

Toby bought his usual large coffee from the concession stall in the atrium and then took the lift up to the second floor. The open-plan office had identical cubicles set around the walls and innumerable hot desks crammed into the large central space. Toby and Adam had adjacent cubicles, and Toby liked to describe their respective roles as Adam doing numbers while he did words. In reality, Adam was an accountant who worked in project finance, while Toby was part of the bid team. They were of similar age and had joined the company within a month of each other.

Adam was already at his desk, although as yet he had been unable to begin work as the company's systems were still running their weekly update sessions. Toby dropped his bag onto his chair, and the sound caused Adam to glance up from the three neat piles of filing arranged on his otherwise empty desk: in his ideal world all paper would be banished so everything existed only in cyberspace. Toby's desk in the adjacent cubicle looked somewhat different: tottering piles of proposals in various stages of drafting covered nearly the entire surface. Toby could always locate any document he needed to refer to more or less immediately, but Adam had once confided in him that if he worked at Toby's desk for more than half a day he would end up as a gibbering wreck.

Toby had been in an offsite meeting for the whole of Friday, so the thick folder of new work in the centre of his desk added to the general confusion. He glanced briefly at this as he began to unpack his bag. 'Morning.'

'Morning. Welcome to another wonderful week of work. I trust you had an enjoyable time on Saturday night.'

Toby grinned. 'I did.' His grin lost some conviction. 'Yes, I did.' He fell silent as he tried to convince himself and then took a large sip of coffee.

Adam realised Toby had a story to share with him. 'And?'

Toby's grin returned. 'I had an unexpected encounter with a mysterious woman backstage at the theatre.'

Adam waited for Toby to provide more details, but after a prolonged period of silence, his impatience finally won. 'What happened?'

'She disappeared.'

'Disappeared?'

'I met her backstage close to the end of the second act and invited her to the cast party. She said she'd come—and then she disappeared.'

Adam laughed. 'I think you're a little confused. It's Cinderella who disappears. It's a key plot point in the story. I was there, and I saw it. Remember?'

How could Toby forget? After a slow start to ticket sales, the anxious director had begged the entire company to help bring in an audience, and Toby had persuaded Adam to buy a ticket. Toby still felt guilty about this and had no desire to find out what Adam thought of the production. 'She was definitely real. I spoke to her for about five minutes—but I didn't find out her name or how to contact her again.'

'Why does nothing like that happen to me? If I ever met Cinderella's Fairy Godmother, all she'd have to do is wave her wand at me, and I'd die happy.'

Toby remembered George's request and snapped out of his self-pity: there would be no need for him to persuade Adam to come to the audition if he had his own reason to turn up. He therefore adopted a tone that he hoped sounded appropriately innocent. 'What if I fixed things so you *could* meet her? Not just once, but regularly over two or three months.'

The long pause while Adam considered the question made Toby think he had taken the bait, but as so often in Toby's life, his optimism had been misplaced. 'What's the catch?'

Toby realised that bringing his plan to a successful conclusion would be more of a challenge than he had initially thought: he would need to use all his powers of persuasion to encourage Adam to come to the audition. He took a deep breath and began. 'Have you ever been in a play?'

'A play?'

Adam's look of confusion made Toby wonder if he should reconsider his plan, but he remembered his promise to George and ploughed on. 'As in "performed in front of an audience".'

'You might be surprised to hear that my performance as an Angel received rave reviews.'

Toby's voice revealed his genuine amazement. 'When was that?'

'Nativity play at primary school. My mum said I was the star of the show.'

'I don't think that counts.'

'Me neither. I only told you because I wanted you to see that beneath this boring accountant exterior, I possess innumerable layers of hidden depths. But what play are you talking about?'

Toby breathed a sigh of relief as he realised Adam had indeed taken the bait. Then he looked again at the thick folder of new work and grimaced: being away from the office for a whole day always carried the same penalty. 'I need to take a look at this straightaway, so I'll have to be quick.'

He opened the folder and scanned its contents while he told Adam what he knew. 'It's an open-air production in the gardens of Somerton Court, a big house in East Upbury, and the play's about the history of the village during the First World War. I can guarantee that Cinderella's Fairy Godmother, who in the real-world answers to the name of Kate, will be at the audition and is very likely to be cast in a significant role. Therefore, I wondered if you might like to come along to the audition as well. It'll take place sometime in early April.'

Adam frowned for a moment and then grinned broadly. 'I admire your powers of persuasion. Let me check my busy schedule and see if I have any space.' He opened up his diary, put on his glasses, and scrutinised the screen for a few moments. Then he raised his head again. 'Oh, what luck! All my weekends in April are free so I can definitely fit you in.' He paused, and a shadow of panic crossed his face. 'But what exactly will I have to do?'

Toby realised if Adam was to stand a chance of being cast in the production he would require careful mentoring, and from what he knew of Adam, this would involve a great deal of additional work. Then, as he started to look in detail through the first document, he had a sudden vision of his hero and trusty sidekick as they set off on an epic quest into unknown territory together. He scribbled a note to himself on a scrap of paper; he could work out the purpose of their quest later on.

Chapter 4
The Village

'The next settlement the Company approached was little more than a squalid collection of roughly built cottages around a green on which a small flock of scrawny sheep grazed. Despite the interest that their arrival provoked among the gaggle of villagers, Duncan instructed his unkempt convoy to keep moving: the potential audience here was far too small to make any performance profitable.'

The Musician's Destiny

The village of East Upbury, sprawling along the foot of the Berkshire Downs, straddled a former turnpike road leading from the honey-stoned market towns of the Cotswolds directly to the capital. However, with the turnpike long since superseded by a motorway, the main road through the village had dwindled to nothing more than a byway used mostly by local traffic. All the residents valued the tranquillity they now enjoyed in their picturesque and characterful community.

During the week, the village lost many of its working-age residents in a daily exodus of commuters who returned too late to enjoy the simple pleasures of country life. Meanwhile, local children disappeared to school on a daily—or termly—basis. As a result of these absences, the village only truly came to life at weekends and on public holidays; at such times, proud householders made the most of these brief respites from the demands of the world outside to indulge in every aspect of the good life that their small community could offer.

Within the village, a group of retired professionals, keen to make a positive contribution to their community, had established the Village Society to oversee the smooth running of every aspect of local life. In their pursuit of this simple objective, the society's members, known formally as the Village Elders, had also created the Culture Committee, known informally as the Ministry of Love, to ensure all communal events, from the Church Fete to the Annual Wassail, from the Produce Show to the Summer Play, took place on time and without mishap. With Easter over, local attention now turned towards the Summer Play as residents began to prepare for the auditions, the first stage in an annual journey that would consume so much of their collective energy for the next three or so months.

On a cool Saturday morning in early April, George had taken refuge in his study, a pleasant room full of light wooden furniture and with framed posters of his past productions decorating its walls. As he turned the pages of the script on the desk in front of him, he heard the distant sounds of Peggy working on her audition piece in the lounge. In previous years, Beech Cottage had been a maelstrom of activity as George coordinated the preparations for his production, but today his study was an oasis of tranquillity. Later in the morning, he would attend the auditions in the Village Hall and then participate in the production meeting that Maggie, as director, had arranged for the afternoon, but currently he had no pressing actions.

Despite his continued hostility towards the members of the Culture Committee who had instigated the coup against him, George had quickly warmed to Maggie, an energetic and attractive woman in her early forties, and now looked forward to working with her. They had met for the first time when the Chairman of the Culture Committee, known to his acolytes as "Freddie" and to other villagers as "Frederick", had summoned them both to an introductory meeting in the Jubilee Room of the Village Hall.

Frederick and his wife had moved to the village last year after his retirement from the Army. Once they had settled into Eulalie, a brick built aberration inflicted on the village in the 1930s, Frederick decided the local population could benefit from his organisational skills and thus had immediately volunteered to join the Village Society. Although not a natural choice for membership of the Culture Committee, after the sudden death of its elderly chairman, he had lobbied hard to secure membership of that as well. Subsequently, he ended up as chairman when the committee's two rival factions failed to secure a majority for either of their own preferred candidates. In his new role, he led the opposition to George's proposed Shakespearean production and then appointed himself as overseer to ensure the summer production properly reflected what the Culture

Committee believed it had voted for.

George had not been in the least surprised when Frederick monopolised their meeting, reminding both him and Maggie at length that the play needed to be true to the heritage of the village; ultimately, only some astute teamwork on their part had enabled them to win back control of the session. Maggie appeared coy when Frederick, wary of reports of the inventive productions George had directed in previous years, demanded the play should be a traditional production with no surprises. In response, Maggie pointed out the play told a true story about real people, some of whose names appeared on the war memorial outside the church, and as such her production would be authentic to their legacy.

George's admiration for Maggie grew as he watched her deal with Frederick's numerous demands: "authentic" was a wonderfully opaque word hinting at strict historical fidelity while allowing her to stage the production exactly as she wanted. Nonetheless, her careful answer placated Frederick who probed no further. As a result of Frederick's interminable lectures the meeting dragged on all morning, and once they finally escaped from the Village Hall, George invited Maggie home for a restorative drink and an al fresco lunch.

Safe within the confines of Beech Cottage, Maggie regaled George with the story of the strange journey that had delivered her to East Upbury. 'I still feel a little dizzy after the unexpected summons from the Culture Committee, and currently I'm so far behind in my preparations, quite unlike all my previous productions. To tell you the truth, I hadn't actually planned to direct anything this summer as I wanted a break after such a heavy teaching commitment at college.'

'So why did you agree?'

'I've known Sheila since university. Our lives have taken very different paths since then, but we've stayed in touch, and I was flattered when she contacted me on behalf of the committee. I've always enjoyed community drama, so there's no way I'd turn down a chance to direct villagers performing a play about their own history. My only concern is that I might have offended you by usurping your rightful position as founder of the festival.'

'Not in the least. The way some members of the Ministry behaved during their coup upset me, but that's strictly between them and me. Now I've met you, I know my festival is in excellent hands. A year off will give me a chance to recharge my creative batteries.'

'Thank you, you're very forgiving. One of the elements I like about the script is the range of parts it offers to women of all ages: it's a real pleasure to see so many positive female roles beyond romantic lead, best friend and mother.' She turned to Peggy who had returned to the dining room with a tray of coffee. 'Do you have any idea which role you'll audition for? I can't promise you anything, but I always aim to be fair in my casting.'

'To be honest, I haven't really thought about it. When George told me about the coup, I initially planned to display solidarity with him and boycott the show completely.'

'That would definitely be a waste of your talents. When it comes to more mature female roles, I need to cast three quite separate types: above stairs, below stairs, and village matriarchs. The above stairs roles are fine for those who like to waft around in gorgeous frocks while the men carry the story, but the dramatic meat comes with the roles below stairs. These women were the unsung heroines of the time: without their managerial experience, life in the big houses would have ground to a halt. My advice to you is to think about the role of Mrs Wilson: she's the housekeeper, and it's a role of significance that would give you a chance to act rather than just react.'

'If that's your advice, I'll certainly take a look. I've heard a rumour that a coterie of Frederick's most fervent stalwarts will audition to play the ladies of the big house, so a role of significance well away from them has a double attraction.'

George coughed hesitantly. 'I hate to bring this up, but I wonder if you have any thoughts on how we can deal with the machinations of the Ministry of Love. My instinct tells me they'll watch what we do like hawks, and they're bound to have numerous willing spies throughout the cast.'

'If I can face down a bunch of disaffected students in a back corridor on a midweek November morning, then a few self-important village functionaries shouldn't be too much of a challenge. As far as I'm concerned, from this point on the play's the thing, and I won't let anyone prevent us from producing exactly the show we want.' By the time they had finished lunch, all three had completely bonded.

In a subsequent meeting with the Culture Committee, Maggie outlined her vision for the production before taking the members through her initial budget, and George watched in amazement as she won point after point without even the slightest pushback. The treasurer always managed the plentiful finances of the Culture Committee as if it teetered on the brink of insolvency and had subjected all of George's previous budgets to forensic scrutiny before he signed them off. However, he immediately agreed to Maggie's request for a free hand to stage the production exactly as she had outlined provided she did not exceed the overall budget. Following the coup, George had begun to plot an as-yet-unspecified act of revenge against the assembled tweed and brogues of the committee, and after seeing Maggie in action on several occasions, he realised he now had a formidable ally on his side.

For his previous productions, George had sometimes been bruised by difficult casting decisions as he struggled to match the limited number of major roles available against the significantly larger number of actors keen to play them. Therefore, this year he made sure villagers knew the constraints his new role placed on him, and subsequently far fewer people bought him and Peggy drinks when they visited the Puppy and Duckling for their usual Sunday morning aperitifs. From his own painful experience, George knew the selection of any cast involved an awkward trade-off between talent and village politics. If Maggie asked for his advice, he would place his local knowledge at her disposal, but from what he had seen of her in action so far, he did not think she would require his counsel.

Toby had expected Adam would be apprehensive as the day of the audition approached, but he had been surprised when Adam arrived in the office one morning with five closely printed pages of questions about what would happen. He had no idea what form the audition would take and, as a result, wanted to find out from Toby as much as possible about every aspect of both the audition and the production so he would be ready to answer any difficult questions. Toby still felt guilty about what he might have let Adam in for by inviting him to the audition, so they spent a long evening working through all of Adam's questions until he had taken pages of notes and felt reassured by the mass of information he had accumulated.

The unexpected nature of this preparatory work made Toby realise Adam would be in no state to get to the audition unaided, so he offered Adam a lift. Adam accepted the offer with alacrity, but then insisted that Toby collect him far earlier than necessary for the short journey to East Upbury. Consequently, they turned into the car park behind the Village Hall more than half an hour before the scheduled start of the audition.

As Toby switched off the engine, Adam looked around in alarm at the vacant parking spaces surrounding them on all sides. 'Are you sure this is the right day? I've been building myself up for this all week, and I can't go through all that stress again.'

'Don't worry. This is a village show, so most people live locally and don't need to drive. We're a bit early too, so let's see if anyone else has arrived yet.'

Once inside the heavy front door, Toby and Adam made their way along a narrow corridor and through an internal door leading into the main hall. In front of the stage stood a large wooden table with three plastic chairs behind it, with further rows of plastic chairs set out towards the rear on either side. The hall looked ready for the audition to begin, but currently the pair had the building to themselves.

As he surveyed the empty space, the worry returned to Adam's face. 'Where is everybody? This feels like the *Marie Celeste*.'

'Perhaps they've been kidnapped by aliens, who plan to replace them all with clones as the first step in their cunning plan to secure global domination.'

'If you visit some of the villages around here, you'll realise aliens have been among us for some time. It's either an unknown alien invasion or the consequence of unreliable local bus services.'

The sound of the front door banging open made them both jump, and Toby giggled as they heard light footsteps coming down the corridor towards the hall. 'Watch out. This could be one of the aliens. Keep your back to the wall and look out for any extraterrestrial probes.'

The door opened, and a slim, blonde figure in a pink T-shirt and immaculate jeans drifted into the hall. As soon as she saw Toby, Kate came over to greet him, hug him, and then kiss him gently on the cheek. Toby returned the hug and gave her an awkward kiss, while Adam looked on open-mouthed.

'Hello, Toby, we meet once more. What a small world we inhabit!'

'Decidedly minuscule. And thanks again for the spell—although, in the end, nothing happened.'

'Don't worry. I used a long-lasting enchantment, so you need to be patient.'

'Do I?'

She extended a palm towards his chest and concentrated for a moment. 'It's definitely still working.'

'That's good news then. I'll let you know when something happens.'

Adam had been clutching his folder like a security blanket as he watched their exchange, but now it slipped from his hand, crashed to the ground, and spread his thick pile of notes across the polished wood of the floor. He fell to his knees and began to gather up the papers as Kate turned and smiled in his direction.

'Who's your friend? Aren't you going to introduce us?'

'Sorry. This is Adam. He's an actor, rather than a lowly techie like me.'

Adam tried to work out if he should stand up and see if Kate would kiss him as well, but after an intense internal struggle he decided that remaining on his knees was the safer option; as a compromise, he gave her a feeble wave. 'Hello.'

Kate waved back. 'Hello, Adam. Nice to meet you. What are you up for?'

Adam realised he now had to string together an entire sentence, and underwent a further massive struggle before he managed to reply. 'I'm not really sure…'

Watching their exchange, Toby realised the magnitude of the challenge he had set himself by bringing Adam to the audition and swiftly moved in to take control. 'He's being modest. He's up for one of the farm workers, so a decent role. What about you?'

'George suggested I read for Maud, the squire's older daughter. He says she needs my skills to make her sympathetic. As it's a big part and she's on stage for most of the first act, I'm inclined to believe him. All I need to do now is convince Maggie to give it to me. If George was directing the show, I'd have it in the bag already.'

Adam had finally remembered how to use his legs, and as he climbed to his feet, he laughed. 'If I had my way, I'd definitely give it to you straightaway too.'

'That's extremely generous of you, but as we've only just met and you've not heard me read for the part, then perhaps your offer's a little precipitous.'

Adam blushed a deep scarlet, but the sound of the front door banging open again followed by many footsteps and voices in the corridor saved him from further embarrassment. After a moment, Maggie swept into the hall, closely followed by George and a stream of anxious villagers.

After taking the central chair, Maggie placed her production folder on the table in front of her, opened it up, and then indicated to George and Toby that they should sit on either side. Once the throng of aspiring actors had settled themselves into the rows of chairs behind her, she began the audition. As the session progressed, George admired the skilful way she separated those with real talent from the rest. Once she has done this, she asked them all to read again for the parts she thought they were best suited to play.

George quickly realised Maggie's casting of the three young village women, who played a central role in the play, appeared to follow his mental cast list to the letter. Louise, Helen, and Jane had played the witches in his modern-dress production of *Macbeth* and had worked well together as a team. The three of them clearly enjoyed their time on the production, as afterwards they adopted the name of the Coven as a badge of honour. With Louise always in charge and Helen as her sidekick and partner in crime, Jane did her best to keep up with the numerous schemes the other two hatched on a regular basis.

Louise had worked briefly in the City but had returned to the village three years ago when her marriage ended, and she now ran a local yard. Helen, an old school friend of Louise, had never quite managed to leave East Upbury, and had recently emerged from the most recent of a series of disastrous relationships. Meanwhile, Jane helped Louise at the yard while living at home with her widowed mother. They came from very different backgrounds, but their personal circumstances had brought them together, and the three were staunch supporters of every event in the village calendar.

Most of the Coven's social life revolved around the Puppy and Duckling: not an ideal location to find a partner, but at least it offered an extensive wine list. The members of the Coven were supporting characters in the ongoing drama of village life, but each was the star of her own story although at this point none of them knew whether this would turn out to be comedy, tragedy or, like the lives of most people, a mixture of the two.

George also noted Maggie had pencilled in the most prominent members of the Culture Committee for parts combining a significant amount of time on stage with very few lines of dialogue: with every passing moment, her skills impressed him even more. When Toby called Peggy and two other women to read for the role of Mrs Wilson, George excused himself and went outside for a breath of fresh air.

As George stood outside the Village Hall in the late morning sunshine, he wondered how Maggie would resolve her biggest remaining challenge; she still had to cast three young male leads, and here she had a far smaller pool to work with. Despite their talent, or in one specific case the lack of it, the majority of those who had read for these parts were either too young or too old for the three to work together effectively as a team. He assumed she would cast Josh in one of these roles. Toby's friend was a similar age and, despite his lack of experience, had performed reasonably well during the audition; thus, he would be good as the third member of the trio. But this still left Maggie with one significant role outstanding, and he wondered how she planned to handle it. The casting of such a key role would be crucial to the success of the production, but Maggie did not seem in the least concerned by the lack of suitable talent so far displayed.

The throaty roar of a powerful engine broke his chain of thought, and George leapt out of the way as a red sports car swung off the main road and into the parking space adjacent to the front door of the Village Hall. As the driver straightened up the car in the confined space, the resulting cloud of exhaust fumes made George cough. Once the engine had died, the fumes dispersed, and tranquillity returned to the main street, the driver opened the door, climbed out of the car, and extracted a piece of paper from his pocket as if he needed to check on his destination. Before George could offer the benefit of his local knowledge, the front door opened and Maggie emerged to greet the new arrival, who immediately wrapped her in an excessively intimate hug.

'Chris, I'm so glad you're here at last. I was worried something had happened to you.'

'Only life—and all its many complications. Your message sounded interesting, so here I am—better late than never.'

'It's been far too long since we've worked together.'

'You should direct more plays with decent roles for me. How's the audition going?'

'We're making good progress, but I still have a few gaps to fill.'

'A few? That's not like you.'

'Most of the gaps are minor roles, and I need to cast them wisely to keep the locals happy. Then there's the role I mentioned in my message. It's perfect for you, and I've already pencilled your name in—the keystone to my casting arch. If you don't take the part, then the whole show falls to pieces, so there's no pressure.'

'How could I refuse such a generous offer?'

'Good, we have a deal. Come in and meet the others.'

George watched in silence as the pair disappeared into the Village Hall.

After Maggie had concluded the second session of the audition, she led George and Toby out of the main hall and into the privacy of the Jubilee Room, and in less than half an hour they had finalised the entire cast list. During this session Maggie proved to be open to advice from George but had already pencilled in names for most of the major roles, and he was delighted to discover she had cast Peggy as Mrs Wilson. Toby took no part in their discussions; he merely produced the final cast list, which Maggie then read out to the expectant horde waiting back in the main hall.

When Louise, Helen, and Jane discovered which roles they would be playing, their priority was to find out who Maggie had cast as David, Herbert, and Lawrence. In last year's production, they had played the goddesses in the wedding masque for Miranda and Ferdinand, and throughout the entire period of the production Helen had cherished an unrequited passion for Josh. Meanwhile, Josh had ignored all her overtures and instead had flirted outrageously with Kate, who had proved entirely impervious to his charms.

Delighted to be working so closely with Josh on this production, Helen immediately scheduled a meeting of the Coven at the Puppy and Duckling to plan her strategy. The presence of Adam had been an unexpected bonus, and Louise agreed to initiate a thorough investigation into his background and circumstances, with a promise to report back once she had any news; for the moment, they pencilled him in for Jane. Meanwhile, Louise provisionally reserved whoever had been cast as David for herself.

Maggie asked Toby to move the chairs closer to the stage so she could address the whole cast and let them know her plans for the production. Adam and Josh helped him with this, but the other actors were too busy discussing their new roles with each other to offer any help. Meanwhile, Maggie circulated between the various groups and finally introduced Chris to a delighted Louise, Helen, and Jane.

With the chairs in position, Maggie clapped her hands to summon the cast to sit down. Chris took a seat in the front row and Louise sat next to him, but he paid her no attention.

Once the actors were seated, Maggie jumped up onto the stage and launched into her pep talk. 'I feel privileged to be here today, to be faced with so much talent from which to cast this wonderful play.'

George had chosen to sit in the back row, and Toby took a seat next to him. As Maggie began to speak, George turned to Toby in amazement. 'Was she at the same audition as us?'

Oblivious to their comments, Maggie quickly got into her stride. 'It was a difficult challenge to finalise the cast list, but the good news is that no one here goes home empty-handed, as I'll need all those who didn't get a speaking part to portray the other inhabitants of the village. Our challenge with this play will be nothing less than to present the heart and soul of this small community a century ago, to be true to the history of that time. In order to make this happen, you'll all need to find your character, to "become" your character, to live the daily life of your character. No matter how many or how few lines you have—or even if you have no lines—you must find your character.'

George turned to Toby again. 'Some of them have difficulty in finding their way to rehearsals. Anything else is a bonus.'

Maggie moved on to the next stage of her oration. 'I want us all to be one hundred per cent committed to this play. We will work hard, but we will also have fun. However, in order to make the most of our limited rehearsal time, I need you all to be word-perfect from day one.'

George remembered some of the challenges he had faced in previous productions and shook his head sadly. 'Fat chance of that.'

'I'll need you all to feel comfortable with your costumes when you put them on for the dress rehearsal, so I want all women to rehearse in long skirts, and all men to rehearse in trousers and shirts with collars. There will be no shorts and no T-shirts for anyone.' Maggie paused and scrutinised her eager audience, who nodded or grunted their consent to her words of wisdom.

After a few moments, she continued. 'I have one final point: before we start rehearsals, I want you all to discover what life was like for your characters at the time they lived, so I need you to carry out some research on the period. The guiding principle that will govern all our work on this production will be authenticity. That's all for now. I look forward to seeing you all again for our first rehearsal. Thank you.'

The session began to break up, and a small group of actors clustered around Maggie, keen to ask questions or engage her in conversation. No one showed any inclination to clear the hall, so Toby began to gather up the chairs by himself.

After a few moments, Adam, still excited by everything he had experienced, came over to help him. 'I'm amazed I got such a big part.'

'You got what you deserved. You did well. Extremely well for a first time.'

Josh joined them as they stacked the chairs in a small anteroom, well out of earshot of all those still in the hall. 'Toby, a few questions if I may. Who the fuck is Chris? Where did he come from? And why did he end up with David while I got stuck with Herbert?' He picked up a chair and crashed it onto the pile that Adam had meticulously assembled.

Toby placed a finger to his lips. 'Our deliberations were confidential, so I can't divulge the secrets of the audition process. All I *will* say is that the casting was entirely Maggie's decision.'

Josh crashed another chair onto Adam's neat pile. 'But it's the best part. He turned up out of the blue, and she cast him without even an audition. She's made the wrong decision, and I'll show her the error of her ways. As soon as we start rehearsing, I'll do whatever Chris does—but much better.'

'I suppose it was too much to hope she'd ban egos as well.'

Adam returned to the room staggering under the weight of yet more chairs. 'Toby, I'd like to borrow some books if you don't mind.'

Even at a distance, Toby could sense his anxiety, and wondered what had happened. 'Anything in particular?'

'History. That's your subject, isn't it? I'll need them for the research Maggie wants us to do.'

'You can borrow whatever you want. But some of them are left over from my degree so are pretty heavy going.'

'I'll take your advice and tackle any you think appropriate. I'm generally fine with books—it's the rest of life that's the challenge.'

Josh put his arms around their shoulders and steered them firmly towards the door. 'I'm starving, so let's grab some lunch at the pub. It'll also give us a chance to find out what the rest of the cast are like before rehearsals start.'

There had been a settlement at East Upbury for more than a millennium, but previous generations, lacking both the sense of history and cultural sensibilities of current residents, had failed to appreciate the value of their heritage. Thus, few half-timbered buildings had survived to the present day, and all had been renovated, restored, and remodelled to a degree completely undreamt of by those who first erected them.

The most prominent of the surviving relics, a three-storey building with numerous outbuildings of brick and stone, stood adjacent to the church in the heart of the village. In the sixteenth century, a prosperous yeoman farmer had built the property to house his family and household staff, but over succeeding centuries the building had undergone numerous metamorphoses and endured the addition of numerous carbuncular extensions of variable quality. In its most recent incarnation, the Puppy and Duckling had been reborn as an award-winning gastropub, which, in the absence of any rival within walking distance, had established itself as the de facto centre of village social life.

In an attempt to reflect the timeless heritage of the village, the current owners had re-styled the interior of the pub to emulate the ambience of a cluttered Edwardian establishment. However, the carefully distressed furniture and faded artefacts crammed onto mantelpieces and shelves were not relics from the clearance of a derelict country house, but rather came from an anonymous warehouse situated on a local business park. Similarly, the dark beams in the ceilings possessed knotholes and imperfections at intervals far too regular to make them the product of organic growth.

The large garden once surrounding the building on three sides had produced vegetables to sustain the yeoman's large household throughout the year. The garden had disappeared under grass and tarmac many decades ago, and the section that had escaped conversion into a car park had now been crammed with numerous wooden tables and benches to allow diners and drinkers to enjoy their refreshments in the open air. In the far corner stood an ancient apple tree, the sole relic of the original garden, that had survived thanks only to a tree preservation order initiated by the Village Gardening Club. To those who dined here now, "local food" merely meant food they ate at their local.

George had stopped Toby as he left the Village Hall to check on his availability for the production meetings he needed to arrange. It had not taken them long to agree on the schedule of dates, but by the time Toby arrived at the Puppy and Duckling, villagers celebrating their success or drowning their sorrows filled the entire garden.

Josh and Adam had commandeered the last vacant table, which stood in the shade of the ancient apple tree. However, they no longer had the table to themselves as the Coven had occupied three of the remaining places. Louise and Jane had mounted an astute flanking movement to place themselves on either side of Adam so he could not escape, while Helen had slipped into an empty seat next to Josh. Helen had immediately launched into an extended paean on the pleasures of working with him again, but while his ears heard her words, his eyes scoured the garden in a desperate search for reinforcements, and the moment Toby arrived, Josh waved a frantic invitation for him to join their party.

Toby squeezed between the crowds of drinkers as he set off towards the distant table, and after standing to one side while a pair of vacant-looking teenage waiters with trays full of food ambled past, he eventually reached his destination.

A welcome beer awaited him on the table, and after some desultory small talk and a none-too-subtle hint from the Coven as to how thirsty they still were after the rigours of the audition, he set off towards the bar to order his lunch and buy a second round of drinks.

Inside the crowded bar, Toby ducked under a low beam and then stood aside to allow Chris, laden down with a tray of drinks, to pass. Chris gave Toby no acknowledgement and swiftly made his way out of the front door and back towards Maggie, who had secured a table in the sunniest part of the garden. However, in his absence, a pair of functionaries from the Ministry of Love had joined her in order to instruct her on how her production should properly reflect the true heritage of the village.

From the antique clock on the wall of the crowded bar, Toby saw he had less than half an hour before the start of the production meeting. Therefore, despite his hunger, he decided to order a made-up baguette from the chiller cabinet behind the bar, although even this simple purchase took far longer than expected.

In front of him, a loud woman, placing a long and complex lunch order for her large extended family, broke off regularly to check menu options and dietary allergies with various relatives and their children. This process took even longer as she interspersed her order with loud complaints to the landlord about villagers who turned out en masse for the audition, occupied all the best seats in the garden, but never showed their faces in church from one year to the next. The landlord, who always displayed the tact and diplomacy of a publican who cannot afford to upset any of his regular customers, smiled apologetically as he finally served Toby his food and round of drinks.

Toby made the return trip back across the crowded garden without mishap. As he approached their table, he heard Adam explaining to Jane, with an almost apologetic tone in his voice, that despite what she might otherwise think about his career choice, he had a secure job with a good salary and reasonable prospects. The look on Jane's face reminded Toby of the expression he had once seen on his family's cat immediately before she pounced on an unsuspecting baby rabbit playing in the sunshine, and he wondered what Jane had asked to prompt such a response. Unfortunately, Josh could not throw any light on the subject, as during Toby's absence Louise had moved into the other vacant seat next to him to relate a long and complex piece of village gossip about a village sex scandal that had prevented five local actors, who had all played major roles in last year's production, from auditioning today.

Toby placed his tray on the table and, deciding that Adam might need reinforcements, moved towards the vacant seat next to him. However, when Louise saw his intended destination, she immediately broke off from her narrative to insist that Jane and Adam should swap places so they could all maintain a proper seating plan.

Shortly after this, the two waiters re-emerged from the kitchen laden down with more trays of food and, after wandering aimlessly around the garden, finally stopped at their table: lunch had arrived. There then followed a period of silence broken only by a few desultory flickers of conversation that resolutely failed to catch fire as they all ate their meals.

After Toby had endured the silence for as long as he could, he finished his baguette, drained his glass, and picked up his folder before excusing himself and setting off back towards the Village Hall for the production meeting. When he reached the gate, he turned to look back at the table he had left and realised the metaphorical shadows enveloping it were far darker than those cast by the ancient tree towering high above. If this was a portent of how the next few months would be, then despite looking forward to the rehearsals themselves, any lunch breaks in the company of the Coven would be heavy weather.

As Toby made the return journey past the gravelled drives, manicured lawns, and immaculate hedges of the properties bordering the main road, he wondered whether he had stumbled on to one of the great truths of life: that the majority of people are attracted to other people who are unattainable—or in his case to a woman who disappeared—while they attract the unwanted attention of other people who are extremely attainable and present all the time. After a moment of objective consideration, he realised this was not an original observation as it provided the plot for far too many films and novels. Then he wondered if he could use the set-up as part of the plot for *The Musician's Destiny*—if a market for romantic comedy novels with a fantasy setting actually existed—but quickly decided it would be better to continue developing his original plot through to some form of conclusion of its own.

When the Village Hall came in sight Toby realised, with a sudden and unexpected flash of self-awareness, that once again he had set himself up as an observer of other people's lives rather than living his own. He had no idea that within the next two hours his own life would change forever.

Chapter 5
The Jubilee Room

'The physical violence that the Guild's Militia meted out to the general populace was nothing compared to the metaphorical violence that all Guild personnel inflicted on each other during the regular schedule of meetings that filled so much of their calendars.'

The Musician's Destiny

When Maggie arrived at the Village Hall for her first encounter with Frederick, she had been amused to discover the cramped reality of the grandly titled Jubilee Room. On the other side of the door, she found a small and shabby space, with faded green paint on its walls and a portrait of the Queen donated by its artist to celebrate the Diamond Jubilee and an ancient recruiting poster for the Army as its sole decorations. A massive oval table almost filled the available floor space, and the dozen large chairs crammed around it meant once all the attendees had taken their seats, any space to move around disappeared: hence local custom dictated that the first arrivals for a meeting always occupied the seats furthest from the door.

As a stranger to the village, Maggie had no knowledge of this house rule. Thus, when she returned to the Village Hall to catch up with George prior to the production meeting, she had deposited her large rucksack on a chair with the large window facing the main road immediately behind her. She knew she needed to make a good impression during this first encounter with the production team, and from this seat she could command the entire room.

In her absence, many of the production team had already taken their places around the table, and while they waited for the meeting to begin they updated each other with the latest village gossip on Maggie's casting decisions. Meanwhile, Maggie and George had been waylaid in the main hall by an elderly member of the Ministry of Love determined to secure a more prominent role for Will, her teenage grandson; she explained that her son and daughter-in-law had spent a fortune on acting classes for him and, as a proud grandmother, she had looked forward to seeing him playing a leading role in the production. Maggie had been impressed by Will's obvious talent during the audition, but with him being at least half a decade too young to play one of the three central roles, she had instead cast him as the younger brother of Kate's character, as his blond hair gave the pair a reasonable family resemblance. Nonetheless, with the innate skill of a practised politician, Maggie promised the anxious supplicant she would review his casting before rehearsals began without saying anything that could be seen as a binding commitment.

While Maggie spoke, she had been watching the second hand of the wall clock move slowly towards the vertical. Then, with an exclamation of 'Gosh, look at the time', she brought the conversation to an abrupt conclusion and swept out of the hall, along the narrow corridor, and into the Jubilee Room. George followed close behind; he bore the scars of numerous similar encounters in previous years and had been impressed by the skilful lack of commitment he had witnessed.

Once safely inside the room, Maggie edged around behind the assorted shapes and sizes of the assembled production team, causing each member to shuffle forward or stand up, until she reached the place she had reserved for herself earlier on. Meanwhile, George slipped into one of the three empty chairs close to the door.

Having secured her seat, Maggie surveyed the circle of expectant faces regarding her with cautious interest. All eyes watched warily as she opened her rucksack and removed a heavily annotated script and three large bundles of production notes, which she placed on the table; first impressions were vital, and these reinforced the message that she meant business. Then, to ensure she had the undivided attention of all those present, she extracted her spectacles from their case, polished them with care, and put them on.

However, before she could launch herself into her opening remarks the door crashed open, and Toby fell awkwardly into the room; he had tripped on the low step and landed on his knees in the doorway. He climbed to his feet and apologised profusely. 'Sorry I'm late, but I got waylaid by the dog outside.'

As Toby approached the Village Hall, he had encountered a large black and white dog tethered outside the front door. The dog had been dozing in the warmth of the afternoon sun, but when he spotted Toby he stood up, walked deliberately over to the red sports car still in the adjacent parking space, and relieved himself copiously and noisily against a rear wheel arch. After completing his business, the dog glanced back at Toby with his head on one side, returned to his patch of sun, and settled down to sleep once again. Toby felt duty-bound to congratulate the dog on his impromptu performance, and thus had missed the start of the meeting.

Maggie gave Toby the kind of stare he had not experienced since his school days when he had once been extremely late for an English class. His teacher had not been impressed by his tardiness, but she had a novel sense of humour; his punishment had been to learn by heart a long speech from the play they were studying. He could still remember just about every word, and after a few drinks had been known to run through the entire opening soliloquy of *Richard III* although he now took care to preface any recital with a disclaimer about the historical inaccuracy of Shakespeare's portrayal of the king.

'Apology accepted—but please ensure you're not late for any of our rehearsals. We all have a great deal of hard work ahead of us before our production will be ready to share with the public.' Her eyes relaxed, and she turned to look once more at the other faces around the table. 'Welcome one and all, and thank you for giving up your time this afternoon. I'll start by outlining what I want for the play and what we have to do to make it work. I'm delighted to be working with this experienced team George has assembled. Combined with our strong cast, I believe that together we will mount a great production.'

Toby had slipped into a vacant seat next to George, who nodded a brief greeting before focussing his attention on Maggie. As she continued in full spate, he began a whispered commentary to Toby in counterpoint. 'I can't wait until she starts rehearsals.'

'I believe every single person involved with the show has a vital role to play in the success of our production. I don't just mean the actors and the stage crew. I'm talking about those who help out front too. I want them all, literally anyone the audience sees once they arrive at Somerton Court, to be in costume.'

A sudden flurry of activity from the furthest corner of the room, as a tiny, grey-haired lady of advanced years sprang into frantic action, made her fall silent. As one of the village's oldest inhabitants, Miss Milton had helped found the Culture Committee, but had long since given up any involvement in its machinations. Nonetheless, she still took an active role in village affairs and greatly enjoyed her annual responsibilities as Wardrobe Mistress for the summer production.

After spreading out an assortment of objects from a battered leather handbag on the table, she retrieved a pair of reading glasses, an ancient notebook, and a ballpoint pen advertising a local farrier. She made a desultory attempt to clean the glasses with a crumpled tissue before she put them on, and then began to write furiously in the notebook.

All those around the table were so absorbed by this unexpected performance that they failed to notice the door open again and someone slip quietly into the last remaining seat next to George until the new arrival spoke. 'I'm so sorry I'm late. We had to take my aunt's cat to the vet, and there was a long queue, so our appointment ran way over schedule.'

Toby had thought about the voice he had heard backstage at the theatre almost every day and, as the weeks passed, had finally accepted he would never hear it again. But now—suddenly and wonderfully—its owner had joined their meeting and taken a seat on the other side of George.

Before Maggie could resume her speech, Miss Milton stopped writing, looked up at the new arrival, and addressed her with a note of real sympathy in her voice. 'I do hope it wasn't bad news.'

'I'm happy to report that all was fine, although she is a bit stressed.'

'I'm not surprised. I always get stressed when one of my little cats is unwell. How is dear Joan now?'

'She's fine—it's her cat who's stressed. Apparently, she needs some pheromones to relax her, so Joan has done the needful.'

Maggie had followed the exchanges with increasing impatience, but her quick glance in George's direction prompted him to take control of the situation. 'Charming as our pets always are, I wonder if we could perhaps postpone these feline discussions until later.' George's default manner was diplomacy itself, but Miss Milton, long accustomed to automatic deference throughout the village, sank back into her chair, her face crumpling.

George saw this and realised he needed to execute an immediate strategic retreat, so he turned to address the new arrival. 'Sarah—welcome. I think you know the village contingent from our last meeting. But you've not had a chance to meet Toby yet. He's our stage manager.'

Toby had so far resisted the urge to look at the new arrival, but George's introduction meant he could delay the moment no longer; he wanted to say so much—but not in front of such a large audience. As he turned towards Sarah, he wondered how she would react when she saw him again. 'Yes, we have. I mean we have met, but it wasn't here, and we didn't get a chance to introduce ourselves.'

The look on Sarah's face revealed her surprise at his unexpected presence at the meeting. Then she smiled, and he hoped this meant she felt similarly about this second encounter.

'Hello—again.'

'Hello.'

A long silence followed. Toby felt the eyes of the whole room on the two of them, all aware they were privileged witnesses to a potentially momentous encounter.

Finally, Maggie ended the silence with an impatient cough, and George resumed his introductions. 'Sarah's aunt is the author of our play, and Sarah has kindly offered to help backstage when she can. If you're happy, I thought she could be your deputy.'

'No. No. No. No. No!' The explosion from the dumpy girl with spiky brown hair and heavy glasses, until this point sitting in silence next to Maggie, made the entire room jump. 'We agreed I was Tobe's deputy, so Sarah has to be something else.'

Sarah had no desire to cause an upset. 'Don't worry about a job title for me. I'm not local, so I'll be happy just to help out whenever I'm here.'

The look of terror that had appeared on George's face as soon as the girl began to speak now dissipated. 'Excellent. Hetty is Toby's deputy, so Sarah can be his assistant. Prizes for everyone. Shall we continue?' When George turned back towards Maggie, he noticed that Toby now had a broad grin on his face.

Maggie looked slowly around the room, took a deep breath, and returned to her agenda. 'I cannot tell you how excited I am by this play. There is so much potential in the script, but overall I want to keep our production simple. I've sketched out my ideas for a flexible set that should cover most of our needs. George, can you take a look at them and see if they'll work?'

From the thick pile of papers on the table she extracted a bundle of drawings, which she passed to George. 'Now costumes. I want real differentiation between the family and staff at the big house and the local people in the village. We'll also need military uniforms for both the village men and the officers.'

By now, Miss Milton had recovered her poise. 'We have some lovely costumes left over from our previous shows, so we'll fix up a meeting for you to view them. Whatever else we need for the main actors, we can hire in.'

'Do we have the budget for this?'

George glanced up from his scrutiny of Maggie's drawings. 'All of my productions played to full houses, and the Culture Committee has always been most generous with its financial support. We have an extremely healthy bank balance, so the budget should not be an issue.'

Maggie had already calculated the likely cost of implementing her plans for the production and felt reassured. 'Then let's hope I can follow your example with this show. The next point is that in addition to the ball scene, there will also be dancing at other points in the play. David, Herbert, and Lawrence will need to learn a Morris Dance.'

George looked puzzled. 'I don't remember seeing those in the script.'

'It is now. I need them to perform in the final scene. Make a note of it, please. I'm sure we can find someone from the local Morris Men to teach them.' She turned back to the room. 'Now furniture and props. I've put together a preliminary list, and we can make any changes once we start rehearsals.' She extracted another long list from her folder and handed the pages to Hetty, who scanned them with a frown of concentration. 'And now for the play itself. Right from the start, it's important we establish a real sense of the countryside, so I want animals on stage: horses, dogs, that kind of thing.'

Hetty put down Maggie's list, and her voice betrayed her surprise. 'Animals?'

'Yes. The fields around here are full of them, so see what you can find for us. There's a wonderful hound outside the front door who'd be perfect.'

'Fenrir's mine, and he'd love to be in the show.'

'Excellent. Consider him cast.'

Maggie returned to her agenda, and Hetty beamed as she resumed her scrutiny of the list. 'Then we come to the play itself. The first act has a perfect ending with the climax of the wedding ball, but the second act just fades away.'

George realised that Maggie, despite her earlier comment about her lack of preparation, had by now thought through the entire production in detail. He sat back in silent expectation, keen to discover what other surprises she planned to spring on the meeting. He did not have to wait long. 'The key scene is the one when the men are getting ready for the Harvest Supper and decide to enlist. We hear all their hopes and plans for the future, but we also know what will happen to them.'

Toby scribbled a note in his folder that retrospective historical inevitability was not authentic, but Miss Milton nodded her agreement. 'It's so sad. I want to cry as soon as I think about it.'

'Yes, but currently, the scene doesn't quite work. Think about it. They've been working all day, every day—for weeks—on the harvest. This is the biggest celebration of their year, so they'll want to look their best. After all their hard work, the men will be tired and hot and dirty and sweaty.'

She paused and looked around the room. 'So rather than merely washing their hands and faces, they need to take baths. On a symbolic level, it's an act of purification as it's the last time we see them alive. It'll also give us a solid bridge to build towards the emotions of the final scene. If we can make these scenes work as well as I think we can, there won't be a dry eye in the house.'

George turned to Toby with a broad grin on his face. 'Let's do something non-controversial this year. I can't wait to find out what the Ministry of Love thinks about this.'

Maggie continued to outline her vision, oblivious to George's comment. 'It's already there in the dialogue, so we don't need to change a word. The scene begins with David in the bath. Herbert is telling him to hurry up—he has a line about the water getting cold—and then, when the women arrive, Herbert grabs his towel and jumps out.'

A long moment of silence followed before George, as the most senior member of the production team, decided he should speak on behalf of all those present. 'As executive producer, I'm happy to do whatever I can to help you realise your vision, but before we can set this in concrete, I think we should find out what Chris and Josh think about your plans.'

'All they'll have to do is get in and out of a bath, so they'll only appear naked for a moment. I've worked with Chris before, and I'm sure he won't have a problem with it. Toby, you know Josh. Do you think he'll agree to do it?'

Toby took a deep breath. After Josh's extended tirades about Maggie's casting, he knew what answer Josh would have to give, but he had no desire to be present when Maggie asked him. 'If Chris will do it, then I don't think Josh will refuse.'

'Good. I'll speak to them both when we start rehearsals to make sure they're happy with what I want to do with the scene. Next, I need to know what we have in the way of lighting rigs and sound systems. Then I must talk to Toby and Hetty about the props and furniture we'll need for rehearsals.'

The final item on the agenda was the after-show party, and once the catering manager agreed her team would provide a similar range of dishes to those everyone had enjoyed so much last year, Maggie closed her folder, people began to stand up, and the meeting broke up.

The narrow corridor outside the Jubilee Room quickly filled with a stream of people inching their way towards the front door. When Toby reached the main road he could see no sign of Sarah, and when he looked back along the corridor he spotted her waiting in the main hall. After struggling against the slow tide of villagers obstructing the passage and undertaking a quick detour through the adjacent kitchen, he finally reached the hall without mishap.

As he approached Sarah she gave him a nervous smile. 'I'm sorry about what happened after I met you at the pantomime. I felt so bad about missing your cast party. My lift had an urgent domestic emergency and was in no state to drive home alone, so I couldn't abandon her. We had to set off straight after the final curtain, and as I didn't know your name, I couldn't leave a message.'

Toby decided not to mention the weeks he had spent wondering why she had disappeared—and what might have happened if she had stayed for the party. 'You obviously did the right thing. I just hope your lift managed to resolve her emergency.'

'Actually, it resolved itself. Her new puppy squeezed behind the sofa shortly after she left, her dog sitter couldn't persuade him to come out, and over the course of the evening convinced herself he was badly injured. Then, as soon as he heard us arrive, he reversed himself out and demanded an extra dinner. In summary, everything turned out fine, and yet again I'm sorry about what happened.'

'Apology accepted—absolutely and unconditionally. In the end, the party wasn't very good. The main thing now though is that you turned up here in the Village Hall for the Production Meeting.'

'And you too. It's quite a coincidence.'

Toby had no belief in coincidence or any form of predestination, but realised this was neither the time nor the place for pointless metaphysical speculation. He also knew he could not afford to waste a moment of this unexpected encounter. 'How long are you staying in the village?'

'I'm visiting for the day, and my aunt asked me to come along to the meeting and report back on how things went: she didn't want to cramp Maggie's style by turning up herself. I'm heading off home later on, and then I'll be back here on and off until the play is over.'

'That's brilliant news. Is it too early to invite you to thc after-show party?'

'No. I will come, I promise. But I hope I'll get my own invitation too.'

'Of course you will. But the party's months away, so what about…?'

Toby tried to think of somewhere local they could escape to for the rest of the afternoon, but before he could suggest anything specific, Maggie's voice from the Jubilee Room broke his chain of thought. 'Toby, we need you back here to run through the props list.'

Toby gave an apologetic shrug. 'Sorry, I think I'm needed. Let me give you my contact details.' He scribbled on an empty page in his folder, tore it out, and handed it to her.

Sarah took the paper and placed it carefully in her bag. 'Thank you. Here are mine.' She took his pen and carefully wrote her contact details on the front page of his folder.

Toby wanted to ask so much more, but their time together—at least for today—had come to an end. Above and beyond everything else, he needed to find out when he could see her again. 'When will you be here next?' He hoped she would be back soon but did not want to appear too pushy. However, he need not have worried.

'I'd wondered about coming back for the first rehearsal so I could be involved right from the start of the production. But after what I've seen today, I'll definitely be here for it.'

'I'll see you there then.'

'Yes.'

'And until then I'll make sure I keep you up to date with all the production news.'

'Thank you. That would be very useful.'

Despite the urgency of the summons from Maggie, they had both lost the power of movement.

Hetty erupted out of the Jubilee Room to interrupt their tableau. 'You need to get a move on Tobe. We haven't got all day.'

'I'd better go. I'll call you soon.'

'Yes. Please do.'

Toby turned back along the corridor and disappeared into the Jubilee Room with Hetty, who gave Sarah a long and meaningful look before she closed the door behind them. Sarah then left the Village Hall and set off on the short walk back to her aunt's house.

When Sarah had moved to London last year, her aunt had issued her with an open invitation to escape to the country if she ever had a free weekend. Initially, Sarah had been too busy to take up her offer, but after last autumn, the prospect of a weekend away from a city full of painful memories had become an increasingly attractive proposition.

On Sarah's first visit in February, Joan had been suffering from a heavy cold and, despite Sarah's protestations about the childish nature of pantomime, insisted that Sarah use her ticket for a village outing to the production of *Cinderella*: this led to her first meeting with Toby. Their encounter was entirely unexpected and in no way unwelcome; she only regretted she had been unable to let him know she would not be able to come to the party after all.

During this visit, Joan had told her that the villagers would be performing her play as their summer production. Her aunt's enthusiasm as she broke the news had been contagious, and Sarah decided she would like to be involved as well. However, this second meeting with Toby unsettled her; the rational part of her mind knew his presence in the Village Hall was coincidental, but the irrational part wondered if some unseen force was trying to bring the two of them together. As she walked back along the lane leading to her aunt's house, she tried to decide whether she should mention to her aunt that she and Toby had met once before during her visit in February.

Chapter 6
The First Rehearsal

'When preparing a new production, Duncan never held with a long period of rehearsal. In order to avoid any trouble from the Guild, the actors needed to know the script and stick to every word of it, but they could only work out where to stand on stage once they knew where they would be performing.'

The Musician's Destiny

Josh turned into the lane running along the side of Somerton Court and parked in a space behind a red sports car, immaculate apart from the stream of fluid running down a rear wheel arch and puddling on the tarmac around the tyre. A wooden gate in the thick hedge bordering the lane gave him access to the extensive grounds. Once through the gate, he took the public footpath leading towards the string of paddocks adjacent to the formal gardens and the open-air theatre, all now basking in the warm sunshine of an early May morning.

Ahead of him, a sizeable crowd had already assembled in the largest paddock, everyone eager and ready for the first rehearsal to begin. Despite the sunshine, all the women wore long skirts, and none of the men had turned up in shorts; everyone had taken Maggie's instructions to heart and was keen to make a good first impression. As he walked towards the disparate mass of humanity on display, Josh regarded them with astonishment, and wondered yet again about the strange alchemical process that, over the forthcoming weeks of rehearsal, would transform the disparate mass into the inhabitants of the same village over a century ago.

Josh knew he was a good actor, and in previous productions he had often coasted through rehearsals in order to save his energy for performances. However, with Chris in the cast for this production, he planned to perform at full pitch from day one. He had even made time to watch several documentaries about the First World War, although he had skipped forward through the boring bits. He still felt resentful that Maggie had cast Chris without an audition, and he planned to do whatever he could to show her what she had missed by not casting him as David.

On the far side of the adjacent paddock and standing close to the path that continued towards the open-air theatre, he spotted Chris in conversation with Kate, both laughing at whatever he had just said. Adam, skulking close to the tightly clipped hedge separating the theatre from the garden, gazed at the pair with a deep scowl on his face, completely oblivious to Louise, Helen, and Jane slowly converging on him from different directions. Meanwhile, the other cast members continued with their important conversations as they watched Toby and his team carry the heavy wooden furniture the actors would use for rehearsals out of the large, restored barn situated between the paddocks. During performances the cast would use the barn as their communal dressing room, but for the moment it served as a useful store for rehearsal props and furniture.

As the clock in the stable yard approached the hour, he saw Maggie emerge from the big house, make her way down through the formal gardens, and then call the cast together in the largest paddock. He then watched as she launched into a pre-rehearsal pep talk. 'Welcome one and all as we take our first faltering steps on this epic journey we are about to undertake. We have but two simple objectives that will govern all our work over the next few weeks. Our first task will be to discover the play concealed within the script. Then, once we have located it, we will set it free for our audiences to experience.'

These comments provoked quizzical faces from several of the less experienced actors, who assumed Maggie had cast them to perform in the village play rather than set off on a journey of discovery and liberation.

Oblivious to their confusion, Maggie continued with her speech. 'This will be an ensemble production, and to me you are all equal. Our challenge is to portray the whole range of village society on our small stage, and to do this, our production must be fluid in every respect. Thus you, my actors, must work as a united team with Toby and his stage crew. Your challenge, as you help them move props and furniture, will be to remain in character so you do not interrupt the action of the play as it continues around you.' The shocked faces of the cast as they took in this bombshell made Josh smile; clearly, many regarded such menial work as beneath them.

Once Maggie had finished speaking, it amused Josh to see those unhappy with her words muttering darkly to each other. However, Maggie had already established her authority by her pep talk after the audition, so for the moment no one dared to disagree with her openly. Nonetheless, Josh knew Toby and his team would face numerous skirmishes with the most recalcitrant of the actors before they all accepted Maggie's intended style of production and worked together as an effective ensemble. He was, as a rule, not a betting man, but somehow, he knew Maggie would ultimately get her own way.

The play opened with a large crowd scene introducing the major characters in the village and establishing the local community. Maggie planned to spend the morning working on this, and her instructions to the cast were simple: work out the village hierarchy by finding out 'who's screwing who and who pays the rent—the rest is merely window-dressing'. Once again, Josh saw several veterans of past productions, accustomed to George's gentle touch and liberal flattery to obtain the results he wanted, mutter unhappily to each other. However, despite a few raised eyebrows at her choice of language, their owners soon set to work along with everyone else.

The opening scene also set up the story of the struggle between David and Herbert for the favours of Rose, a young village woman, played by Louise. While they waited for their first entrance, Josh asked Chris and Adam for their thoughts as to how the three of them could best work together within the larger ensemble. Adam looked worried and remained silent, but Chris immediately pointed out that although they all appeared in the same number of scenes, he had far more lines, and as such, Josh and Adam were merely supporting characters to his starring role. This unexpected exchange set the tone for the rest of the day, and as soon as the three began work on the scene, the escalating displays of macho rivalry between Josh and Chris made their mutual antagonism clear to all.

The scene took place as the villagers made their way home after a church service, and the script called for a minor scuffle as David, Herbert, and Lawrence encountered Rose and her two friends. Maggie instructed Chris and Josh to work out some horseplay that felt natural and unforced, but as the pair rehearsed the scene, this minor scuffle grew into a display of physical force that increased with each run-through.

In the final session before they were due to break for lunch, Chris completely abandoned the choreographed horseplay they had worked on earlier, brutally shoved into Josh, and almost knocked him over. In response, Josh jumped onto

Chris's back, thereby causing him to lose his footing on a patch of damp grass. Chris had not been hurt by his fall, but when he stood up, dark stains had appeared on the knees of his trousers, and from the look on his face, Josh saw he planned a retaliation that went far beyond what Maggie had requested.

Maggie had been moving around the two actors as she scrutinised their performances from every angle, but suddenly she forced herself between them, pushed them apart, and brought the rehearsal to an abrupt halt. They were strong performers, but she was more powerful than the pair of them. 'I think this is a good time for us to take a break. I appreciate the way you've both inhabited your roles so quickly, but that was a little too authentic for my liking. I don't have the luxury of understudies, so I can't afford any permanent damage to my actors.'

Chris and Josh continued to glare at each other while Maggie addressed the rest of the cast. 'Thank you for all your hard work this morning. We've made good progress already. We'll break for lunch now, but please make sure you're back on time this afternoon as we have a great deal more we need to cover before we finish tonight.'

The rehearsal broke up, and people began to drift off home or set off towards the Puppy and Duckling in search of refreshment, all glad of a break after the energetic movement exercises Maggie had insisted on to start the rehearsal. This first morning session had involved far more physical work than they had ever experienced under the benevolent regime of George. Josh and Adam waited while Toby and Sarah, who had sat together throughout the whole session as he made numerous notes in the prompt copy, set up the wooden table, benches, and stools for the afternoon session. By the time they had finished this work, most of the other actors had left the paddock.

The four were finally ready to leave themselves when Maggie called over to Josh and Adam. 'Before you two go, I'd like a quick word if you don't mind. There's something I need to discuss with you and Chris.'

As he followed Maggie back towards the furniture Toby and Sarah had set out, Josh wondered what she wanted to say; he assumed it would be a few words of reprimand about their behaviour during the rehearsal. If she mentioned the scene they had just been rehearsing, he would explain he had been keen to explore the latent violence inherent in the society of the period, a line he remembered from one of the documentaries he had watched.

Chris had sprawled out on one of the long benches, so Josh made a great play of sitting next to him while Adam perched on a small stool off to one side. They did not have to wait long to discover the reason for their unexpected summons.

Throughout the morning's rehearsal, Maggie had displayed an effervescent confidence that had inspired the cast to work hard, but she paused for a moment before she spoke and initially appeared almost nervous. 'I need to talk to you three together because I want to make a change to the way we play the scene where you're getting ready for the Harvest Supper.' She scrutinised Chris and Josh carefully, keen to gauge their reaction to her request. 'I'll come straight to the point: rather than washing in a basin, I want you both to take a bath, so I need to know how you feel about appearing naked. It'll only be for a moment, and of course, I'm not putting any pressure on you. However, in my view, this is one of the key scenes of the play…'

As he heard Maggie's words, Josh immediately thought that being sacked from the production would be far preferable to what she had proposed. Then his brain went into overdrive as he tried to work out how he and Chris could reject what she had asked, although of course only for valid artistic reasons. He wondered if, despite the obvious antagonism between the pair of them, they might somehow establish some form of temporary alliance and suggest a different way to play the scene.

This faint hope vanished the moment he heard Chris's reply. 'It's nice of you to ask, but you saw me perform the Full Monty, so you probably already know my answer.'

Maggie laughed. 'I'll take that as a "yes" then.'

Josh knew even the smallest scrap of information might direct him towards a safe escape route: he needed to find out more about the performance Chris had mentioned. 'Was that the play or the musical?'

'Neither: merely an ad hoc routine at our office Christmas party.'

'And what did you do?'

'Me and a couple of mates decided to perform the Full Monty. We did the full version—and someone filmed us for posterity.'

Maggie laughed. 'It was an extremely revealing performance.'

Josh had only recently met Maggie and had no idea of her background but could not imagine her working in the same organisation as Chris. 'Were you there too?'

‘I directed a production of the play last year, and when Chris heard about it, he sent me the recording as his audition piece. Unfortunately, I’d already cast the show.’

‘It was your loss, not mine.’ Chris turned to Josh. ‘If you want to see it for yourself, it’s still online somewhere.’

Josh grimaced. ‘I think I’ll pass if it’s all the same with you.’

Maggie laughed again. ‘And what about you, Josh?’

Every life includes at least one moment when a coherent and immediate response is required summing up an entirely reasonable but total opposition to what has been asked without causing offence—and Josh now faced such a moment. But he knew that even if he could think of such a response, he would be unable to use it: Chris had already agreed to Maggie’s request, so he had no choice over his answer. He therefore summoned all his ability as an actor and tried to give the appearance of someone without a care in the world. ‘Well, I’ve not appeared naked on stage before, but I’ve always believed there has to be a first time for everything. So, if that’s what you want for this scene, then it’s fine by me as well.’ He paused and swallowed hard. ‘After all, you’re the director, and it’s your show.’

He noticed a look of sudden relief on Maggie’s face. ‘Thank you. I appreciate your commitment very much. That’s all I had to say, so enjoy your lunch, and please be back here promptly.’

Chris accompanied Maggie out of the paddock, and the pair immediately set off towards the Puppy and Duckling at a swift walk. Josh watched until they were out of sight and then turned to Adam, a look of utter desperation on his face. ‘I need a large drink—now.’

Adam had followed the various exchanges with open-mouthed horror, terrified that Maggie might have similar plans for him as well. But, with Maggie safely gone, he regained the power of speech, and he had just one question on his mind. ‘Are you actually going to do it?’

By now, all of Josh’s earlier calm had evaporated. ‘I’ll have to. Chris said he’d do it, so I had to say “Yes” as well. All I have to do now is convince myself I *can* do it. Then I’ll have to do it for real, first in front of the whole cast and then in front of what’s likely to be a sell-out audience every night.’ He turned to Adam. ‘Have *you* ever done anything like this?’

‘No. Never.’

‘Lucky you!’

Adam decided he had to come clean; after everything he had experienced since the rehearsal started, his life had become far too complicated for him to do anything other than to tell the truth, the whole truth, and nothing but the truth. 'What I mean is I've never been in a play before, or at least not a proper one. Toby persuaded me to come to the audition, and then suddenly here I am with a big part in it.'

Josh tried to laugh, but the attempt died on his lips. 'I hadn't realised Toby could be so persuasive. What on earth did he say?'

'He told me Kate would be at the audition. She was, and she's brilliant. Then Chris turned up, and he's brilliant too, far better than I could ever be.'

Despite his gnawing anxiety, Josh could not let Adam's praise pass without qualification. 'He's good, I'll give him that, but he's not brilliant.'

Adam carried on regardless. 'Now I'm in the play, along with Kate and Chris. We all saw this morning he fancies her, and they spent ages together talking and smiling, so she's bound to like him too. It's the story of my life all over again; I see someone I like, for once I manage to meet up with her, and then she goes off with someone else.'

Even in his current state of post-traumatic shock, Josh could not overlook this small chance for revenge on Chris, and a note of determination crept into his voice. 'Just because the bastard walks in and grabs the best part in the play doesn't mean he gets the girl as well.'

Adam looked at Josh in amazement: it had never occurred to him that he could change the course of what he had always regarded as his preordained future. 'No?'

'We need to work together on how you behave during rehearsals to make sure you don't blow it with Kate. There are plenty of other people in the cast who haven't been in one of these village shows before, so no one needs to know this is your first play. Most of the actors will be busy trying to steal scenes from each other so that shouldn't be too difficult—as long as you don't mention it.'

'But I thought being in this play was going to be a quiet, relaxing experience.'

'Quiet? Relaxing? Don't you believe it! Beneath the tranquil surface of rehearsals, this production is a seething mass of jealousy, treachery, lust and lechery—like so many other aspects of everyday life in this wonderful village. Despite all this, I wouldn't miss a chance to be in this show for the world—even after what I've just agreed to.' Josh fell silent and then gave a hysterical giggle.

'If I'm going to have the family jewels on display, they'll need to look their best, so I need to get myself off to the gym pretty damn fast.'

He paused again and scrutinised Adam carefully. 'I don't want to appear personal, but even though you keep your towel on, you might like to come along as well—to make sure you look your best for Kate. While we're there, we can start your training. There's a massive amount we need to cover if you're going to stand a chance of getting the girl in the final scene.'

By now, Adam had travelled so far out of his comfort zone that he had lost the power of speech and had to indicate his consent with a nod. After everything he had experienced over the course of the morning, he needed a large drink as well.

It did not take Adam and Josh long to reach the Puppy and Duckling, and Adam immediately spotted Toby deep in conversation with Sarah at a table in the far corner of the garden. Josh, his state of shock deepening with every passing moment, could do no more than gaze unseeingly around the crowded space, so Adam began to lead him through the maze of crowded tables towards Toby and Sarah. However, loud voices calling his name from elsewhere in the garden made Adam stop, causing Josh to bump into him. Adam turned round to see the Coven waving and pointing at the empty seats around the table they had commandeered near the front door, a clear invitation for Adam and Josh to join them. Adam reluctantly changed direction, and Josh followed behind as before.

The inevitable question came from Jane even before they sat down. 'So what did Maggie want to talk to you about?'

Despite his state of shock, Josh knew what he had agreed to do would soon be common knowledge throughout the village. However, determined to keep the news to himself for as long as possible, he did his best to delay the inevitable by using ambiguity and playing the matter down. 'Oh, nothing much. She only wanted to run a few ideas past us for one of our scenes in Act Two.'

As a relative stranger to the world of drama, Jane did not understand much about the process of direction and always relied on Louise and Helen to tell her where to stand, when to move, and when to speak. Therefore, she merely gazed brightly at Josh, and for a few seconds he thought he might have succeeded in delaying the moment of truth.

However, he had overlooked Adam, still mightily relieved by his own narrow escape, who had never possessed even the slightest appreciation of ambiguity.

'Her idea is that for the scene where we're all getting ready for the Harvest Supper, rather than just washing in a bowl, he and Chris are going to take a bath.'

Louise snorted loudly as she choked on her wine, and it took her a moment to recover her poise. 'So soon we'll see which of you two *really* has the biggest parts.'

Josh gave a sickly grin; he knew that from this moment on his life would be hell, and he wondered how he could escape from the conversation. He glanced in desperation towards the door of the pub and wondered if an offer of a round of drinks might allow him at least a temporary respite. While his addled brain struggled to analyse the merits of this plan, Chris stepped out through the door and then turned back to speak to someone still inside the bar.

Louise followed his gaze and, as Chris walked out into the garden with Kate close behind, her face lit up and she called over to him. 'Chris, if you have a moment I wonder if you could confirm a small matter for us?' Either Chris had not heard her call above the general babble of conversation in the crowded garden or had chosen to ignore her, so she tried again. 'We need to know if it's true.'

Chris had so far managed to avoid any more conversation with the Coven than had been necessary for the purpose of the rehearsal, but he could not ignore a direct question. As the pair reached the group, Kate smiled shyly at Adam and then glanced happily at the distant sight of Toby and Sarah together at their table. Chris, however, remained as frosty as he had been throughout the whole of the morning session. 'Is what true?'

A broad grin appeared on Louise's face. 'Bath time for you and Josh.'

'If you choose to put it like that, then yes, it is.'

'So when will you two hang your washing on the line?'

'Sorry?'

'When are you going to rehearse it?'

'Maggie only mentioned it before we set off to come here, but I assume we'll do it when we start work on Act Two.'

'But when are you going to do it for real? You know, *au naturel*.'

'Whenever she wants us to. The sooner, the better as far as I'm concerned, so everyone has time to get used to it.'

Louise beamed at Helen who merely nodded her approval as she had still not recovered the power of speech. Meanwhile, Jane sat immobile and open-mouthed. 'It's a pleasure to work with someone who's so committed to this production.'

Chris absorbed the compliment without difficulty. 'We can't spoil the scene by having anyone feel awkward or embarrassed about it.'

Even the thought of the scene made Josh feel both awkward and embarrassed, and in yet another attempt to reassure himself, he tried to put Maggie's request into perspective. 'All we have to do is get in and out of a bath, and it'll be over in a moment. We're not doing a song and dance number or anything like that.'

His voice could not conceal his anxiety, and Chris turned on him. 'You're absolutely right. But we'll need to work out the moves for every single element of the scene, and if this morning's session is anything to go by, it'll be a long, slow, repetitive process.'

The morning's rehearsal had ground to a halt several times as Kate tried out different readings of her lines during each run-through of the opening scene. Her experiments had confused some of the less experienced actors, but she always behaved like this during early rehearsals. 'We all need to find our characters. It wasn't bad for a first run-through.'

Chris looked at her. 'No, and from the way you're playing the scene now, you've definitely cracked it. You were brilliant.' He turned to address the entire group. 'But we have to get all our scenes up to the same level. We need to rehearse the bath scene so many times that you don't even notice Josh and I have our kit off.' He glanced at Louise. 'It would spoil all our hard work if you laugh when Josh jumps out of the bath, so you need to get used to us doing it for real.'

Louise's grin grew even broader. 'We'll definitely need plenty of time to see you both with your kit off. We're all one hundred per cent committed to this production, but we're only amateurs, so sometimes we can be slow learners.'

Helen and Jane nodded their agreement, and Josh, who had followed the exchanges in silence, went pale. Chris noticed this and turned to him. 'What's the matter, Josh? You're not getting cold feet, are you?'

Josh's fevered brain had worked out that it might be possible for him, if not to avoid the inevitable, then at least to delay it. 'I'm not getting cold anything.' He turned to the Coven. 'This is not a criticism of your obvious talents as actors, but my instinct tells me your characters need to be surprised when they see me in the bath. Don't forget Maggie wants us to perform every scene with authenticity.'

Louise looked puzzled. 'So what are you proposing?'

'We need to retain the element of novelty. I'll do the scene bollock naked exactly like Maggie asked, but only when the weather's warmed up a bit. I don't want my old man to die of indecent exposure, so you'll have to wait until the dress rehearsal for me to introduce him.'

Chris ignored his desperate attempt at humour. 'We need to rehearse the scene properly. We all have some complicated moves, and we owe it to Maggie—and the rest of the cast—to get the details right.'

'I couldn't agree more. I'm happy to jump in and out of the bath as many times as I need to until we get every single move right—as long as I keep my boxers on.'

An ominous silence followed, and Josh, sensing he had almost managed to delay the dreaded day, looked around for support. 'Adam, what do you think?'

Adam carefully considered everything he had heard. 'You've both missed something important.'

Chris turned on him with a monosyllabic snarl. 'What?'

'We can't rehearse the scene at all until we have a bath.'

He had made a valid point, so Chris turned and shouted over to Toby, still deep in conversation with Sarah at their distant table. 'Toby, we need to check something with you.'

Toby put down his papers and threaded his way between the tables of lunchtime diners to join them, while Chris waited impatiently.

'We need a bath full of hot water for Act Two.'

'I know. We're trying to locate one at the moment, but the bath is only one item on a long list of props and furniture that Maggie adds to each time we see her. We also need to work out how to fill it with warm water as the taps in the garden only supply cold.'

Josh realised although he had not found an escape route, he at least now had a valid reason to delay the rehearsal. 'All those other items on your list are bound to be much more important, so we don't want to burden you unnecessarily. How long do you think it'll take to locate a bath for us to rehearse the scene?'

'It's difficult to tell. I've left the search for props to Hetty as she has good local contacts, but probably a week or two at most.'

Josh put on a reasonable display of disappointment. 'There's your answer. What a shame! Looks like we'll have to delay our work on the scene for a while after all.'

Louise opened her handbag and extracted her diary. 'Shall we set a date then? Two weeks from today?'

Chris nodded. 'Fine by me.'

Josh rccognised that, against the odds, he had somehow managed to win today's battle even though he had already conceded the war. 'Okay then.'

Louise returned her diary to her bag. 'Good. That's settled then. I'll let Maggie know when we go back to Somerton Court. I'd hate to think she didn't add it to the schedule.'

Josh made a mental note to follow the long-range weather forecast on a daily basis.

Chapter 7
The Production Meeting

'The Guild did not actively promote the use of torture. Nonetheless it possessed an enviable range of torture instruments and, for the most part, merely the sight of these was sufficient to loosen all but the most recalcitrant of tongues. The torture chamber was also open for guided tours at weekends and public holidays, subject to the payment of a small emolument to the caretaker.'

The Musician's Destiny

Each hour contains precisely sixty minutes, and at the end of twenty-four such periods what has been the present becomes the past. Then the rigid and unceasing process begins once more, and thus is history made. But, when you look forward, time can be more flexible; sometimes, a whole month passes as quickly as a week, while at other times, a single hour can feel as long as a day. In the end, it all depends on how soon you want your future to arrive.

For Toby, the next two weeks could not pass quickly enough. In long working days tied to his desk, he juggled numerous deadlines for the massive proposal currently edging its way through the uncharted labyrinth known as corporate governance, while he filled his evenings attempting to resolve the actions resulting from George's production meetings. George regarded his role of executive producer as essentially managerial, and as such delegated all the real work to the members of his team.

Outside of these commitments, Toby tried to devote any spare time to his writing. The encounter with Sarah had fired his imagination, and he had now drafted three new chapters that unexpectedly reunited his hero with the mysterious woman. However, despite this welcome progress he struggled to work out how to develop their embryonic relationship any further, let alone bring it to an appropriate resolution. After another long evening exploring numerous fruitless scenarios that all led nowhere, he decided to leave a space in his draft and return to the issue later.

Toby's recent inspiration had been further boosted by an unexpected invitation from Sarah, or rather an invitation from her aunt that Sarah had delivered, for him to come for dinner after the rehearsal on Saturday. As a bonus, Sarah planned to spend a long weekend in East Upbury so she could attend George's next production meeting due to take place that evening. Toby regarded this as a meaningful decision on her part, and ever since she told him of her plans, he had been counting the days until they could meet up again.

Tonight's meeting involved only Toby and his immediate team, so George had suggested they should meet at his house rather than at the Puppy and Duckling, the venue for their previous sessions. As Toby drove along the familiar roads towards East Upbury, he thought yet again about the invitation for dinner. He felt he should not underestimate the significance of the event as it would be the first time he and Sarah spent any time together not directly related to the play. He would also be meeting Sarah's aunt for the first time; he knew Sarah held her aunt in high regard, so he needed to make a good impression on her as well.

When Toby arrived in the village, he could see no sign of Sarah's car outside George's house, a carefully extended brick cottage in a quiet lane on the outskirts of the village, but he assumed she would have walked the short distance from Joan's house. When he rang the doorbell, Peggy opened the door and greeted him with her customary hug and generous kisses on both cheeks, before escorting him to the lounge. George and Hetty faced each on the two massive sofas dominating the room, but of Sarah, there was no sign. Toby sat down next to Hetty, and George immediately proposed they should start their business.

Toby's face could not hide his disappointment. 'Is it only us then?'

'Indeed it is. Sarah called me just now to let me know that a crisis at work has kept her in the office all day. She'll be needed tomorrow as well, so she won't arrive until Saturday morning.'

Over the course of the rehearsals, Hetty had, much to Toby's surprise as George had warned him about her reputation, taken him under her wing; she now gave him a reassuring pat on his leg. 'Don't worry, Tobe. She'll be here in time for your date on Saturday evening. Remember what they say about absence making the heart grow fonder: it works both ways.'

Toby had shared his delight in the unexpected invitation with Hetty the previous weekend, and now noticed a quizzical look on George's face as he disappeared into the kitchen. He soon returned with a tray of drinks but made no mention of what he had heard because, despite her relaxed demeanour with Toby, Hetty still terrified him.

After serving the drinks, George moved towards the fireplace and turned to face them, an unhappy look on his face. 'Before we start on our business for the evening, there's a matter of some delicacy I need to raise with you both. Under no circumstances must my words go beyond these four walls. Do you understand?'

Hetty nodded, and Toby muttered his consent. 'Thank you. I need to speak frankly about the Ministry of Love. They hold the purse strings for this production, and as executive producer, they're making my life an absolute misery.'

This sudden diversion into village politics surprised Toby. He knew nothing about the subject but felt he should, at a minimum, express some sympathy. 'I'm sorry to hear that.'

Inevitably, Hetty, always fully briefed on all such local machinations, offered a more practical response. 'Do you want me to sort them out? My mate Percy has several friends who could arrange something appropriate for you—advance payment in cash and complete discretion guaranteed.'

George looked pensive. 'Your offer is tempting, but I'm afraid I'll have to decline it. However, I digress: the news I need to share with you is that last week the committee formally instructed me to remind Maggie, in the politest possible terms of course, that this is a community production, and as such she needs to involve the whole community.'

This made no sense to Toby. 'I thought she already had. She was extremely diplomatic in her casting; she even gave Jane a good part.'

George nodded appreciatively. 'Speaking as both a local resident and a fellow director, I believe her casting has been exemplary throughout. She kindly gave Peggy the perfect role as Mrs Wilson: a chance for her to display her considerable talents as she marshals the domestic staff to prepare for the family wedding.'

Now Hetty looked puzzled. 'So what, exactly, are they complaining about this time?'

'The way the production is going to look. Malcolm and Cynthia have a beautiful home full of furniture from exactly this period. They were keen to lend a few of the less valuable pieces, subject to full insurance cover and a prominent acknowledgement in the programme. But when they made the offer to Maggie in the Puppy and Duckling, she turned them down flat: she said they weren't authentic. After Cynthia had recovered, Malcolm told me they felt Maggie had accused them of having reproduction furniture. There's no way the Ministry of Love could sack Maggie as it's far too late to change horses at this point in the production. So, earlier this week, Cynthia's cronies convened an extraordinary committee meeting that resulted in yours truly getting it in the neck.'

Toby had no idea who these people were, but he did know, as with most issues relating to the play, that Maggie had made the right call. 'I've not seen the furniture you mentioned, but I'm with Maggie on this. Most of the antiques we have from this period didn't come from houses like those in this village—even though that's where they ended up. The majority of villagers were labourers, farm workers, or in some form of domestic service. Whatever furniture they had would be absolutely basic.'

George regarded Toby over the top of his reading glasses. 'Ah! The voice of the historian. I'd forgotten about your fascination with matters long past. So tell me, what are your thoughts on the matter?'

Toby had expected an evening of routine but necessary conversation about the outstanding technical issues of the production and jumped at this chance to discuss his favourite subject. 'Maggie wants to do full justice to the story we're telling and to show the reality of daily life—not provide a showcase for a load of antiques. The play's about history, not heritage.'

'Forgive me for asking, but aren't they the same?'

'No. History is what happened. Heritage is what people *think* happened: bourgeois nostalgia looking back through rose-tinted spectacles at a time and a place that never existed.'

Hetty let out a low whistle. 'Careful, Tobe! If the Ministry of Love hears views like those, they'll be after you for thought crime.'

'This period wasn't the long hot Edwardian summer with daily life played out against a soundtrack by Elgar. Everyone agrees on what happened in the summer of 1914, but war broke out after more than a decade of political unrest, a raft of strikes, and a whole string of international crises.'

Peggy never entered a room if she could make an entrance, and Toby fell silent as she swept magnificently into the lounge, dressed to go out for the evening. George glanced up at her. 'It's a shame you have to leave us as this is rather interesting. Toby's been explaining what life was like for those who lived around here in the years before 1914.'

Toby tried to summarise what he had discovered about the history of the village from his research in the local library. 'East Upbury was a small agricultural community dominated by a few moneyed families in the big houses.'

Peggy laughed. 'In that regard, the place has never changed: this village is stuck in a perpetual time warp. Once you scrape off the veneer of modernity, the feudal structure soon shows through.'

Toby had no desire to broaden their discussion to examine the ongoing legacy of feudalism, so he steered the conversation back to the early twentieth century. 'The people in the big houses before the Great War hadn't been there very long themselves. A few generations earlier their forebears had made their fortunes in the industrial revolution. Then they escaped from the smoke up north, bought country estates down here from hard up squires, and then hired the locals as domestic staff and estate workers.'

As the implications of Toby's words sunk in, a look of delight appeared on Peggy's face. 'So, despite all their airs, our friends—and I use the term advisedly—in the Ministry of Love are actually the descendants of tradespeople. If that's the case, they certainly keep their ancestry pretty quiet.'

Toby had not encountered this idiosyncratic interpretation of history before, but he could not discount it completely. 'In a manner of speaking—yes.'

A look of triumph filled Peggy's face. 'Marvellous. Would you like to give a talk about this to our History Society? I'd love to see the reaction it provokes when our members find out where their ancestors came from.'

George had followed their exchange with interest, but knew they still had a great deal they needed to discuss on all the outstanding work required for the play. 'Perhaps you could suggest it for next season's programme?' He turned to Toby. 'The point is the Ministry of Love has a stranglehold on this village, and as a result, they're trying to impose their own view of what they see as our glorious heritage on the play.'

He paused and struck mock heroic pose. 'But, as founder of the festival, I feel it my duty to support a fellow director realise her authentic vision for the production. I therefore intend to help Maggie achieve her aims at whatever personal cost to myself, especially if her vision puts the collective noses of the Ministry of Love out of joint. I'll do whatever I can to make sure every single costume, prop, and piece of furniture is properly authentic, and I'll be honoured to share the credit for the success of her show.' He looked at Peggy. 'Then next year, with Maggie well away from here and the Ministry of Love still in shock from her radical naturalism, we can stage whatever we want.'

'My vote is we go back to Shakespeare. I've never understood why people see him as elitist; his plays have been around for centuries and never failed to pull in a sell-out audience when you staged them in previous years.' She turned to Toby. 'I can't believe all this fuss they're making about events that happened over a hundred years ago. It's so in the past.'

'But that's the point: in terms of history, a hundred years is nothing.'

As this unexpected digression continued, Hetty became increasingly exasperated: in her world, everyone agreed what had to be done and who would do it, and then it happened. Unfortunately, the rest of the village preferred talking about an issue while waiting for it to give up and go away of its own accord. 'You know what, Tobe, you're a nice guy, and I really like you. However, I think you'd enjoy your life a whole lot more if you focussed on living in the present rather than worrying about all those dead people.'

'But it's important. Someone has to remember what really happened. You can never let anyone rewrite history—or even worse make up their own.'

This remark sowed a new seed of confusion within Peggy. 'But how can you rewrite history—or even make it up? It's not like Shakespeare where you can cut a few lines or extemporise a little if you misremember a speech because the original text will always still be there. In history, once an event happens, it's happened for all time.'

George tried to explain. 'I think what Toby means is that you have to interpret the historical record objectively and not twist the facts, or even invent a few new ones, merely to justify a pre-agreed conclusion.'

'Then perhaps Toby should come along to my meeting. Our talk tonight is *Dykes through the Ages: An Illustrated History of Local Ditches*. He can make sure our speaker is telling the truth. Apparently, some of the ditches round here go back centuries.'

'It sounds fascinating, but it's not really my period. There wasn't much call for ditches in twentieth-century history, although there were plenty of trenches after 1914.'

'What a shame! If I can't tempt you, then I shall have to go alone. No doubt I shall see you all again soon. A bientot.' She gave George a dazzling smile.

‘After the talk, we plan to continue our ditching discussions in the Puppy and Duckling, so I may be a little late.’

George watched as Peggy swept from the room and waited until he heard the front door close before he spoke. ‘Does the house seem suddenly emptier to you? I think we should finally make a start on the business of the evening.’

Hetty picked up her notebook and turned to Toby. ‘I’ve already told George what we’ve sourced so far. Everyone I approached has ransacked their attics and sheds, and I’ve been able to tick off nearly all the props and furniture Maggie wants—although she still thinks some of the items are too good.’ She scanned her list again. ‘The one major item still missing is a proper tin bath; the only one I’ve found so far is probably too small and looks like it’s come from a nursery. The Coven have been looking forward to next weekend for ages, and I’ve got a reputation to live up to, so I urgently need to find something bigger. Do either of you have any ideas?’

George laughed. ‘I think I can do better than that. We have a galvanised bath I use to capture rainwater in the garden. I’m not sure of its provenance, but it’s fairly ancient, and more importantly, it’s absolutely watertight.’

Toby looked at them both. ‘We’re unlikely to have any experts in early twentieth-century domestic appliances in the audience, so it could be exactly what we want.’

George stood up. ‘Let’s take a look while it’s still light. It would be good to tick the item off your list while you’re both here.’

Toby and Hetty followed George out into his well-kept garden, and the bath proved to be entirely suitable for their needs. Toby had never encountered such an object at close quarters before, and as he examined the cold metal surfaces, he was glad he had been born into an age of indoor plumbing and separate bathrooms so there had never been any need for him to use one. He wondered what Josh would think when he saw the bath for the first time.

Josh felt like a condemned man who has exhausted every right of appeal against a capital sentence: with every passing day the date of his execution drew inexorably closer. In the first of many sleepless nights since Maggie had detonated her bombshell, he had calculated that in the time left before the dress rehearsal, he could visit the gym at least five times each week. If he also gave up all forms of carbohydrate and alcohol, then, all things considered, he might be in marginally better shape by the dress rehearsal. Nobody could describe Josh as in any way overweight or even noticeably unfit. However, as the Coven had delighted in pointing out to him, Chris clearly worked out regularly, and they had probed him mercilessly on the details of his own fitness regime. When the day of the dress rehearsal finally dawned, he knew the Coven would offer forthright feedback on everything they saw.

In fact, Josh also used a gym on a regular basis, but in his case, 'regular' meant 'fortnightly' and then only to swim in the pool for half an hour or so. However, he now planned to make daily visits after work and acquaint himself in detail with the various pieces of technology filling the main hall. He knew it was not much of a plan, but at least it occupied his mind and helped reduce the permanent state of panic that threatened to turn him into a gibbering wreck. Needless to say, he had made no mention of the play at work; his friends and colleagues there had never shown any enthusiasm for purchasing tickets for any previous plays in which he had performed, but this time he had remained uncharacteristically silent about every aspect of the production.

He somehow managed to reach the end of the first week with his plan still on track. However, the weekend had brought no relief: the Coven spent both days bombarding him with endless questions about his workout schedule, which he attempted to deflect without disclosing any specific details.

Meanwhile, Chris ignored every overture from the Coven and instead did his best to spend any spare time in the company of Kate. However, despite all his efforts, she paid him no attention as her desperate search for her character consumed all her spare time: although she shared the same geographical location as the other actors, she now spent most of her time visualising life about a hundred years earlier. Despite Chris's failure, the mere fact of his continued proximity to Kate had filled Adam with gloomy thoughts all weekend. Consequently, he had accepted Josh's invitation to meet up for a joint planning session at the gym; he knew to stand any chance with Kate he needed all the help he could get—even if this involved accepting assistance from Josh.

On Thursday evening, Josh drove into the gym car park for his fourth visit of the week. As he walked towards the entrance, he spotted Adam's car parked close to the door, so he hurried into the locker room to change. Until today, his new regime had resulted in an acceptable level of ongoing pain, but when he crawled out of bed that morning every muscle in his body had screamed in agony. As he climbed the stairs to the gym hall, his legs hurt even more, and only the thought of the looming dress rehearsal kept him going. Since the beginning of the week, he had even used a running machine during each visit, but regardless of his fitness level, he knew he would be unable to run away from the dress rehearsal.

He found Adam deeply engrossed with a weights machine in the gym hall. Despite being a member of the gym for several years, Josh had until last week always steered clear of all such machines, as he regarded them as medieval instruments of torture with some modern high-tech additions. However, he realised Adam appeared to be completely at home with the machine: after straddling the padded seat and placing a pair of thick rubber straps over his shoulders, he had started a series of actions that involved straining forward to pull on the straps, which, in their turn, raised a stack of weights behind him. As Josh approached the machine, Adam made no move to interrupt his workout. Josh therefore lowered himself carefully onto a nearby rowing machine to rest his aching legs and watched as Adam continued with what to him looked like an excessively strenuous session.

After a further minute, Adam still showed no sign of slowing down, so Josh decided to begin his training programme. 'Now we're both here it's time to start your lessons on how to be an actor. The first point is that in addition to your character in the play, you also need a character for rehearsals.'

Despite displaying some signs of struggle with his ongoing exertions, Adam could still talk. 'What?'

Josh realised he needed to take matters slowly, so he explained what he meant. 'Maggie's told us what we need to find out about the background of our characters.'

In the face of such continued heavy exertion, Adam found it impossible to engage in any form of coherent speech, so he slowed down for a moment. 'I know. I'm ploughing through a pile of Toby's books at the moment. I more or less understand the origins of the war, but it's complicated stuff.'

'When Maggie said she wanted us to carry out some research, I don't think she meant us to submit a dissertation.'

'You do it your way, and I'll do it mine. I feel comfortable doing it like this.' Adam resumed the vigorous activity, a clear sign their discussion, at least for the moment, had come to an end.

Josh took the hint and decided to return to his lesson plan. 'But, for rehearsals, you need another character—let's call him "Adam"—who can suggest a range of experience from previous productions without giving too much away.'

Adam paused for a moment to give greater emphasis to his response. 'I'm not telling lies.'

He took a deep breath and resumed his workout while Josh hastened to clarify what he meant. 'You don't need to tell lies. All you have to do is market yourself a bit better. Have you ever been in a play before? Of course I have, but it was a while ago. Be vague, don't mention the school nativity play, and no one will ever check up on you. Got it?'

A slight smile appeared on Adam's face. 'Yes. I can do that.'

Josh allowed himself to relax. Now he had established his first principle he could move on. 'Good. Then we need to establish your character. You know all your lines, but you also need to know the jargon we all use. I mean like "stage right" means "left" and "stage left" means "right".'

Adam stopped again and looked at him with real confusion. 'Why?'

'It's a long story, and in any case, the reason doesn't matter. But, when Maggie tells you to move, you need to make sure you go in the right direction.'

'So left means right and right means left.' He shook his head. 'Illogical, but not difficult to remember.'

Josh decided to build on this success. 'Excellent. Now we move on to upstaging.'

'Let me guess: that means downstaging.' The confusion returned. 'Whatever that means.'

Josh put him out of his misery. 'No downstaging means nothing, at least nothing we need to worry about here. But upstaging is what you do to steal the attention of the audience from another actor, especially when said actor has a big speech.'

'And will this happen?'

'It's bound to. Some people are past masters at it, and they do it without even thinking.' Josh had been guilty of such crimes many times himself, and generally loved to talk at length about his roles in other productions. For the moment, however, he knew he could not afford to be diverted into sharing any such war stories, as he still needed to cover one final key part of his first lesson. 'You also need to be aware of what else is going on during rehearsals.'

He looked around to check the area, but despite the gym still being full of activity, they had the immediate area to themselves with no one else within earshot. 'Do you realise you and Chris are being auditioned for other roles beyond those you have in the play?'

'No. Not at all.'

Josh dropped his voice to a conspiratorial whisper. 'Let me explain. You'll have noted there are a number of unattached women in the cast; for our purposes here tonight, I'm referring specifically to Louise, Helen, and Jane.'

Adam nodded but said nothing, so Josh continued with caution. 'What I mean is if you fail with Kate, then, as long as you play your cards right, you have a fall-back position. If you're lucky, you can even take your pick from among the Coven. Do I make myself clear?'

Adam suddenly became upset. 'I don't want a fall-back position. It's Kate or nothing.'

Josh realised he had pushed his pupil too far for this first session; there would be time enough to explore the other complexities he still had to master during later sessions. 'Good. An excellent attitude. You need to stay focussed.'

A look of determination appeared on Adam's face. 'I'm always focussed. I set a target, and then I meet it. It's always been like that for work. All I need now is to find out how to do the same in what passes for my personal life.' He released himself from the straps and climbed unsteadily to his feet. 'Now it's your turn. Then you can tell me who *your* fall-back position is.'

Josh paused for a moment and then grimaced. 'My problem is I know the Coven too well—and they all know me too. It would be like getting involved with my own sister—if I had a sister.' He pointed to the schematic on the thick metal upright displaying a male torso with prominent abdominal muscles highlighted. 'If I use this machine, will it give me a body like the one on the diagram?'

Adam leant forward and read the text underneath. 'In the long term—yes. But only if you combine it with a change of diet and lifestyle and commit to regular workouts.'

'So it definitely won't have any effect by the time of the show?'

'No way.'

'Shit. Not much use in me wasting my time here then. I think I'll get back to the running machine.' Josh walked slowly across the floor of the gym and made a great play of adjusting the speed of the running machine before pressing the start button, although what he wished he could find was the setting for a downhill incline.

Chapter 8
The Garden

'When on tour with his company, Duncan always accepted invitations for dinner—or indeed for any other meal—offered by local Guild Officials. He knew that once everyone had eaten he would be asked to sing for his supper; in fact, it was impossible to persuade him not to do so.'

The Musician's Destiny

Toby had kept Friday evening free in the hope he might be able to spend it with Sarah, so her delayed arrival meant he now had some unexpected free time. After his initial disappointment when he heard the news from George, he decided to be positive and to devote the evening to working on his novel: the tin bath from the garden of Beech Cottage had allowed him and Hetty to tick off the final item on their long list of props and furniture, so there should be no more urgent issues for them to deal with until closer to the dress rehearsal.

To spend the evening working on his novel had seemed like a good plan, but Toby found it to be far less so when he came to put it into practice; as he began to work his way through his most recent draft, he immediately found his train of thought derailed by thoughts of Sarah. He did his best to ignore these and carry on, but numerous repeat derailments prevented him from making any real progress, and he finally admitted defeat. Abandoning his attempt to make sense of a cryptic comment he had scribbled in the margin a week ago, he instead allowed himself to speculate what might have happened if they had been able to spend the evening together. Each time they met up, something or someone had interrupted them, but this time circumstances had prevented them from meeting up at all.

Toby knew that one of the standard plots of a fantasy novel involved the hero embarking on a quest and overcoming a series of challenges before fulfilling his destiny in the final chapter, and wondered if he had finally put his finger on the reason why he found it so difficult to spend any time alone with Sarah. He then realised he might be able to use this idea to help him untangle his own plotting issues, and decided to devote the remainder of the evening to identifying various challenges his hero might face while undertaking his own quest. After a long and productive session, which resulted in several pages of detailed notes, he ended up going to bed far later than he had planned.

The next morning Toby re-read his notes while he ate a hurried breakfast and laughed at the absurdity of comparing his recent experiences with those of a fantasy hero. He laughed even more when he arrived at Somerton Court to find Sarah, full of apologies, waiting for him with a large bag of croissants she had bought from London and a flask of hot coffee provided by Joan. They enjoyed their late breakfast together, but as the day progressed, Toby began to wonder whether there might, after all, be some truth in his theory about the unknown challenges he still had to face.

After lunch, the cast ran through the whole of Act One for the first time. The experience turned out to be painful in places, but the actors eventually staggered through to the end and Maggie congratulated them on their achievement. Toby hoped this might mean an early end to the rehearsal. However, Maggie then announced she wanted to use the final hour of the afternoon session to allow the principal actors to share one historical fact relevant to their character they had discovered during their research. Maggie and Toby had discussed the history of the period on several occasions, and she now asked him to judge the individual efforts and to award prizes for the most relevant contributions.

Toby generally enjoyed any opportunity to discuss history, but today he had no time to indulge himself as he needed to get home to shower, change, and then return to East Upbury in time for dinner with Joan and Sarah. He began by briefly congratulating everyone on the range of their research. Then he awarded the third prize to Louise for describing the introduction of licensing hours for public houses and the second prize to Adam for a statistically accurate account of casualty rates during the Battle of the Somme: by now, he had read and absorbed most of the books he had borrowed from Toby.

However, Toby caused an outcry when he awarded the first prize to Kate, as she initially announced she could not carry out any research until she had found her character. To Toby's genuine surprise, Adam, now an unexpected expert on the history of the period, came to her rescue; he suggested that an intelligent woman like Maud would have known about the struggle for women's votes, and therefore would have been a suffragette. Kate thanked Adam profusely for his suggestion, an action that caused him to blush deeply. Then she announced she knew a bit about the suffragettes and gave a brief summary of what the movement had achieved.

Despite the spontaneity of Kate's contribution, Toby awarded her the first prize for introducing an important new strand of history into the play. Maggie immediately endorsed his comments and instructed Miss Milton and her team to include suffragette colours in the costumes for Maud and several other female characters, both in the big house and in the village. Toby followed this by answering several questions from other cast members about the history of the period although he tried, for once, to keep his answers as short as possible.

When Toby parked his car outside Joan's house early that evening his hair was still damp, but at least he had arrived on time. As he picked up the bottle of French wine, the recommendation of the manager of his favourite off-licence, and the bunch of variegated poppies, ordered from a local florist, he was relieved to discover they had both survived the short journey unscathed. He hoped Joan would appreciate these delicate allusions to the subject of her play.

There had been little chance for him to have any private conversations with Sarah during the day, as numerous requests from Maggie and George and the endless demands of the cast had kept them both busy. When they finally managed to snatch a moment together as they cleared up after the unexpected history seminar, Sarah only had time to tell him to arrive after half past seven. The clock on the dashboard indicated one minute past that time and, as he locked his car, Toby wondered what the evening would bring.

Joan's house stood at the end of one of the quiet lanes lined with individual properties of very different sizes, ages, and architectural styles leading off from the main road through the village. In front of the house, immaculate stretches of lawn contained several well-stocked flower beds, with the property separated from its neighbours by tall beech hedges on both sides. Toby had no real knowledge of architectural history, but from the large porch, impressive double front, and sash windows, he assumed the property had probably been built in the late Victorian period. A low beech hedge stood between the front garden and the lane, with a small picket gate part way along; behind this, a gravel path bisected the lawns and led straight to the front porch.

Further along the hedge, a five-bar gate opened onto a drive where Toby could see Sarah's car. To the left of the house, a tall trellis covered with wisteria screened the back garden, and beyond this, a large tree and the top of a high brick wall appeared to mark the rear boundary of the property.

As Toby crunched up the path, he brushed past thick borders of lavender hanging over the gravel on both sides, with a similar bed stretching along the base of the trellis; the layout and contents of both the beds and the trellis complemented the style of the house perfectly. The overall effect reminded him of Philip Larkin's line about the men of 1914 "leaving the gardens tidy", and inevitably this made him wonder how the war had affected the family who had once lived here.

However, he had no time to consider the matter further, as before he could lift the knocker, a slim woman in late middle age, wearing a purple tunic over loose yellow trousers, opened the door to greet him. She scrutinised him in silence for a moment with a broad smile on her face. Then she opened her arms in a gesture of welcome. 'Hello, Toby. I've heard so much about you from Sarah, so I'm delighted to finally meet you in person.'

Toby muttered an anodyne 'It's nice to meet you too' in response. He would have liked to have followed this with a string of questions to discover precisely what Sarah had said about him, but instead he merely handed over the wine and the flowers.

Joan made appropriate expressions of thanks for his gifts, and after placing them on the hall table, she enveloped him in a broad hug before kissing him on both cheeks. After this unexpectedly physical first encounter, she took a step back as if to examine him from a distance. This scrutiny unsettled Toby, and her question, when it came, confused him further. 'Tell me—are you Scottish?'

Toby had never encountered such a geographically specific interest in his ancestry at a first meeting; he had lived all his life in England although his father's family originally came from Scotland, and with his own fair hair and pale skin, he sometimes wondered if any of his forebears had arrived there in a longship. Before he could work out how to answer Sarah, a large cotton apron covering her fuchsia pink dress, emerged from the kitchen to rescue him. She wiped the flour off her hands with a cloth, unfastened her apron, and then, much to Toby's surprise and pleasure, kissed him on his cheek before leading him into the lounge. Meanwhile, Joan disappeared into the kitchen with the flowers and the wine.

Observing the look of confusion remaining on Toby's face, Sarah provided an explanation for her aunt's question. 'Joan remembers several of her earlier incarnations. She often meets people she's known in previous lives.'

Toby had no idea how to respond to this comment either and, based on his experience so far, he realised the evening would not be at all as he had anticipated. He decided his safest course of action from now on would be to stick to the truth. 'Actually, I am part Scots.'

As Joan came into the room carrying his flowers, now artfully displayed in a simple glass vase, she nodded in triumph. 'I thought so. You probably don't remember the last time we met, but you were drenched in blood and wearing a kilt.'

Toby would have liked to have learnt more about their previous meeting, but Joan had already moved on. 'Whenever I visit a place, I can feel its history. That's what's so wonderful about this village—the whole place has a real history. I began my play after I'd visited the war memorial. The voices of all those it commemorates started telling me their stories, and I simply had to write them down.'

Despite this insight into the unusual nature of Joan's creative processes, Toby felt he had finally reached safer territory. 'It's a good play, and we're fortunate to have Maggie as director. She has some great ideas, and if all goes well and the weather stays fair, the production should be excellent.'

'I'm glad to hear it. I've stayed away from Somerton Court up to now so as not to cramp Maggie's style. But I need to talk to an impartial witness who can tell me the truth about how rehearsals are going, so be warned as I plan to cross-examine you later.'

'I'll be happy to share everything I know.' Toby smiled, but his uncertainty returned as he glanced across the hall towards the dining room, where the sight of the immaculate linen cloth on the solid wooden table set for six made him wonder who else had been invited. There had been no sound of footsteps on the gravel path outside, so the unexpected tap on the front door made them jump.

Joan went out into the hall to investigate, and an awkward silence ensued that Toby finally broke with an embarrassed laugh. 'I was just thinking about the whole string of coincidences that's led to us both being here tonight. If you hadn't ended up backstage on the last night of the pantomime and so on.'

'Of all the theatres in all the towns in all the world, and I walked into yours?'

Toby glanced at Sarah in delight; he had always felt an immediate affinity with anyone who could quote from his favourite film. 'What in heaven's name brought you to Casablanca?'

'My health. I came to Casablanca for the waters.' He was impressed that she knew the screenplay as well as he did.

'Waters? What waters? We're in the desert.'

'I was misinformed.'

'Huh!'

Joan's return to the room with Miss Milton trailing behind brought their impromptu performance to an end. In honour of the occasion, Miss Milton had exchanged her usual tweed skirt, cream blouse, and cameo brooch for a bright floral print dress that could have doubled as curtain fabric. 'Come in, my dear. I think you know Toby and Sarah from their involvement with our play.'

Toby and Sarah stood up as Miss Milton advanced slowly into the room, extended a thin arm, and gently shook hands with them both. Toby had been in awe of her when George first introduced them after the Production Meeting, and he later told Toby her full story: born in the village, she had never married and still lived in her parents' house, which had not been updated for more than half a century. To Toby, she looked like an elderly member of the aristocracy, and her accent made her sound like a relic from a long-vanished world.

'What a small world this is! We keep bumping into each other everywhere we go.'

'Currently, this village is the extent of my world. I spend so much time in the place I almost feel I live here.'

'Perhaps one day you will.'

'I'd certainly like to. The whole village feels so full of history, especially after our final session this afternoon. Once again, we made excellent progress with our rehearsal.'

'I agree. I do hope tomorrow goes just as well! I look forward to our rehearsals all week. Despite the hard work, I so much enjoy the shows we put on each year. Without our summer festival, the village would be full of strangers: so very different from how the place was when I was a girl. It gives us all a real chance to get to know each other a little better.'

Toby, who would have given anything to get to know Sarah better, glanced briefly at her and wondered if she harboured similar thoughts about him.

However, he decided, as a guest in Joan's house, he should say nothing more himself.

Joan's return with a tray of snacks broke the silence. 'Hopefully, we can all get to know each other a little better before this evening is over as well. But, while we're waiting for our other guests, I think a drink is called for. It's been a busy day, and the sun is well and truly over the yardarm. Sarah, I wonder if you could give me a hand, please.'

Once in the kitchen, Joan closed the door and turned to Sarah. 'I like Toby. He'll do his best for my play. I know it.'

'I like him too.'

'Only "like"?'

Sarah bent down to retrieve the wine from the fridge. 'Yes. I like him because he makes me laugh.' She steered the conversation back into neutral territory. 'He's so knowledgeable about what we have to do to make the play work. He has a real challenge with some of the actors as they can be so difficult, but the production will be a success, I'm sure of that.'

'Let's hope so—for all our sakes.' Joan picked up a tray of glasses, and Sarah followed her out of the kitchen with the wine. As they entered the lounge, the heavy silence and the look of anguish on Toby's face made Sarah realise they had returned in the nick of time.

Joan handed round the drinks and, after proposing a brief toast to the success of her play, turned to Sarah. 'Now, before the sun gets too low, perhaps you'd like to give Toby a tour of my garden. I need to catch up on some village gossip with Miss Milton, and George and Peggy are never on time for anything. Everything in the kitchen is under control thanks to all your work earlier on, so for the moment, there's nothing more for either of us to do.'

Sarah led Toby out into the enclosed garden and took a narrow brick path snaking towards a large flagstone terrace in a far corner. Walls of ancient brick enclosed the terrace on two sides, with a heavy wooden door giving access to one of the numerous footpaths running through the village set into one of them. On the terrace, which perfectly caught the last rays of the evening sun, a pair of solid wooden chairs and matching table, all bleached silver from years of sunshine, stood ready for them.

The mingled scents of the pots of herbs and blossoms fringing the edge of the terrace hung in the still air and, within the seclusion of the garden, the sound of the many insects drifting slowly between the pots drowned out any faint noise from the world outside. Only the body of the dead rabbit laid neatly on the edge of the terrace detracted from the perfection of the moment: Joan's cat had obviously recovered from her earlier stress.

While Sarah deftly upended an empty flowerpot to conceal the corpse, Toby sat down at the table and looked around at the garden in awe. He had hoped the evening would allow him some time to be alone with Sarah, and now, for the first time since they had met, they were by themselves.

The beauty of the location made the occasion even better, and he realised he had been stupid to imagine any malign conspiracy aiming to prevent them from meeting. He even knew what he wanted to say, although as ever he needed more time to work out the right words. In order to cover his lack of preparation time, he fell back on small talk. 'This is an amazing garden. It's so peaceful out here.'

'It's difficult to believe my aunt has lived here for such a short time. She must have the greenest of fingers because everything is so well established.'

'And it was kind of her to invite me for dinner tonight.'

He saw Sarah turn away and glance back towards the house. 'I'm afraid she had an ulterior motive: she's desperate to discover the truth about how rehearsals are going. No one in the village, especially anyone associated with the Culture Committee, can give an opinion that's anything other than biased—one way or the other. She wanted to talk to someone we could trust.' She turned and looked directly at him. 'So I suggested she should talk to you.'

This spontaneous vote of confidence delighted Toby. 'And do you trust me?' He had meant his question to apply to them both, but Sarah gave an answer that was both unexpected and welcome.

'Yes, I do.'

'Thank you.'

'All I hope is that tonight won't be too awful for you.'

After everything Toby had experienced so far, this made no sense. 'Awful? Why do you say that?'

'Because we've been rehearsing all day and we'll be busy with the play again tomorrow, so you'll hardly want to spend the whole evening talking about it too. Surely you need time to do something different. Don't you have a life outside of this production?'

Toby jumped to his feet. 'Of course I have a life, although most of the time it can be pretty ordinary. But believe me, at this moment, there's nothing else in the world I'd prefer to be doing more than being here with you.'

'Really? I was worried you'd find Miss Milton heavy going. She's a bit of an acquired taste, but Joan likes her and promised me she'll mellow after a glass or two of wine.'

'I'll watch out for that later on. I thought she looked a little surprised to see me when she arrived as I'm not actually a resident. I get the feeling some of the villagers regard anyone involved with the play who doesn't live locally as an interloper.'

'Joan would agree with you about that. She's lived here for seven years and still doesn't feel completely accepted. That's why the play is so important for her.'

'Miss Milton seemed a little confused as to why Joan had invited me tonight. Just before you returned with the drinks, she asked me if I was "walking out" with you.'

He saw Sarah glance sharply at him but found it impossible to read anything into her expression. 'And what did you say?'

'I told her Joan had invited me because I was your friend. I hope I said the right thing.'

'Was that all?'

He wondered if he heard a note of disappointment in her voice. 'And then you both came back with the drinks, so I didn't get the chance to tell her that I'm not currently "walking out" with anyone.'

'No?'

'No.'

'Same as me.'

Toby took a deep breath. He knew this would not be the most eloquent invitation in the world, but he could not let the opportunity pass. 'Then perhaps we could go out somewhere together. Sometime when we're not rehearsing. If we have some time when we're not rehearsing, having production meetings, or doing something else linked to the show. If we're lucky, we might even be able to find a screening of *Casablanca*.'

'That would be wonderful. I haven't seen it on a big screen for ages.'

The heavy door behind them swung open without warning and knocked into Sarah. The force of the blow caused her to stumble forward, but as she fell towards a large ceramic planter filled with jasmine, Toby stepped forward and caught her in his arms. George, immaculate in a cream linen shirt and dark blue chinos, stepped through the open doorway and, as he took in the situation, gave them both a knowing look. After a moment, Peggy, resplendent in a summer dress of vibrant primary colours with a matching scarf and sunglasses, followed him into the garden. In her hand, she held a wicker trug basket in which Toby could see two bottles of wine and a small tray of seedlings: they too had arrived laden with gifts.

'Evening, Toby. Evening, Sarah. Hope we didn't injure you, but Joan suggested we should use the footpath and the back gate instead of tramping all the way along the main road. She told me the door needed a good shove to open it, but please accept my most profound apologies: I hadn't expected to find someone lurking on the other side.'

Sarah smiled as she and Toby disentangled themselves from their unexpected proximity. 'Don't worry. You made us jump, but you haven't hurt us. I was just giving Toby a tour of the garden while we waited for you.'

Peggy placed the trug on the table and gazed around the garden. 'It's a wonderful place. Joan must have her work cut out to keep it looking like this, and it's so romantic at this time of night.'

Toby gave Sarah a meaningful glance. 'Yes.'

Sarah stifled a giggle. 'Joan is inside with Miss Milton. They've started on the nibbles, and Joan has just opened a bottle of wine. If you'd like to go on into the house, we'll join you shortly.'

'Excellent. In this hot weather, even a short walk gives one a thirst.' Peggy picked up the trug. 'Come along, George. We're wasting valuable drinking time.'

While they had been talking, the sun had slipped below the roofline of the house, and now darkness engulfed much of the garden. Toby watched George and Peggy disappear into the gloom as they followed the curves of the path back towards the house. 'Suddenly, it seems very dark.'

Toby sensed Sarah move closer to him. 'It's the best part of the day. I love being out here at this time so I can enjoy all the wonderful evening perfumes. Close your eyes and take a deep breath, and you'll see what I mean.'

'I daren't. I always get hay fever for a few weeks, although it'll be over well before the play.'

'In that case, we'd better go in as well. I'd hate you to be smitten tonight.'

Toby had no desire to be smitten either. Up to now, the evening had proved to be so much better than he had dared hope, and he did not want their time alone together to end. 'Where's the path? I can't see anything in all the gloom.'

Sarah moved forward into the darkness. 'Follow me. I know my way around here blindfolded, so I'll lead you.'

Toby moved towards the sound of Sarah's voice and took her outstretched hand, and she then led him back along the winding path. Neither saw the face observing their progress through the kitchen window.

While serving the aperitifs, Joan had been dismissive of the dinner she had prepared, describing it as a simple supper thrown together to share with friends. However, when they sat down to eat, Toby thought it the best meal he had eaten in months: after enjoying a goat's cheese salad as a starter, Toby struggled to choose between the poached salmon or the asparagus quiche as his main course, so Joan insisted on serving him generous portions of both. She seated him next to Sarah at the table, but they had no opportunity to carry on any further private conversation once the wine began to flow.

Toby did his best to follow the conversations underway around the table, but as Peggy and Miss Milton gossiped about villagers he had never met, their exchanges made little sense to him. Meanwhile, George outlined to Joan the various technical challenges her play had posed for the production team and explained how they had overcome them. Toby made an occasional contribution to this discussion, and was delighted when Joan promised to lend him the privately printed history of the village she had used to research the background of her play.

As the evening progressed, Toby felt relieved he had managed to escape without being questioned too much about the progress of rehearsals. However, once Joan had cleared away the dessert plates and returned to the table with a large jug of coffee and a tray of liqueurs, she turned to him. 'Now Toby, it's time to sing for your supper. I'm dying to find out how you think rehearsals are going. Don't be shy; tell me everything.' She sat back with an expectant look on her face, and Toby realised that Peggy and Miss Milton had fallen silent as well.

Toby had dreaded this moment all evening, but a meaningful glance from Sarah gave him confidence so he took a deep breath and began. 'Today we ran through the whole of Act One with music for the first time. We now have a three-piece band plus a singer, all thanks to my trusty deputy who has contacts everywhere. She's an absolute miracle worker.' He saw George nod his appreciation as he continued. 'The guests are all dancing to something upbeat while the groom makes his farewells and prepares to re-join his regiment in Flanders. Then the music changes to *The Roses of Picardy*.'

Over the course of the meal, Miss Milton had enjoyed two large glasses of wine, and in a quavering soprano voice, she now sang the final couplet of the song:

'But there's one rose that dies not in Picardy
'Tis the rose that I keep in my heart.'

As she finished singing, she became pensive. After a moment of contemplative silence, she explained the reason for her change of mood. 'That was my dear mama's favourite song. It always reminded her of her first fiancé who died at Ypres.'

Her disclosure prompted immediate expressions of condolence. However, she gently reminded them this happened over a century ago, and if her mother's fiancé had not been killed, then her mother's life would have been very different, she would not have been born herself, and thus would not be sitting around the table to share the story with them.

Toby paused for a moment while everyone analysed the irrefutable logic of her statement. Then he carried on. 'The music continues, but gradually everyone stops dancing to watch the groom as he leaves. The song finishes as he exits, and the scene ends in stillness and absolute silence. Even today, in broad daylight and with the actors in their rehearsal clothes, you could feel the chill it produced. It hadn't been easy to see the bride and groom's relationship so strongly in the script, but Maggie's put it all right there on the stage.'

Joan looked directly at him. 'You don't need words when two people are attracted to each other. It's all in the body language.'

Peggy joined in the cross-examination. 'What do you think of Martin as the dashing young groom?'

Toby thought for a moment, remembering the issues Maggie had encountered in some of the earlier rehearsals, and decided to be diplomatic. 'He's very good—now.'

Peggy snorted. 'To show *any* interest in a woman is a real achievement for him.' She took a large sip of the brandy she had poured for herself. 'And what about Ruth as his blushing bride?'

Miss Milton smiled happily. 'She'll look stunning in the antique dress we've found for the wedding scene. She'll be wearing my mama's lace with it.'

Joan was impressed. 'In that case, I'm sure she'll look absolutely beautiful, every inch the pure young bride.'

Peggy knew most of the local actors from George's previous productions and had her own views on Maggie's casting decisions. 'Don't you believe it! Ruth had a small part in last year's show, and during rehearsals she tried it on with almost every male in the cast. Maggie definitely believes in casting against type.'

Joan realised it would be wise to bring this excavation of past productions to an end, so she turned to Toby and attempted to direct the conversation towards what she hoped would be a safer subject. 'And what will you be rehearsing tomorrow?'

'Tomorrow will be interesting.' Toby paused and glanced again at Sarah, who gave him a reassuring smile. 'We'll be working on Act Two again, but there's one scene we haven't actually rehearsed yet.'

'Why ever not? It's just over two weeks until the first night. Aren't you cutting things a little fine?'

'We are, but what Maggie wants to do with the scene has given us...' He paused while he searched for the most appropriate words. '...a significant logistical challenge.'

A look of sudden interest appeared on Joan's face. 'I'm intrigued. What on earth has Maggie done to my script?'

'Nothing; don't worry. She hasn't changed a word of the script: merely some of the action.'

'That sounds fascinating. Tell me all.'

Toby swallowed hard; he had dreaded this moment all evening. 'It's towards the end of the act. Our logistical challenge requires us to get a bath full of warm water onto the stage.'

'Why on earth do you need it?'

'Because in the scene before the Harvest Supper, instead of just washing their hands and faces as you wrote in your script, Maggie wants two of the men to take a bath.'

Joan laughed and clapped her hands in delight. 'What an excellent idea!'

'You don't mind?'

'I wish I'd thought of it myself.'

Peggy joined in their conversation. 'I'm only in Act One, albeit with a major role, and for reasons of authenticity, I decided I should know nothing about what takes place in the village during Act Two. Could you therefore please enlighten me as to what will happen tomorrow?'

Toby could not think of any appropriate euphemisms so realised he had no choice other than to be direct. 'Tomorrow Josh and Chris rehearse the scene for the first time with a bath full of water, although they'll be keeping their boxers on while they work out all the moves. Chris is an exhibitionist and would have stripped off tomorrow, but Josh persuaded Maggie they shouldn't perform *au naturel* until the dress rehearsal so as to preserve the element of surprise.'

Peggy took another large sip of brandy to help her recover from the shock of this unexpected news. 'My God, I've known Josh ever since he turned up in one of my English classes as a young lad. He's always been a good actor, and the last time I saw him on stage he played the romantic lead; he gave such a poetic performance, the height of sensitivity. But now you say he's playing a farm labourer and stripping off on stage. That sounds a bit out of character for him.'

'It is. He's a bit apprehensive about it.' Toby paused and reminded himself of his decision to stick to the facts. 'No, he's extremely apprehensive about it, and I don't blame him. But he and Chris both agreed to do the scene as Maggie wanted, and so tomorrow we have what the Coven are calling our undress rehearsal.'

Peggy placed her glass carefully on the table. 'When Maggie generously offered me the role of Mrs Wilson, I decided a woman of her status would have nothing to do with the common people of the village. As such, I've kept away from all rehearsals and forbidden everyone—even dear George—from telling me what was going on outside of the confines of the big house. But now, as our first performance looms ever closer, I feel I need to immerse myself fully in the historical world we've all worked so hard to create. I owe it to Maggie to fine-tune my character, and to ensure I bring every shred of authenticity to my own performance.' She gazed around the table. 'From now on, I shall attend every rehearsal.'

Joan smiled innocently at her. 'I have an open invitation from Maggie to drop into rehearsals whenever I want. I've kept away up to now as I had no desire to interfere, but I think I might accept her offer for tomorrow. Apart from anything else, it would be a gesture of solidarity in support of all her hard work, especially after the unpleasantness from the Culture Committee. I'd be honoured if you'd accompany me as my guest.'

Peggy reached over and patted her hand. 'Thank you, my dear. I cannot tell you how much your kind invitation means to me. It will clearly be a challenging scene for the actors to rehearse, but hopefully, our joint presence will help accustom them to performing it in front of an audience.'

She glanced at George, who had remained silent while the conversation flowed around him. 'On that happy note, we two should think about heading home, as we have another early start tomorrow.' She drained her glass and stood up, and George promptly followed her. Joan led the pair out into the hall, and once there Peggy hugged her warmly. 'Thank you so much for a wonderful evening. It's been marvellous. Until tomorrow.'

George also embraced Joan. 'Thank you for such a superb meal. We will reciprocate soon, I promise.' He turned to Miss Milton, who had wandered out of the dining room after them, and now stood uncertainly by the front door. 'We'll be walking right past your house and never travel anywhere in this village at night without our torches. If you're ready to leave, we can escort you safely to your front door.'

'That's very kind of you. I've never worried about there being no streetlights in the village as I don't go out much at night. However, at times like this, I can see they have their advantages.'

Joan watched her visitors make their way down the gravel path, and when she returned to the dining room, Toby stood up. 'I think I should be off as well. I daren't oversleep as tomorrow is likely to be yet another busy day.'

'You too? What a shame. But don't forget the book I promised you. With your interest in local history, I think you'll find it fascinating.' She turned to Sarah. 'I wonder if you could fetch the book from my study. I think you'll find it somewhere on my desk.'

Toby watched Sarah disappear along the corridor. 'A big thank you from me as well. It's been such an enjoyable evening, very different from my usual Saturday nights.'

'Good, I'm glad. I enjoyed our evening as well. I'd hoped matters were going well, but now I've met you I can see they are.'

'We still have a long way to go.'

'Yes, but you will get there.'

'The next two weeks will be critical.'

'I agree.'

Sarah returned with the book in her hand. 'I'm sorry I was so long. Your desk is a disaster area, so it wasn't immediately obvious.'

'Out of chaos comes creativity: never trust anyone with a tidy desk.' She handed the book to Toby. 'I think you'll find this interesting. It gave me a great deal of useful background for my play.'

'All I hope is we give your script the production it deserves.'

'After everything I've heard from you tonight, I don't have any worries about the play.'

'I'll look forward to reading the book once the play is over and I have some spare time again, but for now, I must go.'

'Come here and say goodnight properly.' She hugged Toby and then to his surprise kissed him on both cheeks. He decided to reciprocate.

Sarah smiled at him. 'Goodnight, Toby. I'll see you tomorrow morning.'

'Goodnight.' Toby decided to kiss Sarah too, and they engaged in an awkward dance while Joan watched.

Once Joan had closed the door behind Toby, she turned to Sarah. 'What a splendid evening! And now we have tomorrow's rehearsal to look forward to as well.'

She walked back into the dining room and began to clear the table.

Chapter 9
The Undress Rehearsal

'Duncan knew that the slightest hint of impropriety always guaranteed the Company a full house, so when the actors saw he had added The Creation of the World *to the repertoire they realised that the rumours of financial problems were true.'*

The Musician's Destiny

Sarah enjoyed the feel of the fresh morning air on her walk through the quiet village streets, and she arrived at Somerton Court as the clock in the stable yard began to strike the quarter to the hour. During her previous visit to East Upbury she had decided the relaxed pace of life in the country made her feel good, and this morning she felt even better. Today, the village itself had also changed: she saw posters for the play covering every public surface, and felt a palpable sense of excitement about the imminent production from everyone she spoke to. But, as Sarah made her way along the footpath towards the paddock, she knew both cast and crew still had a great deal of hard work ahead of them before the opening night.

By the time she and Joan had cleared up after the dinner party it had been late, but nonetheless Sarah had woken early and thought again about the events of the previous evening. Joan had planned to hold a dinner party for friends in the village for some time and, after enduring a slew of unsubstantiated rumours about the production from disaffected members of the Culture Committee and their supporters, had asked Sarah who she could invite to discover the truth about the rehearsals. Inevitably, Sarah suggested Toby, and Joan agreed at once. When Sarah subsequently delivered the invitation to Toby, his eager acceptance delighted her far more than she would have been willing to admit to anyone.

Following their unexpected second encounter at the Production Meeting, Sarah and Toby spoke to each other by phone on a regular basis; he also sent her long emails, mostly written late at night, with witty descriptions of the production meetings he had attended. However, whenever she returned to East Upbury for rehearsals, they spent most of their time together. However, a seemingly endless list of issues concerning the play always kept them both busy, for the most part with Hetty in close attendance. As the weeks passed, the way Toby dealt with the problems that Maggie, George, and the cast threw at him impressed Sarah, but with all these commitments, they never had any space for themselves.

Last night, they had discussed seeking out a screening of *Casablanca*, but the arrival of George and Peggy had prevented them from considering anything else they could do together away from the all-encompassing demands of the production. Sarah realised, with the first night of the production just over a fortnight away, this situation was unlikely to improve in the short term. She felt she knew Toby a little better from their regular phone conversations and all his emails. However, during weekend rehearsals, her lack of experience sometimes made her feel a little superfluous when everyone else demanded so much from him.

She had hoped the dinner party last night would allow them some time to be alone together, and clearly the same idea had occurred to her aunt. However, even safe within the protective sanctuary of Joan's garden, they had been unable to escape completely from the clutches of the play. After what had happened on the terrace, she felt certain Toby liked her, and then she realised she had known this from their first brief meeting backstage at the theatre. After further extended deliberation with herself, she acknowledged she liked him too, and Joan's unsolicited endorsement had been an unexpected bonus. But, although a mutual liking for *Casablanca* showed they agreed on certain important matters, she could not treat this in isolation as a solid foundation for anything more substantial.

Many of the cast were already gathered in small groups in the paddock while they waited for the rehearsal to begin. Some had begun the warm-up exercises Maggie insisted they carry out before each session, while others practised the formal dances for the extended ball scene ending the first act. Several waved to her and wished her a good morning; she smiled at them all and returned their good wishes, but despite this outward show, she felt an inner trepidation as she thought again about the events scheduled for later in the day.

As Sarah made her way across the paddock, she spotted Louise, Helen, and Jane standing outside the barn where Toby and his team now stored the heavy furniture they used during rehearsals. The three had always done their best to avoid any participation in Maggie's warm-up exercises, and as their characters were villagers, they were not required for the dance during the ball scene. However, at least today they had arrived on time; all three had regularly arrived late for rehearsals and, despite Toby's repeated reminders of the need for punctuality, until this morning had made no attempt to change their ways.

Louise noticed Sarah at once, waved frantically, and then rushed over, a sheaf of papers in her hand and a broad grin on her face. 'Hi, Sarah. Do you want to join our sweepstake? I've had a hot tip Chris is planning to rehearse *au naturel* today, and we're hoping Josh will feel he'd lose face if he doesn't do the same. We're running a book on it.'

Until now, Sarah had spoken to Louise only occasionally and found this unexpected intimacy a little unsettling. 'Dare I ask what we're betting on?'

'On how long it will be.'

Sarah chose her words with care. 'And who gets to measure?'

The grin on Louise's face grew broader. 'I do.' She opened the large bag slung over her shoulder, rummaged in its depths for a moment, and pulled out an antique stopwatch. 'How long do you think it'll be before their boxers come off? I'll start the clock once the bath is full of water and Maggie begins the rehearsal. The bet closest to both times wins, and the umpire's decision is final: that's me by the way. Are you in?'

Sarah had no wish to be regarded as a prude, so she chose two times at random and handed over her stake. As Louise added her details to the form, Sarah looked with surprise at the long list of names already there: what might happen during the day's rehearsal had certainly generated a great deal of interest among both cast and crew.

From her perspective as an objective spectator to all such village activities, Sarah found this fascinating to observe. Despite all the hard work of the Coven, Chris had so far proved resolutely impervious to their combined charms. From the very first rehearsal, he had shown interest only in Kate who, safe within her own time zone, for the most part, failed even to acknowledge his existence.

Meanwhile Josh, focussed entirely on his campaign against Chris, had no time for anyone other than himself. Sarah realised the majority of those involved in the production regarded this as a two-horse race, with Adam, in life as in the play, cast in a supporting role. However, she could not overlook how Kate had spoken so enthusiastically to her about his suffragette suggestion after yesterday's rehearsal. She looked forward to seeing how all these different strands resolved themselves over the remaining weeks of the hermetic environment the production had created; with so many variables in play, it would be impossible to offer realistic odds on any sensible resolution.

A century ago, the large barn standing between the paddocks had stored the vast quantities of hay needed for the numerous horses kept at Somerton Court, but currently the random pieces of heavy furniture spread across its stone floor gave the place the appearance of a junk shop. When Sarah entered the dark interior, she found Toby perched on a solid wooden chair while he focussed on his first challenge of the day. He had spread out a tangle of leather straps and assorted pieces of steel on the long table in front of him, but from the blank glaze on his face, he clearly had no idea what to do with them.

Hetty watched his struggle with an expression of long-suffering patience on her face, and finally offered him a hint. 'With a bridle, it's easier if you start with the bit.'

Toby's look of confusion grew more intense. 'Which bit? There are so many of them.'

Hetty said nothing, and instead picked up the tangle of leather and steel from the table. Then, in a few easy moves, she connected the buckles together and, in a moment, she held a splendid antique bridle in her hands.

Toby looked impressed. 'I feel like an absolute idiot. You made it look so easy.'

'When you live in a village like this, you can't escape ponies, even if you don't ride yourself. It's how I managed to find Mr Big for us. I only hope the bridle will fit him, as he's rather small.'

'How small?'

'He's a Shetland.'

'Can I assume he's the right shade of brown?'

'He's chestnut.'

'But Maggie specifically wanted a brown one—to match the set.'

‘Chestnut is brown in horses.’

Sarah laughed. ‘And grey is white.’

Toby smiled a greeting before the look of confusion returned. ‘Why?’

Hetty sighed. ‘It is because it is. Take my advice and yet again don’t waste your life worrying about something you don’t need to.’ She acknowledged Sarah with a knowing grin. ‘Morning, Sarah. Hope you both had a good evening together. Can you and Tobe make sure we’re all set up for the rehearsal while I’m away? I need to check that this bridle fits Mr Big. I shouldn’t be away too long.’

‘We’ll be fine. We’re both adults with responsible day jobs, so I’m sure we can manage without your supervision for at least an hour.’

Toby watched Hetty as she trotted out of the barn. ‘I feel honoured she thinks we can cope in her absence. I don’t know why she decided to get involved with this show, but without her, nothing would ever get off the ground. She’s a force of nature. No one in the village can deny her anything.’

‘Joan says she’s desperate to escape from here once she finishes school next year. I wonder where she’ll end up.’

‘Parliament or prison; possibly both.’ Toby yawned and immediately apologised. ‘Sorry, I’ve lost count of the late nights and early mornings I’ve had since rehearsals started, and today my sleep debt seems to be demanding an urgent down payment. In terms of the hours of actual sleep I’ve had, I feel I’m still way back in the middle of last week.’

He realised he had strayed too far from his intended route, so he executed a rapid change of direction. ‘That dinner last night was the best meal I’ve eaten in months.’ He paused again. He had decided to ask this on his drive home last night and hoped his pre-planned question still sounded sufficiently spontaneous. ‘If you’re willing to risk my culinary skills and fancy a return match, I’d like to invite you for dinner in my flat.’

‘That would be lovely. If you can suggest some dates, I’ll check with Joan and get back to you.’

An invitation for both Sarah and Joan had not been part of Toby’s plan. ‘Actually, I meant just you by yourself. Of course, I’ll invite both of you some other time, but I’d need to practice a bit before I could do that, as I wouldn’t want to disappoint your aunt with my cooking skills.’

Earlier that morning Sarah had wondered how Toby really felt about her, as the endless demands of the play meant he never had time to open up to her about anything. She realised this unexpected invitation was a far more momentous step than the potential cinema trip they had discussed last night, but from all she had seen of the rehearsals so far, she knew the next few weeks would be even busier than those that had gone before.

Above and beyond this, a looming family commitment meant she would have even less free time. 'I'm here all next weekend, and then I'll be away for a cousin's wedding on the Saturday before the play. I haven't seen him for years, but I sent my acceptance months ago, so my parents would never forgive me if I pulled out now. I'll be back in time for some of the rehearsal on Sunday, and then of course, I'm staying here all week for the performances.'

'Next Saturday is good for me, assuming Maggie doesn't let the session overrun. What sort of food do you like?'

'Anything—eggs, cheese or whatever. Obviously no meat or fish.'

'Obviously.' Last night, Toby had enjoyed the generous slice of asparagus quiche Joan had pressed on him but, as with so many events in his life, at the time had not appreciated its real significance. When he decided to invite Sarah for dinner, he did not realise the additional challenge he had set himself: he would have to move away from his signature dish of chilli con carne. Toby always regarded time spent in the kitchen as an adventure, but cooking a three-course vegetarian dinner would mean a trip into uncharted territory. In order to make this expedition a success, he urgently needed to acquire some new maps—or at least buy a new recipe book.

He glanced at Sarah and saw a bemused expression on her face. 'Sorry, I started to think about menus and got distracted. As you're vegetarian, I'll need to begin my planning a bit earlier than usual.'

'Please don't say any more about what you're planning in case you spoil the surprise.' Then she remembered why she had come into the barn. 'By the way, have you seen Miss Milton? She left her reading glasses behind last night, and Joan asked me to return them. I thought I might find her here.'

'I saw her earlier on, but then one of her ladies summoned her up to the big house to check out some towels. Maggie wants them to be not too big and not too small. I think she's aiming for the Goldilocks look.'

'Thanks. I'd better head off up there right away, as she'll probably need her glasses to help her make her selection.' She paused and then appeared anxious. 'Before I go, I'd appreciate your honest opinion about what we're rehearsing today.'

'Ask away. I'm full of opinions about everything. If you don't like them—well, I have others.'

Sarah gave him a pained smile. 'Do you think the bath scene is gratuitous?'

Toby paused for a moment while he analysed Sarah's question. He realised they had recently passed a hopefully significant milestone in their potential relationship, so he needed to choose his words with care: he had far too much experience of what happened when he said the wrong thing. 'I don't think so. I've known other directors who've had some crazy ideas, not all of which involved nudity. But, from what I've seen of her so far, Maggie seems very well grounded. She said at the first rehearsal she wanted to liberate the play from the script, so I assume that's why she's decided to change this scene.'

Sarah remained silent, so he tried to explain what he meant. 'Well, Joan certainly seemed relaxed when we discussed the scene last night. I assume it wasn't merely good manners on her part.'

'Good. She means a great deal to me, and I wouldn't want anyone to hurt her, especially those monsters on the Culture Committee. I'd hate it if someone tried to spoil her play.'

'So would I. As stage manager, my job description is simple: do anything and everything needed to make every performance a success.'

'Excellent! With you in charge and Hetty on our side as well, what could possibly go wrong?'

Sarah left the barn to resume her search for Miss Milton, while Toby picked up a box of props and set off towards the stage to prepare for the rehearsal. Now the technical team had completed their work on the set, Maggie had decided to hold all remaining rehearsals on the stage so the actors could familiarise themselves with its layout. The theatre lay beyond the paddock, separated from the open space by a thick beech hedge. As Toby made his way through a gap, he spotted a solitary figure slumped on the far end of the highest tier of seats. Josh had a glazed look on his face, and although he faced the stage, he gazed unseeingly at the finished set.

Initially, Josh did not respond to Toby's call of good morning, but eventually he managed to force a slight smile onto his face. 'Sorry, I was miles away.' The smile increased. 'How's love's young dream? I hope you had a good time last night.'

'I had dinner with Sarah and her aunt, and several of the great and the good from this wonderful village were also in attendance. Over the course of the evening, industrial quantities of a whole range of excellent alcoholic beverages were taken by the locals, but I abstained as I had to drive myself home. It was hardly a romantic assignation.'

'But you'd have liked it to have been.'

'Of course. In fact, the breaking news is that I've just invited Sarah for dinner at my flat—and she's accepted.'

'Good man! Have you given her the standard health warning yet? You need to make sure she knows what she's letting herself in for?'

'That mistake with the chilli powder was not my fault: there was a typo in the recipe.'

'But didn't you think a heaped tablespoon was a bit much?'

'I was using a new recipe, so I followed it to the letter!' Toby cringed at the memory. 'Anyway, it didn't do us any permanent damage. But Sarah is vegetarian so I can't cook a chilli.'

'Do you know any other recipes?'

'Not yet, but this is neither the time nor the place to discuss menu options for a hopefully intimate three-course vegetarian dinner for two.'

'No. Today, there are other matters prompting a great deal of local discussion. I've even heard a rumour from Martin that someone's running a book. I've no idea what they're betting on, but I don't trust Chris an inch and wouldn't be surprised if he had something up his sleeve.'

'Don't forget I am but a humble stage manager. As such, I have no idea what you actors have been talking about.'

'Today is but the happy prologue to the act itself in which I reveal my all to the watching world.' This made no sense to Toby either, and he remained silent as Josh attempted to explain his previous statement. 'What I mean is that this afternoon everyone will see a family-friendly trailer for my subsequent performance as a bare, forked animal, totally exposed to the gaze of all and sundry.'

Toby finally understood Josh's concerns about the rehearsal, but before he could offer any appropriate words of comfort, a flurry of activity at the far side of the theatre brought their conversation to an end. They watched as two figures, laden down with a folding table and a picnic basket, made their way through the hedge and set up the table in front of the first row of seats. Peggy waved enthusiastically to Josh, while Joan gave Toby a regal wave that he acknowledged with a deferential nod of his head.

Josh had been pale before, but now the final shades of colour drained from his face as he made a desultory wave in return. 'I've spent all week thinking today was going to be bad, but never in my worst dreams did I think I'd be performing in front of an audience as well. Everything has just got worse, much worse.' With a despairing sigh, he buried his head in his hands.

At this point in the production, Maggie insisted on being involved in every key decision and, with so much activity underway in parallel all over Somerton Court, for once the rehearsal began later than scheduled. Once she had approved the towels the wardrobe team had selected for her, Maggie returned from the big house and the actors and crew then followed her into the theatre, all finally ready for the rehearsal to begin. The actors spread out in small groups across the curved rows of tiered seats, while Maggie reviewed the positioning of the furniture that Toby and his team had set out on the stage. They had followed the same process for every other scene since they had moved into the theatre.

Sitting together with Hetty in the furthest corner of the front row while they waited for Maggie to confirm her approval, Sarah watched with curiosity the various dramas playing out among the waiting actors. Chris, persistent as ever, had taken a seat next to Kate, but once again, she had not even acknowledged his presence. Instead, she and Adam were deep in conversation as they worked their way through his thick folder of notes.

Sarah made a mental note to mention this unexpected proximity to Toby, as he had told her all about Adam's fascination with Kate as well as his endless worries about every aspect of his involvement with the production. Eventually, Chris became bored with Kate's failure to engage with him, and, to Sarah's surprise, he wandered over to Hetty and began to question her about where she had sourced the antique set of poaching traps and knives his character had to carry.

As their discussion continued and Hetty resolutely refused to disclose any information about the provenance of the items, Chris tried to draw Sarah into their conversation, but she merely gave him a frosty smile. She had witnessed the numerous problems he had caused for Toby during rehearsals and had no desire to become involved in his issues. Instead, she continued with her self-appointed task of converting Toby's scribbled notes on the pages of the prompt copy into clear instructions for her and Hetty to follow. Toby claimed his handwriting was always entirely legible, but to anyone else who picked up the folder, his notes looked as if he used a private cipher.

Sarah made slow progress with her work, but she eventually reached the final page, placed the folder on the floor, and glanced around again at the assembled actors: most continued their quiet conversations in small groups as Maggie and Toby neared the end of their work, but Josh remained in splendid isolation in the back row. Sarah thought his face looked gaunt, and the dark shadows under his eyes made her hope that with the production so close he had not fallen ill. She had no means of knowing that, above and beyond his dread of the looming dress rehearsal, his self-imposed regime of diet and daily trips to the gym had finally taken their toll, and today every single muscle in his body ached.

In the centre of the stage, Toby and Maggie scrutinised the large tin bath that Hetty had delivered earlier on. Toby, in his supplementary role as historical advisor, confirmed the authenticity of the bath to Maggie, and she immediately gave it her approval. Toby had already positioned two simple wooden benches on either side of the bath, and apart from these few items, the stage was empty. Maggie then walked off the front of the stage and roamed around the tiers of seats as she checked the layout from all sides.

Having satisfied herself with the sightlines, Maggie ran back to the centre of the stage and called the cast to order. 'Welcome, my actors, once again. Today we will finally complete our work on Act Two. I intend to spend as much time as we need to bring this final scene up to the same high standard as the rest of our work. We'll treat it just like every other scene we've rehearsed already. We'll work out the moves and run through the scene as many times as we need until we're all comfortable with what we've achieved. Then then we'll take a break.'

She paused and glanced around at the expectant faces spread out in front of her. 'After that, we'll fill the bath with water and run through the entire scene again, as we cannot afford to arrive at the dress rehearsal and discover we have any issues in such an important scene.' She looked around at the cast again. 'Before we make a start today, I want to thank Chris and Josh both for their massive commitment to this production and for their agreement to perform this scene as I requested. They are excellent actors, and I'd like us all to show our appreciation for their hard work in the usual way.'

A polite round of applause rippled through the assembled throng of actors, interspersed with giggles from Helen and a wolf whistle from Louise. Maggie silenced them both with a glare before she continued. 'Toby and his team have set up the stage ready for us, so let's get started.'

Chris, Josh, and Adam made their way onto the stage, and the members of the Coven moved into the wings to await their cue. Meanwhile, Joan opened her hamper, extracted a thermos flask of coffee and two china cups and saucers, and placed them all on the table. Then she poured the coffee, added milk from another flask, and handed one of the cups to Peggy: she believed in living her life to her own exacting standards. Meanwhile, Peggy, determined to be prepared for whatever sights the day might bring, reached into her bag and withdrew a pair of opera glasses, which she proceeded to hang around her neck.

Josh prowled around the stage, familiarising himself with the layout of the furniture and looking out at the two hundred individual seats rising on tiered semi-circular rows in front of him. Once he had confirmed his worst fears by calculating that every seat had an unrestricted view of the bath, he sat on the bench nearest the front of the stage. Despite his terror at the thought of using the bath for real, as an actor, he instinctively chose the position giving him best visibility to the audience. Adam had followed Josh as he explored the set, and he now sat down carefully on the other bench. Finally, Chris strolled across the stage, jumped into the empty bath, and pretended to wash himself all over.

Adam giggled, and Josh glared at him. 'Be serious. This is our big scene.'

'Sorry.'

Maggie clapped her hands to attract their attention. 'And action when you gentlemen are ready.'

Josh switched his accent to the generic rural burr all the actors had adopted. *'You need to get a move on; otherwise, we'll all be late. It's not just you that's got a date tonight. If you don't hurry up, that water's going to be cold. You've both made it dirty enough as it is.'*

Chris did his best to lie back in the small bath. *'I need time for a proper wash. After all our work in that heat today, I'm even more filthy than usual.'* He paused and then addressed both Josh and Adam. *'You know there must be something better for us three than this. All we have to look forward to every week for the rest of our lives is work, work, and more work.'*

Josh had no problem delivering his next line with the level of contempt it required. *'Like what? You're always so good at talking. When are you going to do something about it for real?'*

Chris glared back at him. *'Soon. Very soon. I've got a chance to escape from this. We've all got a chance—it's right here in front of us. All we have to do is reach out and grasp it.'*

Adam only had one line in the scene but made the most of it. *'Grasp what?'*

Chris turned to him. *'I'm going to join up. That's what I'm going to do. I'm going to show everyone in this village what I'm really made of. The squire's son returned to his regiment straight after his wedding, so what's there to stop us from joining up as well now we've got the harvest in? We're all as good as he is, better if you ask me, and this is our chance to prove it. This is our country, not just his. This is our chance to win a better future for us all, and I'm planning to go off and fight for it. I'm going to join up first thing tomorrow, and once I'm gone from here, I'm never coming back. If you're men rather than worms, then you'll both come along with me.'*

Chris stopped and turned to Maggie. 'Do I need to stay in the bath for this whole sequence? I'd feel better if I could move around the stage a bit.'

Maggie scanned her script. 'Get out of the bath when you feel it's right to do so, and make sure you do it before your line about showing what you're made of. We don't want any cheap laughs.'

Josh raised his hand. 'Can I check a point too, please? My next line is about the water being cold, so I need to be in the bath for it to make sense. Should I get into the bath during Chris's big speech? I'm only asking, as I'd hate to distract the audience by revealing my all at the wrong moment.'

Chris glared at him. 'Don't kid yourself. The audience will be so focussed on my performance they wouldn't notice if you cartwheeled naked around the stage.'

Josh feigned innocence. 'All I want is for the scene to work as well as possible. We're in a hurry to get ready for the Harvest Supper, so none of us can afford to hang around.'

Maggie brought their discussion to a swift end. 'Don't forget this is only our first run-through. I value all your contributions—as I always do—but we need to battle through to the end of the scene. We can focus on the detail in our next run-through, and we have the whole of this session to get the scene right. By the time we finish tonight, you all need to be totally relaxed about what you're doing—both in and out of the bath. As long as you're all comfortable in your own skins, the audience won't even notice your lack of clothes.'

Several cast members unburdened by pressing domestic responsibilities adjourned to the Puppy and Duckling after rehearsals each Sunday, both to review the events of the weekend and to fortify themselves for the rigours of the forthcoming week. As usual, Louise, Helen, and Jane arrived first; the former sped off to the bar with their order while the other two took possession of their favourite table in the window.

Louise quickly returned with a tray of drinks. As she poured the wine, she chided Helen and Jane who, in her absence, had lapsed into rapt and silent contemplation of what they had witnessed earlier on. 'Wake up, you two. It wasn't a dream. I saw it too. It definitely happened.'

A happy smile appeared on Helen's face. 'I know, and we still have the dress rehearsal and all the performances to go.'

'I trust you were suitably impressed by my hot tip?'

Helen nodded. 'Definitely. I'll never forget the look on Jane's face when Chris announced he couldn't feel authentic unless he rehearsed *au naturel*, dropped his boxers and got into the bath. That man doesn't have a shred of modesty about him.'

Louise laughed loudly. 'No. But he does have a lot not to be modest about.'

Helen turned to Jane. 'And what did you think about Josh?'

Jane could still recall every moment of the rehearsal. 'He looked nervous enough before they started on the final run-through, and when he saw what Chris had done, I thought he was going to faint. So full marks to him for rehearsing *au naturel* as well. Mind you, Chris must have been nervous too; up to now, he's been almost word-perfect, but today he kept messing up his big speech so poor Josh had to keep getting in and out of the bath.'

Helen shook her head. 'When he stopped halfway into the bath and began shouting at Chris for messing up his lines yet again, I didn't know where to look.'

Louise laughed again. 'I did.'

Behind them the door of the bar opened, and all conversation immediately died. The room remained in total silence as Hetty walked slowly over to the Coven, an expectant grin on her face. 'Don't worry, I'm not stopping so you don't need to buy me a drink. All I need to know is who won the sweepstake?'

Louise pulled a sheaf of papers from her bag and placed them on the table. 'Helen is my scrutineer, so I can let you know once she's signed off on the results.' She pushed the papers towards Helen. 'Do you agree with my adjudication?'

Helen scanned the list, checked the three names Louise had highlighted, and nodded her assent. 'Absolutely.'

Louise retrieved her papers and glanced up at Hetty. 'So here are the results: in reverse order as ever. The third place goes to Peggy: as she hadn't seen Act Two before today, I guess we should call it beginner's luck. The second place goes to me: damn close for Chris, but a bit optimistic when it came to Josh. I'm therefore pleased to confirm that you're the winner.'

Hetty took the money that Louise offered to her. 'Thanks. By the way, purely as a matter of professional interest, how close was I?'

Helen checked the list. 'God! You were spot on for both. To the second.'

Hetty grinned. 'Good, I like winning.'

Louise looked puzzled. 'How do you do these tricks?'

Hetty's grin vanished in a moment. 'They're not tricks; they're never tricks. If I told you the truth, I'd have to kill you. I don't want to give Maggie any casting problems at this late stage, so I'll just collect my winnings, take my leave, and see you all at the next rehearsal.' She slipped the money into her bag and left as quickly as she had arrived.

Jane watched in silence until the door had closed behind her. 'I don't know about you, but I find every single aspect of her absolutely terrifying.'

Louise nodded. 'Join the club. After she arrived in East Upbury, she was put into the same class at the village school as my youngest sister, so I've known her, by reputation at least, for about seven years. Until she arrived, all the local kids had been terrified by the West Upbury mafia who ran all the usual playtime protection rackets, but within a week, she'd taken control of everything. No one ever discovered what she said to them, but the violence and extortion ended immediately—and there were never any repercussions afterwards. I don't know about you, but I'd never want to get on the wrong side of her as I value my life too much.' Louise emptied the remnants of the bottle into their glasses and then waved to the barman to bring them another.

Chapter 10
The Dinner Party

'The choices for dinner on the Gaol Menu never changed: brown stuff or grey stuff. Whichever dish you chose, the meals always tasted exactly the same: the only difference was the colour.'

The Musician's Destiny

The rehearsal on the following Saturday went well, but the session had required hard work from everyone involved. Throughout the day, Toby and Sarah had no opportunity for any private conversations, and as they packed away the props and furniture at the end of the rehearsal, they had time only to exchange a quiet "see you later". Sarah then set off to walk back to her aunt's house, and as Toby watched her take the footpath across the paddock towards the gate in the hedge, he mentally crossed off another milestone in his project plan.

Toby's week had been filled with many such moments. If he had a clear set of instructions or access to a reliable guidebook, he usually managed, to a greater or lesser extent, to meet the challenges life threw at him. However, he had decided to invite Sarah for dinner before he had worked out how to prepare for the occasion, and his discovery that she was vegetarian had added a massive extra layer of unexpected complexity to what he already realised would be a monumental task.

He spent the whole of Sunday evening producing a comprehensive list of the tasks he needed to complete over the following six days to prepare for the event. Then, as he reviewed the list and tried to plot a logical course through his notes, he realised the magnitude of the challenge he faced required a change to his approach: rather than spending each day checking off innumerable and unconnected "to-do" lists, he needed to adopt the methodology his company used to deliver complex projects. If he incorporated all the activities required to plan, prepare, and cook the meal into a multi-phase project plan, he would know exactly what he had to complete each day to ensure he could prepare everything in time for Saturday evening.

This appeared to be a sensible strategy, but it contained one fundamental flaw: Toby had no idea how to construct an appropriate menu, and thus had no way of reaching even his first milestone. Several hours of unsuccessful searching online for a vegetarian cookery book for beginners made him wonder if his ambition had for once over-reached itself. However, on the following day, a lunchtime expedition to a local independent bookshop allowed him to make a significant breakthrough. He had no idea what to look for, but he eventually shortlisted several books that showed potential.

After a further review of these, he finally settled on a hardback volume filled with large colour photographs of the finished dishes displayed on artisan pottery set on picturesque country dining tables. He initially baulked at the price of the book but changed his mind once he realised the photographs would give him an idea of what the finished products were supposed to look like.

Toby had deliberately not mentioned his plans to Adam, as he wanted to avoid the inevitable requests for status reports that would follow his announcement. He therefore picked up a copy of a new fantasy novel he had recently seen reviewed as a cover story for his trip out of the office. The reviewer had described the book as an epic quest in which a small but diverse band of heroes ventures into unknown and dangerous territories in order to fulfil their respective destinies, and Toby immediately wanted to read it. However, as he paid for both books, he realised the demands of the production meant he would have no time even to open the novel until after the production had finished.

Despite the comprehensive range of dishes in the book, Toby still found it impossible to reach his first milestone: many of the recipes appeared reasonably achievable, even to a novice like him with no experience, a tiny kitchen, and a complete lack of catering technology, but he had no idea how to combine an appropriate range of the available dishes into a coherent menu. After another long night of indecision, he realised he needed to engage the services of an expert consultant, so the next evening, he called his older sister for advice.

Julia was five years older than Toby, and he had always been in awe of her culinary abilities although he would only have admitted this to her under extreme duress. He was certain Julia would give him good advice, but he knew he risked breaching the confidentiality of his project as he had never been able to keep any secrets from her.

Once Julia had reminded him to call their parents more often and checked he had not forgotten any imminent family birthdays, Toby seized the opportunity to raise the subject he wanted to discuss. 'I've invited some friends for a meal, and one is vegetarian. This is uncharted territory for me, and I wondered if you had any idea what I could cook.'

'Does your guest eat eggs and cheese?'

'Yes, she does. Just no fish or meat.'

'She? How many people have you invited?'

'There'll be just the two of us.'

'And will it be a romantic candle-lit dinner?'

Toby realised he had already breached his self-imposed confidentiality provision, and paused while he gathered his thoughts. 'I'm planning for candles, but I'm not sure about the other bit.'

'Who's the lucky lady?'

'We're both involved with the East Upbury play.'

'Is she in the cast?'

'No, she's backstage like me. An additional complication is that we're rehearsing all weekend, and as she's not local, the only time she can come is on Saturday evening.'

'How much time do you have to cook on the day?'

'Currently, I hardly have time to live—let alone cook a three-course dinner.'

'If you're pushed for time, you'll need to prepare everything in advance. Then, on the day, all you have to do is cook it.'

'I should be able to manage that. My real problem is I don't actually know "what" to cook.'

Julia remained silent for a moment while she considered her response. 'Do you remember the chaos you caused the first time Mum let me cook pancakes on Shrove Tuesday?'

'I wanted to help you.'

'What an interesting definition of the word "help"! If we had the time, we could debate the semantics for hours. But to return to the matter in hand: you can make pancakes, fill them with spinach, ratatouille or whatever well in advance, and store them in the fridge. Then, on Saturday, all you need to do is bake them in the oven and serve them with something simple like new potatoes and a green salad.'

'That sounds achievable, even for a neophyte like me, and there's a recipe for stuffed pancakes in my book. How do you manage to make cooking sound so easy?'

'Because, unlike you, I live in the real world. How's the novel going?'

'Very slowly. Over the past few months, my life has been a bit busy.'

'Well, you need to get a move on. I'm looking forward to seeing it on the shelf in my library, although I'm not sure of the Dewey Decimal category for a first novel by a younger brother who lives in a world of fantasy.'

'And I love you too.'

'Do you have everything you need now?'

'Yes, I mean no. I also need your thoughts on a pudding.'

'That's easy: always go for chocolate. For simplicity, I suggest a mousse.'

'Brilliant. I've seen several recipes for that online.'

'By the way, when's the play?'

'The week after next. Do you fancy coming to see it? It's about the history of East Upbury at the time of the First World War. If you're free, I can probably get you tickets.'

'It's more your period than mine, so regrettably I'll have to pass on your generous invitation. But, apart from that, I hope it's a success.'

'The rehearsals have all gone well, so as long as it doesn't rain the show should be excellent.'

'I meant your dinner party. Bye.'

'Bye.'

Once Toby had finalised the details of the menu and re-checked all the recipes, he produced a master shopping list of all the ingredients. In view of the importance of the event, he decided he ought to test his pancake-making skills by holding a dress rehearsal for the main course, so he then doubled the relevant quantities on his list. He also updated his project plan to include this new stage, although it took him considerably longer than the recipe suggested to prepare the dish.

Nonetheless, when he finally removed the finished product from the oven, it looked recognisably similar to the photograph in his book, even without any artisan pottery on which to display the results of his hard work. More importantly, when he came to eat the meal, it tasted quite good. Even the thought of eating the same meal again the following evening and then, for a third time, with Sarah on Saturday did not put him off; after all, as a stage manager, he regularly witnessed nightly performances of the same production.

In his project plan, Toby had allocated some time on Friday evening to clean his flat. However, an excruciatingly slow review meeting meant he arrived home far later than planned, and by the time he finished making the chocolate mousse, he only had time to tidy away the clean clothes he had hung in the bathroom to dry, remove the draft chapters of his novel from the dining table, and return a pile of books that had set up temporary lodgings on the floor next to the sofa back to his library.

As he set off for the rehearsal on Saturday morning, he felt his flat looked as good as he could make it. He had even managed to iron the tablecloth and napkins he had bought in honour of the event, although he had to abandon the stack of dirty bowls and jugs he had used while making the mousse and leave them unwashed in the sink.

When Toby returned home after the rehearsal, he immediately set to work on the final tasks in his project plan: he removed the pancakes from the fridge, washed some new potatoes, and made the dressing for the green salad. As he ticked off each of the tasks, he realised he felt far more nervous about the forthcoming evening than he had expected and as a result had fallen well behind his schedule. He therefore closed the kitchen door on the chaos inside and headed off to shower: he knew from experience at work that even the best project plans needed regular revision.

Sarah arrived precisely on time, and the sight of her in a summer dress rather than her usual uniform of jeans and polo short made him feel much better. He hoped the smile on her face augured well for the success of their evening together. Once she had made appreciative comments about the skilful conversion of the historic mill building and he had assured her it was neither dark nor satanic, Toby offered her what he called the "guided tour": the wide range of his film collection and the eclectic choice of film posters decorating the walls impressed her, although the number of books in his library left her momentarily speechless.

When they finally sat down to eat, Toby realised that Julia's menu advice had, as ever, been perfect. Sarah enjoyed the first two courses and offered spontaneous praise of his pancake-making skills. However, her subsequent remark that she was glad he had not spent too long cleaning his flat especially for her because of all his commitments with the play left him struggling for an appropriate response. He did his best to thank her for her compliment, but as he surveyed the room, he acknowledged to himself that the place had not been this tidy since he first moved in.

By the time Toby collected their plates after the main course, he finally felt he could relax. He had managed to deliver both courses completely to plan, and with a large bowl of chocolate mousse chilling in the fridge, nothing now could go wrong.

As he moved towards the kitchen door with the plates, Sarah picked up the empty salad bowl and started to follow him. 'Let me save you a trip and bring this.'

Toby stopped in front of the closed door. 'Don't worry, I can manage.'

She gave him a look that made him feel good. 'You can't do everything. You've worked so hard to produce all this delicious food, and after such a long day of rehearsal as well.'

'No, but I can clear the table. Don't forget, you're my guest.'

'Are you trying to keep me out of the kitchen? Do you have a chef concealed in there?'

'Of course not. I prepared every single item myself. I thought I had everything under control, but a few last-minute crises before you arrived meant I ran out of time to finish the washing up, so the kitchen is currently a bit messy.'

'Don't worry, I can cope with a bit of mess.'

'Well actually, it's extremely messy. If it's all the same to you, I'd prefer you not to witness the disaster area. I'd hate to spoil this carefully crafted illusion of competence.'

'As you put it so eloquently, I'll sit down again.'

'Thank you. The dessert is chilling in the fridge, so I won't be a moment. Feel free to browse the books or something.'

He closed the kitchen door behind him, and Sarah walked over to the bookcase, picked up a large hardback book, and opened it. As she glanced at the first few pages, a puzzled frown appeared on her face, and she quickly returned the book to the shelf. After a moment, she picked up a second one and repeated the same process.

Toby soon returned with two soup bowls in his hands, and when he saw Sarah's look of concern, he hastened to reassure her. 'Don't worry, it's all completely vegetarian. I checked every label.'

Sarah returned to the table. 'I'm sure it is. It's just that I've never seen chocolate mousse served in a soup bowl before.'

'I'm not really set up for dinner parties. These were the only bowls left that were clean, so I had to improvise. If it makes it easier, you can think of it as thick cold chocolate soup.'

'Chocolate soup sounds delicious.'

After several mouthfuls and further compliments, Sarah paused, and a serious look appeared on her face. 'I don't want to appear nosy, but several of the books on your shelves appear to be library books.'

Toby nodded. 'They are—or at least they were.' The serious look remained, so he hastened to explain. 'Don't worry, I haven't stolen them. My sister's a librarian, and she doesn't like to discard books—so she rehomes them. Some people rehome animals; she does it for books.'

'That's sweet.'

'I get the history books, especially anything about the First World War.'

'Well, since you're clearly such an expert on the period, I wonder if you could answer a question that's been bugging me.'

'Ask away, I'll do my best.'

'My aunt's filled me in on the local background to the play, but I'm a bit fuzzy about why there was a war at all. Our syllabus didn't cover it when I was in school: we only ever studied the Tudors and Hitler. What I want to know is why the men from the village ended up on a battlefield in France.'

Toby frowned. He could certainly answer the question but had not expected to be called on to do so during their dinner. 'Let me think for a moment. Some people have spent years studying the subject, so I'll need some props to do full justice to the story.' He glanced around the room in a desperate search for inspiration. 'This table is France, I'm the British army, and you're the German army.'

Sarah nodded reassuringly, so he continued. 'Once war broke out, you planned a quick strike in the West against France. You wanted to knock it out and then concentrate your forces against Russia in the East—by the bookcase.' He gestured towards the large pine bookcase where Sarah had found the books. 'But this meant you had to pass through Belgium.'

He pointed at the soup bowl in front of her. 'Your mousse is Belgium. It's Belgian chocolate by the way. I'd guaranteed Belgium's neutrality, so that was how I got involved. You planned to cut off Paris in a pincer movement.'

He moved the wine bottle into position. 'This bottle is Paris. The battle ended in stalemate, so we dug parallel lines of trenches stretching from the mousse down to the Swiss border by the cheese board.' He paused and looked down at the table. 'And there, more or less, we stayed for the next few years.'

He knew the subject well, but the unexpected intimacy of their situation made it increasingly difficult for him to remain focussed on the final stages of his narrative. 'There were several inconclusive battles. Then, in 1916, I deployed numerous regiments, including one with the men from East Upbury, to northern France to take part in what I'd optimistically called the Big Push, a massive battle intended to break the stalemate.' He indicated a spot on the table, and his hand moved closer to hers. 'It opened with a massive artillery barrage, which went on for five days, but which failed to destroy your lines. Then my men advanced across No Man's Land.'

As if under its own volition, his hand moved across the table and took hers. 'And, as the men advanced, they were massacred. On the first day of the Somme, the British Army suffered around sixty thousand casualties.' His narrative ground to a halt as too many distracting thoughts prevented him from continuing any further. 'What happened over the next five months is in all the history books. I can lend you some if you like.'

'What took you so long?'

'I had to wait for the barrage to end. You can't change history.'

'It's not cannon fire. It's the sound of my heart pounding.'

There are moments in every life when time stands still as the individuals involved anticipate what will happen next. Toby knew, more certainly than he had ever known anything in his life, that in the next few moments he would kiss Sarah. He also knew she was going to kiss him.

The loud ring of the doorbell brought their moment of anticipation to an abrupt end.

Toby closed his eyes and breathed out sharply. 'I have no belief in any type of deity in whatever shape or form he, she, or even it is supposed to come in. However I sometimes feel that someone, somewhere, is watching my every move. Ignore it.'

The doorbell rang again.

'Aren't you going to answer the door? It might be important.'

'I'm not expecting anybody. It's probably only the local evangelists again, and I wouldn't want to subject you to a performance of my "being born again only makes you even more of a pain the second time around" routine.'

The doorbell rang again, this time for longer.

'It'll go away.' Toby spoke more in hope than expectation.

After a moment, the unmistakable sound of Adam's voice came through the letterbox. 'Toby, I need to speak to you urgently.'

Sarah looked at Toby. 'I don't think Adam will go away.'

Adam rang the bell again, and for a moment silence reigned. Eventually, Toby shook his head. Almost incapable of speech, he gave a monosyllabic but deeply considered response. 'No.'

'Are you going to let him in?'

'I suppose so.'

Toby walked out into the hall to open the front door, and a visibly upset Adam rushed past him into the living room. 'I knew you were in because I saw your car outside. I need to talk to you urgently. I've got a huge problem with the play.' Despite not being noted for his powers of observation, Adam could not miss Sarah sitting at the table and smiling politely at him. 'Oh, hello. I thought Toby would be here by himself. I'm not interrupting anything, am I?'

Sarah shrugged non-committally. Toby, still struggling to be polite, ignored Adam's question and spoke slowly and deliberately. 'What, exactly, is your huge problem?'

'Everything! Everything is wrong.'

Adam began to pace about the room, and Sarah glanced at her watch. 'I hadn't realised how late it is. I think I'd better leave you both to it.'

Toby turned to her in anguish. 'No. You don't need to go. Please.'

'It's very late, and we all have another long day tomorrow. I need my beauty sleep—even if you don't.'

'Do you have to?'

Sarah stood up. 'For tonight—yes. There'll be time enough for us another day.'

Adam had collapsed onto the sofa, staring in forlorn concentration at the floor, and completely oblivious to their conversation.

'I'll see you out then.' Toby followed Sarah into the hall and opened the front door. As she turned to face him, he laughed. 'I hadn't expected our evening to end like this.'

'Obviously.'

'I wanted our evening together to work out right—nothing more than that.'

'It did. You worked so hard, and you'd cooked such a delicious dinner. I can't wait until next time.'

'What are you doing tomorrow evening?'

'We'll both be busy with the rehearsal again tomorrow, and once it's over, I have to head straight back to London to prepare for work on Monday. We need to save all this until we have the time to enjoy it properly.'

'Are you sure you have to go?'

'Yes, I do. At least for tonight. Goodnight.' She leant forward and kissed him on his cheek.

Even though Toby had always considered himself to be a pacifist, when he heard Adam's voice, he would willingly have killed him on the spot. However, Sarah's kiss dissolved his murderous intent, so he merely closed the front door behind her, and after standing for a moment in the hall to compose himself, he returned to the living room.

With Toby and Sarah in the hall, Adam had wandered into the kitchen, helped himself to a large bowl of chocolate mousse, and now sat at the table eating it. 'I hope you don't mind, but food always helps me calm down.'

'Have as much as you like. It's spare now.'

Adam ate another large spoonful. 'You took your time. Is anything going on?'

Toby looked at him in amazement, wondering how Adam could be so unaware of what he had interrupted. 'Something came up. Something we had to talk about for tomorrow's rehearsal.' He paused and took a deep breath. 'So tell me, what's the huge problem?'

A look of utter despair appeared on Adam's face. 'I have no idea of timing.'

'Really?'

Adam's lack of reaction made Toby realise he also had no appreciation of sarcasm.

'It's the whole dance thing. I can't remember any of it. I've spent the entire evening trying to work out how the Morris Dance is supposed to go, and I just can't get it right. If I carry on with the play, I'll let everyone down.'

'You'll let everyone down if you dropped out now. It's not long before our first night.'

Adam's panicked reaction made Toby realise he needed to offer some urgent reassurance. 'But there's still plenty of time for you to get the Morris Dance right.' This appeared to work as he saw Adam recover a little. Then Toby had another idea. 'And what about Kate? You both seem to be getting on extremely well, and the two of you were together for most of today. It would be a shame for you to blow your chances with her at this point.'

The look of abject despair did not leave Adam's face. 'What chances? I'm currently waiting for her to tell me how much she thinks of me as a "good friend" so I can notch up yet another failure to add to my extensive collection.'

Toby shook his head sadly. 'We can't resolve the issue with Kate, but at least we can work on the dance problem.'

'Now? But it's late.'

'Not now. Tomorrow morning, before the rehearsal. We'd need to get to Somerton Court early, but we should have enough time to rehearse what we need to before the rest of the cast turns up. Where should we start?'

'At the beginning I suppose. I've got it all written down.' Adam jumped up, pulled a crumpled piece of paper from his pocket, and started to read aloud as he attempted to work out the movements.

'Left, right, left right, left, right, turn.

Left, right, left right, left, right, turn.

And so on.'

Seeing Adam's intense frown of concentration, Toby realised he had taken on a far more complex problem than he initially assumed, and knew he needed to probe the matter further. 'And how do these moves fit to the music?'

Adam's confusion intensified. 'Fit? What does "fit" mean?'

Toby saw that to make any progress at all he needed to address the issue one small step at a time. As he had encouraged Adam to audition for the play, he felt an obligation to him, to Maggie, and now of course to Sarah as well. 'The rhythm. Don't think about the tune; just concentrate on the rhythm and remember to count. The music is in four time, so you count in fours. It's like this...

One, two, three, four
Two, two three, and turn
Three, two, three, four,
Four, two three, and turn.'

As he spoke, he jigged around the table.

Adam watched in amazement as if Toby had just performed an elaborate conjuring trick. 'You make everything look so easy in here. But it's completely different in that huge open space with Chris and Josh there as well.'

'So we'll need to get Josh there too. Hopefully, he won't mind an early start too much. I'll call him.' Toby picked up his phone, and Josh soon answered. He seemed to be having a quiet night at home, although Toby could hear another masculine voice in the background.

'Josh? How are you? Good. Yes, it went well—and I didn't serve any chilli. But she's gone home now. Yes. Gone home. I'll tell you the full story tomorrow. Look, Adam's here, and he's a bit worried about the Morris Dance so we thought we might schedule an extra rehearsal at Somerton Court. First thing tomorrow morning. Can you make eight o'clock? How about quarter past? Fine, we'll see you at half past. Done.' He put the phone down and turned to Adam. 'And once you've finished your chocolate mousse you can help me wash up.'

Adam said nothing and instead picked up his spoon and resumed eating.

Chapter 11
The Journalist

'Many locations retain a residual echo of significant events that once occurred there, and those wizards who possess the power can access such traces when they visit the place. This is how wizards track the nefarious deeds of the Guild; if they manage to overcome their innate hostility to each other and work together, a team of wizards can accomplish anything.'

The Musician's Destiny

In the early morning sunlight, a thin mist hung over the sluggish stream meandering through the fields that surrounded East Upbury on three sides. At this time of day, most of the villagers were still indoors; only the distant figure of a jogger on a footpath through a field of wheat, with the burnished gold of the ripening crop dotted with the deep red of poppies, gave an indication of contemporary life to the timeless landscape.

But, as Adam drove along the empty roads, he did not notice the beauty of the countryside around him. Since rehearsals started, each weekend had been an adventure unlike anything he had experienced before. As in all good adventures, there had been moments of fear as well as many thrills, and a sudden terror had prompted last night's panic over the Morris Dance.

Despite the generous helping of reassurance provided by Toby, Adam still had no idea if he could act—let alone dance. He simply had nothing to measure himself against, as he had never experienced anything like the play before, and since the start of rehearsals he had travelled far beyond the familiar landmarks of his daily life. In his career, he had achieved what the world regarded as success, but along the way he had somehow forgotten how to have fun.

As he turned into the lane leading towards Somerton Court, he attempted to settle his nerves by once again reminding himself of Toby's description of the Morris Dance as merely a part of the play rather than a test on which he would be examined. He hoped that after this additional rehearsal, he would be better able to face the ordeal when they rehearsed the scene later in the day.

He also wondered what else the day might bring beyond the Morris Dance, and he now felt almost positive about seeing Kate again. Toby had reminded him that yesterday Kate had joined their table for lunch at the Puppy and Duckling, and he regarded this as a positive development. When she arrived, Adam assumed she wanted to talk to Sarah, and the two of them then spent some time discussing a new romantic comedy they had both recently seen.

However, last night Toby explained Sarah had viewed Kate's arrival very differently. Although Adam always questioned Toby's judgement as a matter of course, discovering what Sarah thought filled him with secret delight, as the way she dealt with the endless demands of the actors without ever upsetting any of them showed her to be an excellent judge of character.

With Kate at their table, Adam had said little as he preferred films with subtitles rather than romantic comedies, and as such could not contribute much to their discussion. However, the mere fact of her continued proximity meant he had struggled to eat his lunch. Afterwards, he decided that Kate was the most wonderful woman he had met in his entire life, and if she ever deigned to ask him, he would gladly worship her forever.

Adam parked his car and then made his way across the paddocks and through the gap in the hedge into the theatre, where Toby had prepared the stage for their impromptu rehearsal. After the events of the previous evening, Toby had hardly slept and had arrived at Somerton Court far earlier than he needed to. Then they both heard the sound of another car engine in the lane, and shortly afterwards Josh ambled into the theatre, carrying a large coffee, yawning ostentatiously, and complaining about how much he had to suffer for his art. Adam and Toby ignored his grumbles, and Adam and Josh then took their places on the stage while they waited for Toby to turn on the music.

As the familiar music began, Toby began to count the time out loud to remind Adam of what they had worked on the previous evening. Unfortunately, this did not produce the desired effect: Toby's late-night tutorial had reassured Adam that he knew all the steps, but he still had little idea how to move around the stage, as Toby's tiny flat had not allowed them to rehearse this additional key element.

Once Josh and Adam had finished their initial run-through, Toby attempted to give them some positive feedback, but Adam interrupted him with despair once more clouding his face. 'The counting makes sense now—ultimately, it's only numbers, and I work with those all week. But I still don't know where to go. I'm supposed to follow Chris, and he's not here.'

Josh laughed. 'You should've invited him as well. I'm sure he'd love such an early start.'

This did not amuse Toby. 'This extra rehearsal is our little secret—and it's going to stay that way.'

'So what's your cunning plan?'

Throughout rehearsals, Adam had been impressed by Toby's ability to resolve most of the issues that everyone, from Maggie on downwards, threw at him on a regular basis. But this morning, possibly due to the early start and a lack of sleep and coffee, he struggled to come up with an answer although Adam, for once, could see the solution immediately. After Toby had stuttered on ineffectually for a few more seconds, Adam interrupted him. 'We need Toby to be Chris.'

A moment of silence followed while Toby attempted to analyse this contribution from such an unexpected source. He ended his moment of reflection with a curt response. 'What?'

'You know all the steps because you showed them to me last night. So you need to be up here too, and then I can follow you around the stage.'

'That was purely in the privacy of my own flat. I'm not an actor—and certainly not a dancer.'

'But, as stage manager, your job is to do everything you can to make the show a success. You've said it enough times.'

Toby knew from experience that he always struggled to argue with Adam once he had facts on his side and conceded the point with reluctance. 'I know.'

'So, for this one rehearsal, you need to stand in for Chris.'

Toby hesitated. He realised he had been backed into a corner and found the feeling unsettling. 'I can't dance—as you know all too well from seeing me at parties.'

'Come on. We've got the place to ourselves, so there's no one else here to witness your debut performance.'

Toby hesitated again while he considered his options. After working out, there were none available to him, he grunted his reluctant consent.

As he walked onto the stage to take his position, Josh gave him a round of applause and made a move to pick up his phone. 'This is amazing: Toby dancing. I need to record this for posterity.'

'No way. If you do, I'll release Hetty's photos of you and Chris rehearsing *au naturel* to the ladies of the cast. She's an excellent photographer, and they leave absolutely nothing to the imagination.'

'But Maggie banned all cameras from the rehearsal.'

'Have you ever tried to stop Hetty from doing anything? She plans to use the photos to get her revenge on Chris for the way he's treated her during rehearsals, but knowing him, he'll just ask for a set for himself as well.'

For once in his life, Josh had no idea how to answer, so Toby turned to Adam. 'Shall we dance?'

Toby liked the music Maggie had selected for the Morris Dance. The Morris Band performed a traditional tune at a village party during the first act, but for the final scene had reworked the piece in a minor key to make the music sound sinister and ethereal. During this scene the three young women returned to the village green where they had first met their partners on an earlier Whitson morning. Maggie wanted the men to appear there as ghosts and perform a Morris Dance; they would be invisible to the women, but she told Louise to sense David's presence and react accordingly.

Despite his familiarity with the music, Toby initially struggled to take the lead. However, as it continued, he realised he knew much of the routine from having watched so many rehearsals and the rest he could improvise by following Josh. By the end of their third run-through, Adam had finally mastered how to move around the stage, while Toby was surprised to discover he had actually enjoyed the experience.

As Toby switched off the music, a round of applause from behind the thick hedge that rose above the topmost tier of seats made him jump. After a moment, Joan stepped through the gap and onto the top of the steps leading down towards the stage. 'That was excellent: a superb ending to the play. You three boys have done my script proud.'

She made her way down the steep steps and joined them on the stage. 'I hope you didn't mind an uninvited audience, but I heard the music and was curious to discover what was happening. This ungodly hour is usually a stranger to me, but I'm here this morning to pay my respects at the war memorial in the garden.'

Toby had not yet read Joan's book on the history of the village, and so had no knowledge of the memorial. 'What does it commemorate?'

'It's a private memorial raised by a grieving Ewart Somerton and his wife to their son and the men of the estate who died in the Great War. Today is the anniversary of the day they went over the top—at about this time too. All were about your age or even younger, and within a few minutes, not much longer than that dance you were rehearsing, most of them were dead. That's why I came here this morning: to make a private homage and let them know what we were doing with their story.'

All three were at a loss how to respond to this unexpected intrusion of reality into their rehearsal, and finally it fell to Adam to break the silence. 'You wouldn't like to know how many books I've read about the history of the war over the past few months. But your story brings the whole nightmare far closer to home than many, many hundreds of pages.'

Joan scrutinised each of them in turn. 'You'll all succeed in what you're doing, and each of you will get what you deserve, I know it. I really struggled to write this scene; in the end, I described what I wanted to happen, and Maggie had the inspired idea to add the Morris Dance. What I saw you rehearsing was exactly the ending I'd hoped for, and you all worked together so well as a team.'

Adam stood in silence, unaccustomed to receive such generous compliments. However, his reverie came to an abrupt end as a large black and white dog bounded out of the bushes and knocked him to the ground.

A short stocky figure, dressed in a camouflage T-shirt and baggy shorts, followed Fenrir onto the stage where, breathing hard, she attempted to remove him from on top of Adam. 'Don't worry. He loves everyone he meets. When he licks your face like that, it's his way of saying hello.' As Hetty attached Fenrir to his lead, she acknowledged the amused audience to the chaos her arrival had created. 'Morning, Tobe. Morning, folks.'

Toby managed to stop laughing for a moment. 'Morning, Hetty. What are you doing here so early?'

'I like to keep an eye on matters around the village. Ever since we started rehearsals, I stop off here on my morning run to make sure everything is still as it should be. No one ever asks me what I'm doing when I have Fenrir with me.' Then she regarded the three of them with suspicion. 'But why are you here already? There's nothing on the schedule this early.'

Toby decided it would be safe to share their plan with her. 'We thought these two could benefit from an extra rehearsal of the Morris Dance, and I've been playing Chris.'

Hetty shook her head dismissively. 'That's way beyond your acting skills. You'd need to be an actor of real talent to play such a pretentious git.' She turned to Adam and Josh. 'But you two might not be rehearsing this scene today anyway, as Maggie's had to change the schedule. All the smart costumes and military uniforms the wardrobe team have hired arrived last night, and Miss Milton's team have dug out the costumes for the villagers and the front-of-house team from the depths of the Village Hall as well. Everything's waiting in the barn, and Maggie needs you all to try them on so Miss Milton's team have time to make any alterations. Then later a journalist and photographer from the local rag will be coming to take some publicity shots of you in costume. They've promised Maggie a big article on the show in next week's edition, what with it being the centenary and the local connection. She hopes the publicity will sell a few more tickets.'

This unexpected disruption to their schedule concerned Adam. 'But why do we need the extra publicity? I thought we'd sold loads of tickets already.'

'We have, but Maggie wants to show the Culture Committee she knows what she's doing: they can't argue with a week of full houses. She'll announce the change to today's schedule before the rehearsal starts.'

Joan smiled round at all of them. 'I think we locals should leave you three lads to finish your rehearsal. Once you're done here, call round to my house, and I'll find you all some breakfast to keep you going. It's a long time to lunch, and you can't rehearse very well on an empty stomach. I need you all to be at your best for our show.'

Adam had no idea of the additional work required during the final weeks of rehearsal to make the production ready for public performance. He hated any change to his expected routine and would spend the day in a state of permanent shock as the stream of unscheduled events swept him along. He quickly decided the only way to survive the disruption would be by sticking closely to Josh, as he should be well used to such chaos and thus would be a safe guide through to the end of the day.

When Toby, Josh, and Adam returned to Somerton Court after their second breakfast, Maggie directed the entire cast to the barn where they found the floor full of so many racks and hampers of costumes that the place looked like a jumble sale.

Until the establishment of the summer production, which always attracted an artistically minded and geographically diverse audience, the annual Wassail, held in the Village Hall in early December, had been the zenith of village cultural life. However, despite the ancient heritage of its name, the Wassail was little more than a parochial pantomime or, more accurately, a drunken pre-Christmas review for villagers. Few of the costumes retrieved from the store in the Village Hall could be regarded as properly authentic and thus suitable for the summer production.

Miss Milton had already assembled her team in the barn, and a plump middle-aged woman, about the same age as Adam's mother, pushed through the crowd of expectant actors towards Adam and Josh and peered at the paper in her hand. 'I see from my list that you two are soldiers. Get undressed down to your underwear, and let's see what we can find for you.'

Adam wondered where they would go to try on their costumes, but as he looked around for a changing room, he saw Josh had already started to unbutton his shirt. Adam had a recurrent nightmare of undressing in public, but all around him people had begun to remove their clothes as well. He forced himself to follow, and only began to relax when he realised no one was taking any notice of him. Then he sensed someone *was* watching him: a few feet away, Kate, framed by a strong shaft of sunlight from the large open doorway, gazed in his direction while a swarm of wardrobe ladies fitted her with a ball gown of ivory silk inlaid with rows of tiny glass beads.

When Kate saw Adam looking back at her, she smiled at him. 'What do you think of my outfit?'

'It's wonderful. You look like a goddess.' Then he blushed a deep crimson all over.

Kate held a finger to her lips. 'That's uncommonly perceptive of you. I am indeed a goddess, but it's supposed to be a secret, so keep it to yourself, and please don't let on to anyone else.'

The wardrobe lady returned with several hangers of khaki uniforms, creased cotton shirts, and pairs of heavy boots for Adam and Josh to try on. After several false starts, the addition of thick leather belts to hold up their trousers, and the judicious application of pins to indicate where the legs needed to be shortened, she finally expressed her satisfaction. She then packed them off to the stage for Maggie to scrutinise their outfits and give them her approval.

As they trudged across the paddock, Adam expressed his concerns to Josh. 'I feel like an idiot in this outfit. These uniforms look ancient.'

'They're not ancient—they're authentic: precisely what Maggie said she wanted when she gave her pep talk after the audition.'

'But we're not authentic, are we? I mean we're only pretending to be farm workers and soldiers and so on. We don't really get killed—otherwise, there'd only be one performance.'

'It's called acting, not pretending.'

In the theatre, Maggie had set up her base in the centre of the front row, with Toby at her side to take notes and record her decisions. The two of them then watched as a stream of costumed actors took turns parading across the stage for directorial approval. Meanwhile, a democratic chaos of villagers and sundry residents of the big house, with the lord of the manor and members of his family deep in conversation with dairy hands, farm workers, and housemaids, all massed together in the wings as they awaited their own turn for Maggie's scrutiny.

Adam and Josh had left Chris in the barn working his way through the rack of uniforms as he attempted to find the one that fitted him best. He eventually joined them in the wings, and the three then stood around in a tense silence while they waited for their call. Since the unscheduled revelations during the undress rehearsal, the overt hostility between Chris and Josh had been replaced by a taciturn non-aggression pact.

From the earliest rehearsals, Maggie had insisted that David, Herbert, and Lawrence should behave like soldiers once they had joined up although Chris, Josh, and Adam had initially struggled to perform in an authentically military manner. In order to remedy this, Maggie had invited a local TA officer to the previous weekend's rehearsal, and he had then subjected the three of them to an hour of basic drill techniques.

Initially, their efforts had been painful both for the actors taking part as well as for all those watching the spectacle, but ultimately his work had achieved the desired objective. The three could now march around the stage with a reasonable degree of military precision. Before Maggie gave her approval to their costumes, she instructed the three of them to display their marching skills, and after she and Toby had a brief discussion about how they moved together, he recorded her decision in his folder.

Maggie then instructed Sarah to summon Peggy and her team of indoor staff to the stage while the photographer and journalist from *The Journal*, who had been deep in conversation with George in the row behind, got to work. To begin with, the photographer instructed Chris, Josh, and Adam to execute yet another brisk display of marching while he photographed them from different angles. After this, the journalist spent a few minutes with Josh and Adam while she recorded their names and asked about their roles as background for her article. As Josh and Adam made their way back to the barn, they could see her still deep in conversation with Chris.

Adam looked back at the pair of them in amazement. 'He's incorrigible. Doesn't he ever give up?'

Josh shook his head. 'Probably not, although despite all his hard work to date, his success rate with Kate has been precisely zero. Having seen how she continues to ignore every display of his abundant charms, I can only assume she's saving herself for someone else.'

'I assume so too. I wonder who the lucky man is.' Adam had long ago persuaded himself that Kate was way out of his league although, after observing her so closely over the weeks of rehearsal, he knew only Chris ever attempted to spend time with her. He decided not to dwell on the matter any further, as merely the thought of the two of them together made him unhappy. 'What do you think he's telling her? It can't take that long for him to give her his name, rank, and serial number. It's not as if she's writing a feature for the Sunday papers.'

'He's probably telling her that, despite Maggie's description of the play as an ensemble production, he's actually the leading man. Let's leave him to his delusions of grandeur so we can get the first pick of the other costumes.'

Adam and Josh found the wardrobe team waiting for them back in the barn, this time with their farm worker costumes. Miss Milton's team had struggled to find many appropriate outfits, and in the bright light of a summer morning, Adam and Josh recognised the forlorn selection displayed on the rail as relics from the Wassail collection. As a result of the judicious combination of collarless shirts with waistcoats and heavy trousers from several superannuated suits, the wardrobe team had assembled two reasonably complete outfits. However, despite their best efforts and the employment of a significant amount of creative ingenuity, they had struggled to combine what remained into a third outfit that would pass muster.

In the continued absence of Chris, who had clearly decided to grant an extended interview to the journalist, Josh and Adam grabbed the two better costumes and tried them on. Neither costume fitted especially well, but the wardrobe lady had prepared herself for their inevitable complaints: she had discussed the history of the period with Toby and reminded them in a period of agricultural recession, farm workers often had to wear such badly fitting hand-me-downs.

When Chris eventually returned to the barn, he had a broad smile on his face, but this vanished the moment he saw the sole remaining costume hanging on the rail. With a look of disbelief, he picked up the shirt, trousers, and waistcoat, examined them carefully, and then, much to the amusement of Josh and Adam, set off at speed towards the main house where Miss Milton had gone to oversee all the required alterations.

He had not returned by the time Toby summoned them to the stage, so Adam and Josh paraded around as before until Maggie gave their costumes her approval. As they left the stage and headed back to the barn, they met Kate, by now properly in character: with her hair up and resplendent in her ball gown, she looked every inch the young debutante ready for her first season. She said nothing but merely lowered her eyes before curtseying demurely and then continuing on her way.

When Josh and Adam arrived back at the barn, they found the place once again full of actors, some still in costume and others changed back into their rehearsal clothes. Adam wondered how much longer it would be before they broke for lunch; their additional rehearsal had necessitated a horribly early start for him, and despite Joan's generous second breakfast, he now felt very hungry. However, at that moment, the wardrobe lady returned, this time with an armful of towels. 'Sorry, my dears. I almost forgot Maggie needs to approve these as well. Choose one each, get changed as soon as possible, and then head back to the stage for her to take a look.'

Despite the mass of people all around him, Adam had by now become used to changing in public, but his fingers struggled as he attempted to untangle the unfamiliar bootlaces. As Adam continued his battle with the knots, he realised Josh had already removed his clothes and placed them on a chair before wrapping one of the towels around his waist and setting off for the stage. Once Adam finally unlaced his boots, he removed his trousers and folded them over a hanger. He then grabbed the larger of the remaining towels, wrapped it around his waist, and rushed out of the barn. He caught up with Josh as he approached the theatre: with the session almost over, theirs were the final costumes still requiring Maggie's approval.

As they stood in the wings, Adam turned to Josh. 'The barn is not the changing room at the gym. What happened to your inhibitions back there?'

'All gone. All long gone. There's no one here who hasn't seen me *au naturel*, so what's the point of false modesty when I'm in a rush to get changed?'

'So you won't mind taking a bath in front of a sell-out audience every night?'

'I'll be scared shitless on the first night, but I'll do the scene anyway.'

Adam laughed, as Josh turned to him. 'Have you kept your boxers on?'

'Yes—of course.'

'You're not being authentic. I think I should report you to Hetty.'

'Please don't. I'm happy to be as authentic as anyone else—as long as my towel stays on—but I'll need time to work up to it.' He decided to change the subject. 'Do you have any friends coming? Toby's sold loads of tickets at work with a promise of me dancing as his USP.'

'It might not surprise you to hear this, but I've tried to keep news of my imminent exposure extremely quiet.'

'I don't blame you. And what about a girlfriend? I suppose she probably wouldn't mind what you do in the bath scene.'

Josh paused for a moment. 'I used to have girlfriends, but that wasn't what I really wanted. I now have a boyfriend.'

Adam blushed. 'Sorry. I shouldn't have made assumptions.'

'Don't worry. It's not a secret. Toby knows, but it's not public knowledge so please keep it to yourself.'

'Of course.'

'By the way, in case you start wondering later on, I think I should give you my standard disclaimer.'

'Disclaimer?'

'Merely the small print: nothing personal, but you're not my type and I don't fancy you.'

'Oh, thanks. I think.'

An urgent summons from Maggie brought their conversation to an end.

Chapter 12
The Journal

'As far as Duncan was concerned, any publicity was good publicity—as long as it sold more tickets for a show.'

The Musician's Destiny

Toby had not been in the world of work for many years but had already experienced his company's concept of "promotion": greater levels of responsibility and all the additional work coming with this, but without any significant increase in salary. Nonetheless, he had been delighted when Maggie, at George's suggestion, appointed him as historical adviser for the production although he knew the job would require a great deal of extra time and effort from him.

Inevitably Maggie chose to interpret the scope of Toby's new role extremely broadly. In addition to reviewing the costumes, props, and furniture to ensure they contained no obvious anachronisms, she also asked him to write an article on the historical background of the play for the programme and to produce a briefing note for her interview with *The Journal.*

Toby had never taken any notice of the local newspaper, as church fetes, produce shows, and local football derbies were of no interest to him, and he knew if an event of significance ever happened in the area, then national media would quickly pick up the story. Nonetheless, if Maggie thought an article in *The Journal* would sell more tickets for the play, then he was willing to sacrifice an evening he had planned to spend working on his novel to produce both the article for the programme and a detailed briefing note for her interview.

The new edition of *The Journal* appeared each Thursday, and Toby duly bought a copy during his lunch break. He then returned to his office to discover what the journalist had written. It took him some time to find her article, but after ploughing through pages of adverts for over-priced character properties in picturesque rural locations and a special photographic supplement covering the recent proms at local schools, he finally located it at the foot of page twenty-three. Beneath a small photograph of Chris, Josh, and Adam as they stood to attention in their uniforms, he spotted a brief article that he could easily have overlooked:

Somme Enchanted Evening

This year, East Upbury is breaking with its recent tradition of open-air Shakespearean productions performed in the magical setting of Somerton Court. To commemorate the centenary of the end of the Great War, the villagers will instead perform a new play about the tragic fate of a group of local men who were killed during the Battle of the Somme.

Even more than usual, the cast are hoping that the weather will stay warm and dry for their performances, as two of the actors will be taking a bath on stage each night.

The article also included full details of the venue, the times and dates of the performances, and a contact number to buy tickets. Toby read the article for a second time, and then let out a loud groan of despair.

Adam could not fail to hear the noise as he returned to his desk in the adjacent cubicle with a packet of sandwiches and a bottle of water. 'That sounded painful. What's the matter?'

'I've just read the so-called article about our show in *The Journal*.'

'What's wrong with it?'

'There's a good photo of you, Josh, and Chris playing soldiers, but after an appalling attempt at a pun in the headline, the article is short to the point of non-existence. It spends almost as much time on the bath scene as describing what the play is actually about. I spent a whole evening preparing a bullet-pointed list of key events to prep Maggie, and the only mention of the history is a throwaway comment about the local connection with the Battle of the Somme.'

As usual, Adam displayed no shred of sympathy for Toby's discomfort. 'From what little I know about journalists, they always look for the human-interest angle in any story. Despite all your excellent work, the risk of goose pimples for a couple of actors is likely to be of far more interest to readers of *The*

Journal than a thorough exposition of the play's historical context.' He paused and grinned. 'But why are you worrying? Isn't any publicity supposed to be good publicity?'

Toby considered this for a moment. 'Yes.'

'So you need to think of it as helping to get bums on seats. Even though the article's not what you expected, I'm sure it'll help sell a few more tickets.'

'Actually, there aren't very many left now. I used the human-interest angle to sell a bunch around here last week. In case you need to prepare yourself, most of our team will be coming on Saturday night.'

Adam groaned. 'Don't worry, I already know all about it. The play got mentioned in just about every meeting I went to last week: no one can believe I'll be appearing on stage. I'm just glad I keep my clothes on.'

'True. But I'd like to know who gave the journalist the story about the bath.'

From this point on, like ripples in the village pond after a stone has disturbed its placid waters, the story in *The Journal* became a major topic of conversation both in East Upbury and beyond. The issue that attracted people's attention was not so much what the article said, as this was old news, but rather the identity of the individual who had given the story to the journalist. Inevitably, the members of the Culture Committee also had their own specific concerns about the article, as its tabloid tone clashed uncomfortably with their own more elevated broadsheet aspirations.

For the most part, George had little time for local papers. He had still not forgotten the unthinking review *The Journal* had given to his production of *The Tempest*. The critic had been more concerned to produce a witty article full of laboured puns instead of a proper review of the production itself; to compound the insult the article appeared a full three weeks after the final performance. However, Maggie had introduced him to the team from *The Journal* when they arrived at Somerton Court, and after the young journalist mentioned she had only recently joined the paper, George decided to give her the benefit of the doubt and *The Journal* one last chance.

In the centre of East Upbury, the General Stores and Post Office stocked any item and offered every service for which the proprietors hoped their customers might be willing to pay good money. In addition to selling basic groceries to villagers and ready-made sandwiches, snacks, and drinks to passing tradespeople, the shop also acted as a newsagent, drop-off point for dry cleaning and Off-Licence (although neither the range nor the quality of its wines appealed to the more discerning palates of the Culture Committee). Within the General Stores, all villagers, irrespective of income, profession, or social status, met on neutral and equal terms. The young couple who managed the shop ran a slick seven-day operation, and thus had no time to become involved in the summer production. However, they had always supported George by acting as a box office for his productions, and for this reason, he tried to patronise their business as much as possible.

Today, George had several large letters he needed to post, and he planned to stop off at the General Stores on his way home after a lunchtime meeting at the Puppy and Duckling. The ostensible purpose of the meeting had been to review outstanding technical issues on the production, but as George already knew his team had every element firmly under control, he enjoyed the opportunity to combine some notional business with a pleasant lunch. As he walked back along the main street, now baking in the early afternoon sun, the sight of so many posters for the play visible in front windows, pasted on to lamp posts, and even taking prime position on the large noticeboard in the front window of the General Stores, filled him with both delight and pride.

George stopped for a moment to read a poster detailing the autumn programme for the Local History Society that had recently appeared on the noticeboard when the front door of the General Stores opened, and the emerging figure hailed him. George recognised the voice immediately: it belonged to Frederick, the Chairman of the Culture Committee, and the enthusiastic conduit for the myriad complaints about the summer production emanating from the great and the good of the village.

After spending his entire career in the Army, Frederick and his wife had moved to East Upbury last year following his retirement. He now filled his days with activities resulting from the numerous positions of responsibility he had subsequently taken on around the village. In addition to his role as Chairman of the Culture Committee, he had also become a Church Warden, School Governor and an active member of the Fete Committee; no event of significance in the village now took place without his involvement in some capacity. Some residents had swallowed their antipathy to Frederick's reactionary views, as few villagers possessed such a keen sense of public duty or worked as hard as he did, but others preferred always to keep him at arm's length.

In view of the season, Frederick had exchanged his familiar tweed jacket for a regimental blazer, but he never left his house without a shirt and tie. He had been born five years after George, but he dressed in the style of a man at least five years older and had the attitudes of a man at least a further decade older again. He was the antithesis of all that George lived for and believed in.

Frederick had led the opposition to George's proposed production, suggesting instead the committee select a play to commemorate the centenary of the Great War. In previous years, the committee had endured numerous lengthy discussions about such a commemoration although no one had ever proposed anything definite, let alone appropriate. Thus, several members had vaguely supported Frederick's suggestion, and when he forced a vote on the issue, the committee ended up evenly balanced, with his casting vote carrying the day.

The committee had been unprepared for Frederick's victory, and their subsequent selection of *Yonder Deep Green Field* had been a last-minute decision to meet the imminent publication date of the next parish magazine. As a result, Frederick and his coterie had approved the production of a play about which they knew nothing and endorsed the appointment of a new director they had never met. The accumulated fall-out resulting from these unknown elements had led to the volume of complaints that gave so much delight to Frederick each time he passed them on to George.

Frederick had a copy of *The Journal* in his hand, and the crimson flush in his cheeks and the way he brandished the paper in George's face made his state of mind immediately clear. 'Have you seen the article about your production in here?'

George noted Frederick's judicious use of the second-person possessive adjective and shook his head. 'Not yet. I'm on my way to pick up a copy.'

'I wouldn't waste your money on it. There's nothing about a commemoration of our heritage, merely a few short paragraphs about some actors taking a bath. Call me naïve, but I'd hoped for a little more from our local paper than this cheap descent into the tabloid gutter.' He folded the paper and slid it under his arm. 'But, apart from that, I'm pleased I've finally caught up with you as we have a number of outstanding issues that require our urgent discussion.'

With his scars from the meeting about the furniture still raw, George had not tried to avoid Frederick, but neither had he gone out of his way to look for him. However, with no obvious escape route available, he decided to play along.

'Discuss away. I'm on my way home after a pleasant lunchtime meeting, so I have all the time in the world.'

'I think I've notified you already that we have numerous concerns with this production of yours.'

'I think you have, and by "we", you mean the committee.'

'Of course, and I speak merely on their behalf, so this is in no way intended to be personal. But, as a committee, we selected this play after we were assured it would be a worthy commemoration of our local heritage.'

George decided to be placatory, at least to begin with. 'As indeed it will be. Maggie's watchword from our very first rehearsal has been "authentic". At my suggestion, she's even appointed a historical adviser to ensure we have no anachronisms. She plans to leave nothing to chance.'

'And what do advisers know?'

'In this case, a great deal. He has a degree in history from one of our older universities. Thus, he is vastly more knowledgeable on this period than either you or I.'

Frederick conceded the first point to George. 'That's all very well, but members of the committee are not happy with the way the production is going. This is definitely not what we voted for.'

He brandished the paper again to emphasise his point, but before he could continue, George moved on to the offensive. During his mauling at the committee meeting, he had not wished to upset those members who had always supported his previous productions and consequently had not caused a fuss. However, if Frederick wanted to continue the fight on a one-to-one basis, then he would defend himself forcefully although, of course, their only weapons would be words.

George resolved to refute each point Frederick made until, on a metaphorical level, he had either beaten him into submission or received his unconditional surrender. 'Don't forget I attended the meeting as well, and I recall how everyone voted: the committee tied five all on the choice of play and only your casting vote swung the day. I wouldn't describe it as a decisive majority; the result definitely didn't give you an overwhelming mandate.'

Frederick glared at him. 'Nonetheless, we won, and so our view must prevail. We selected a production to commemorate the noble sacrifice of our illustrious forebears.'

'From what I know of the history of the battle, it was certainly a sacrifice, but there wasn't much nobility in it—especially for those who died.'

Outside of the protective cocoon of the committee, Frederick struggled to deal with George; during his military career, he had been accustomed only to giving or receiving orders and had never been required to deal with reasoned debate. Now, deprived of his supporters on the committee, he once again resorted to physical display as he brandished the paper in George's face.

'And I see from the article in this rag that the production will include nudity. You certainly kept pretty quiet about that.'

George decided to bring Frederick's new line of attack to an end before he could establish his position. 'I don't want to criticise the journalist unduly, but we need to put this into perspective: there's a scene in which two actors use a bath, and both appear naked for a moment. But the bath is one hundred per cent antique and of the period; our adviser has checked its provenance and confirmed that to us. We're also fortunate that neither of the actors involved sports any anachronistic tattoos, although we did not require a check on that specific point as they both somewhat unexpectedly revealed their all during a recent rehearsal.'

The conversation had not developed in the direction that Frederick had expected, so he decided to initiate a strategic retreat. 'But this is diluting a story of heroism and nobility with a scene that panders to the cheapest of tabloid values.'

'I have to disagree with you. All our director is doing is holding a mirror up to history.'

Frederick realised that to achieve a successful withdrawal without incurring significant further damage he needed to distract George, so he tried another angle. 'And do you know who gave the journalist the story?'

This non sequitur made George realise Frederick was on the point of conceding their skirmish and he laughed out loud. 'Now that indeed is the question. And the simple answer is that no one involved with the production has the slightest idea as to the identity of the culprit. I sat in while the journalist interviewed Maggie, and I heard her get across all her points on the historical background of the play. However, for some reason, the journalist then chose not to use them. In my opinion, she must have picked up her story from someone else after she'd finished with us.'

Frederick decided to cast around for a more tractable enemy. 'Can we at least sue the paper? The article does not cast our community in a good light.'

George stifled another laugh and tried to look serious. 'As the story is true, I'm not sure what legal argument we could use.'

'Perhaps, if we could find out who gave the journalist the story, we could sue for breach of confidence.'

'The subject of the story is an issue that has preoccupied a significant portion of the female population of the village since they first learnt about it. Once again I'm not sure of the legal argument, but I think a claim for breach of confidence would be a little difficult to prove. Both actors have already performed the scene *au naturel* in front of the entire cast, and as far as I know, none of those who witnessed their unexpected exposure had been placed under any obligation of confidentiality.'

Frederick considered George's response for a moment and realised he had no option other than to concede yet another point. He turned and glared at George. 'I'm not happy with the situation at all. I need to review how we've arrived at this sorry state, and I'll present my findings to the committee at our next meeting.'

George accepted what he recognised as Frederick's offer of unconditional surrender with consummate grace; with the summer holiday season about to begin, the next meeting of the Culture Committee would not take place until early September, so neither Frederick nor the committee could interfere any further with the production. 'That's excellent. By then, I'll be ready to present my report on the outcome of our show. I understand we've already sold most of our tickets, so in terms of revenue, I once again expect a healthy profit.' He glanced at Frederick with an innocent look on his face. 'Despite your concerns, I trust you and your good lady will be able to grace us with your presence at our drinks reception before the final performance.'

'It's my duty, and I never miss parade. I never let the side down.'

'Good man. And if you'll excuse me now, I need to make sure these packages catch today's post. If I don't see you before, I'll see you for the final performance.' George gave Frederick a friendly nod, pushed open the door, and disappeared into the cool of the shop.

The identity of the source for the story also preoccupied most of the drinkers who assembled in the Puppy and Duckling on Friday evening. Louise, Jane, and Helen met there each week to make their plans for the weekend's rehearsals, and tonight they had also scheduled an urgent review of the state of their campaigns for Chris, Josh, and Adam. With the first performance fast approaching, none of them had any significant progress to report, and they knew they needed to review their strategies. But, beyond this matter, Louise had one further issue she needed to raise.

All week, or at least until publication of *The Journal* when discussions about the article immediately swamped all available bandwidth, the village network had been preoccupied with a detailed analysis of what Chris had said to the ladies of the wardrobe team when he confronted them over the threadbare state of his costume. The colourful nature of his language meant his comments could not be repeated verbatim in polite company, so all those who contributed to the discussions used a variety of creative euphemisms as they shared their opinions on the matter.

Nonetheless, despite the wide variety of views expressed about what Chris had said, all the contributors agreed Miss Milton had taken the encounter particularly badly; it had cost her several sleepless nights, and she had opened up at length about how she felt to the other members of the Women's Institute during their recent meeting. Her outpouring had primed the local gossip pump, and from this point on, gravity took over as the story spread quickly throughout the village.

Outsiders to East Upbury did not appreciate the complex web of invisible ties entwining so many local families in its strands. As a result of this, some trivial village quarrels had festered for years if not decades, and over time some quarrels had enveloped multiple generations of the affected families in their grasp. The extended threads of this same invisible web meant the descendants of the Royalist inhabitants of East Upbury had never entirely forgiven the villagers of West Upbury for supporting the Roundhead cause during the Civil War.

As a visitor to the village, Chris knew Miss Milton only as an elderly spinster in charge of a team of middle-aged ladies responsible for the play's costumes. Therefore, his lack of local knowledge meant he did not appreciate Miss Milton's great niece had recently married one of Louise's uncles, and despite the distant and tenuous nature of their relationship, Louise had taken Miss Milton's upset as a personal slight on the good name of her entire extended family.

Louise began to lay out her case as she topped up their glasses. 'After his behaviour last weekend, Chris must be punished.'

Helen knew from experience the lengths to which Louise could go when she took on a family quarrel. She would never forget the incendiary consequences of

Louise's revenge on her sister's former boyfriend after he had abandoned her for the captain of the village football team. Louise had only intended the fireworks to spoil his plan for a romantic dinner at his boyfriend's remote cottage, but a stray rocket had landed on a hayrick in an adjacent field, and the subsequent conflagration had required fire engines from three counties to bring it under control. Fortunately, the ferocity of the blaze had destroyed any forensic evidence of Louise's involvement.

With memories of the blaze still strong, Helen wanted to ensure Louise retained a sense of perspective. 'Nothing permanent. We can't do anything to spoil the play otherwise everyone else, us included, will suffer as well.'

Louise acknowledged her concern with a conciliatory gesture. 'True—we need to think of something imaginative.'

For some reason, the image of Chris lying in the bath had remained fixed in Jane's mind. 'We could put ice cubes in the bath water and freeze his assets.'

Once again, it fell to Helen to inject a note of reality. 'But Josh uses the bath as well, and apart from ignoring me completely, he hasn't done anything wrong. He certainly doesn't deserve hypothermia.'

Jane had run out of ideas. 'What then?'

Louise had listened to their exchanges in silence, but now a broad smile lit up her face. 'Got it.'

Jane and Helen waited for Louise to share her words of wisdom, but she maintained her uncharacteristic silence. Finally, Helen could bear the suspense no longer. 'Are you going to share your plan with us?'

Louise shook her head. 'No, at least not for the moment. If you don't know, it'll be a surprise for you as well.' She paused for a moment, glanced at their curious faces, and then posed an innocent question. 'Have either of you ever seen a poltergeist at work?'

This made no sense to Helen, who wondered if Louise planned to seek some form of supernatural help. 'Are you going to organise a séance? You know what happened last time we tried one of those.'

The smile on Louise's face disappeared. 'No, definitely not. I had nightmares for weeks after that.' She took a large sip of wine to quell the memory that had risen unbidden into her mind. 'For the moment, I'm not going to do anything.' She picked up the bottle to top up her glass. 'Oh dear, it's empty already. Do you fancy another?'

'Yes, please. We've got plenty more on the agenda we need to get through before tomorrow.'

Conversations about the identity of the source were not confined to the Puppy and Duckling. On the sheltered patio of Beech Cottage, George was serving drinks to Maggie and Joan while Peggy put the finishing touches to dinner in the kitchen. With the final phase of rehearsals now upon them, George and Peggy had invited Maggie to stay with them for the weekend. George knew from his own experience how difficult it could be to manage the last-minute demands of a production and thought her visible presence might also help defuse any last-minute surprises that Frederick might spring on them. However, after their unexpected encounter earlier in the day, he realised that Frederick, for the moment at least, had shot his bolt.

After he and Frederick had gone their separate ways, George bought a copy of *The Journal* as planned, and once he returned home, he read the article. He had been amused by the strong reaction it had provoked in Frederick, but he regarded the article as nothing more than a typical example of tabloid journalism, in that it hinted at a salacious detail while helping to publicise what it described. George's main concern now was to discover who had given the story to the journalist.

He told Maggie about the encounter with Frederick when she arrived, and he raised the subject again as he refilled her glass. 'Now you've had a chance to read the article, what do you think about it? It's only short, but it's caused a real stir throughout the village.'

'You were there while I spoke with the journalist and heard how we covered all the history, how the war affected the locals, and the way the production seeks to capture the essence of their community. I said nothing more to her after that, never even mentioned the bath, and she didn't ask any other questions. I'm as surprised at the article as you are.'

'Interesting. She must have spoken to someone else after she'd finished with you.'

Joan passed them the tray of canapes that Peggy had just delivered from the kitchen. 'But who was it?'

Maggie turned to her. 'I saw her deep in conversation with Chris for a while, but I can't imagine he was talking about the play. Apart from himself, he has only one interest—and that's definitely not this production.'

George mentally crossed another name off his list. 'Well, she must have spoken to someone else after she'd finished with him.'

Maggie stretched out on the chair as she enjoyed the warmth of the early evening sun. 'In the end, it doesn't matter. The good news is that we've sold out for the whole run, and now even have a waiting list for returns. The thought of some impropriety might have helped shift a few more tickets, but what our sell-out audience will see is a play about a key event in the history of this village. Ultimately, what's important to me is to bring in as large an audience as possible to witness the story we're telling.'

George frowned. 'But there are dark forces at large in our community, and some members of the Ministry of Love aren't at all happy with what we're doing: our show definitely doesn't present the glorious vision of noble sacrifice they announced to the village when they selected the play. Other people are taking sides on the issue too, although I doubt if there will be physical violence.'

Maggie laughed. 'I've never minded people taking sides, as long as our side wins in the end. All we're doing is presenting a living memorial to those who went off to the Great War and never came back, and to those who came back changed in ways not visible to the naked eye. Men like my great-grandfather, who saved the life of his officer under fire and was mentioned in dispatches but never told his family anything about it. He refused to speak about his war service to anyone, and I only discovered what had happened when I started to research my family history.'

Joan picked up her glass. 'I think we should drink a toast to the memory of all the unknown soldiers.'

George stood up. 'And to history rather than heritage, and to the success of your show.'

Maggie raised her glass. 'It's not *my* show: this is a real team effort. Our show belongs to everyone who has worked so hard over the past few months to produce what we are about to share with the world.'

George beamed at them both. He had begun the year full of resentment at the way the Culture Committee had treated him after his years of hard work for the local community, but now he looked forward to seeing what both the village and the wider world made of their production. However well the performances went, and whatever reactions the actors received from their audiences, he knew the next week would be interesting for every single person involved with the production.

Chapter 13
The Wedding

'During previous ages a Royal Wedding, with the most powerful families in the kingdom all assembled to celebrate the happy event, offered the perfect opportunity for murder, plotting, and every form of nefarious intrigue. However, the coming of the Guild put an end to such elitist practices: now murder, plotting, and intrigue occurred at all levels of the Guild every day.'

The Musician's Destiny

In addition to the increasingly wild rumours about the source of the story circulating unchecked around the village, the news now travelled far beyond East Upbury when Toby summarised both the story and the ongoing village reaction to it in one of his emails to Sarah. He framed the search for the source as a country house mystery set in and around Somerton Court; after working out who had given the story to the journalist, he planned to assemble all the suspects in the library before revealing the hitherto unexpected culprit with an appropriate flourish.

Sarah had always enjoyed golden age murder mysteries, and thoughts of his plan amused her as she packed her suitcase for her cousin's wedding. They also helped reduce, at least for the moment, her sense of foreboding about the event. She had no concerns about the wedding itself as she had always regarded her relationship with her cousin Sebastian as semi-detached, had no idea who his bride might be, and felt she had received an invitation only out of a misplaced sense of cousinly obligation. Rather the source of her unease was the thought of an extended encounter with Sebastian's twin sister Viola, who he had appointed as his Best Woman for the ceremony.

Sarah had learnt about Sebastian's unusual appointment several months ago. Although familial loyalty meant her mother did not express an overt opinion about her nephew's choice, her tone when she informed Sarah could not conceal her surprise at this unexpected gender swap of such a traditional role. Sarah did not share her mother's attachment to such traditions, and when she heard the news, she immediately wondered if Sebastian had played any part in the decision. However, whatever the true reason for her appointment, Sarah knew Viola would, as usual, exploit the opportunity to the utmost and attempt to usurp the position of the bride and groom as the centre of attention for the day.

Viola had been born a whole seven minutes ahead of her brother and, even before either of them could speak, had worked out how to use this age difference to dominate every aspect of his life. As a young child she also made Sarah's life a misery, with endless tiny acts of cruelty whenever they met up, although with a bully's innate cunning she always ensured neither set of parents ever witnessed these acts. Fortunately, an unexpected promotion for Sarah's uncle had required a move to Scotland and this had brought such regular family gatherings to an end. Strangers meeting Viola and Sarah as children often assumed they were sisters, but as they grew up, their lives had taken very different paths, and all such similarities had long since vanished.

The wedding would take place in the picturesque Cotswold village where the bride's parents had their family home, and Sarah met up with her parents just before midday outside the ancient church that stood on the edge of the village green. Sarah spotted Viola as soon as she arrived: her cousin's peroxided hair and electric blue trouser suit made her conspicuously visible amid the variegated floral patterns and pastel shades worn by the other female guests. Viola made no attempt to break off from her conversation with a middle-aged woman who Sarah assumed might be the mother of the bride, although she did deign to acknowledge Sarah's arrival with a brief wave.

While waiting outside the church, Sarah and her parents engaged in the usual pre-wedding small talk with other guests until an usher summoned everyone into the cool interior for the ceremony. They had all taken their seats on the hard wooden pews to wait for the service to begin when Sarah, sitting towards the rear of the nave and close to the heavy wooden door, became aware of some unexpected activity and a burst of frantic whispering from the porch outside.

She initially wondered if the bride had developed cold feet and called off the wedding, before immediately reprimanding herself for such an uncharitable thought. However, a flash of electric blue speeding down the aisle, as Viola hastened to explain the unscheduled hiatus to the family members in the front pews, brought an end to her speculation. 'I'm afraid there'll be a bit of a delay before we can get things kicked off, as both the bridesmaids are still back at the hotel.'

Sarah found out the full story at the reception: despite the meticulous planning of every other aspect of the wedding, no one had arranged transport to the church for the bridesmaids, the younger sisters of the bride, and they had struggled to obtain a mobile signal to summon assistance from the remote country hotel where the wedding party had based itself. One of the ushers immediately set off in his car to collect the pair, and while the members of the congregation around her filled in the time with polite conversation, Sarah took the opportunity to study the war memorial mounted high on the wall adjacent to their pew. As she read the long list of names it contained, she wondered what sort of play the villagers here could perform to portray the lives of those listed on it: presumably, there would be similar tales of loss, injury, and death, just as there would be for every other war memorial the length and breadth of the country.

This made her think about the rehearsal back in East Upbury, and she realised how much she missed being there. Maggie planned to spend the entire weekend working on the musical sequences, with the local Morris Band scheduled to play live for the first time on Sunday afternoon. The musicians had a reputation for unquenchable thirsts whenever they performed, and Toby had warned her the session would be chaotic. She decided that once she had discharged the last of her filial duties tomorrow morning, she would leave the hotel as early as possible and return to East Upbury to witness the afternoon session for herself.

The rural hotel, the venue for both the reception and the boisterous pre-wedding party the previous evening, had started life as a late Victorian country house before undergoing an unexpectedly brutal transformation into an executive conference and training venue in the last quarter of the twentieth century. Two massive concrete and plate glass wings now sandwiched the picturesque mansion between them, and these clashed horribly with the Cotswold stone, delicate sash windows, and tiled roof of the original building. The house looked distinctly ill-at-ease with its two modern appendages, but only the corporate conference trade and executive training courses using these facilities each week made the continued existence of the hotel viable.

When the wedding party arrived back at the hotel, the crowded melee meant Sarah easily managed to avoid any meaningful conversation with Viola. They exchanged polite greetings as Sarah and her parents walked into the reception, but Viola's official duties kept her far too busy to waste any quality time with such low-status relations. When Sarah consulted the seating plan, she noted with delight that she and her parents had been allocated seats on a table in a far corner of the dining room together with several of the bride's cousins and distant relatives. The three of them located the table, introduced themselves to the other guests, and took their seats. Once everyone had agreed the bride looked beautiful, the groom looked dashing, and their whirlwind courtship was so romantic, the table settled down to a meal of pleasant banalities while the main action of the afternoon switched to the top table.

Once everyone had eaten, the father of the bride launched into an unmemorable speech that meandered on interminably before ending abruptly, almost as if he had lost the final page, with an ambiguous toast to the future happiness of the bride and groom. Sebastian then responded with a rambling and innuendo-laced performance that concluded with a fervent wish from the happy couple for their guests to use the imminent evening reception in order to get to know each other better. After several noticeable winces from elderly female relatives as they endured his more risqué jokes, this final section received a generous round of applause from all those present.

However, as the end of the afternoon approached and a further tier of more distant relatives, friends, and work colleagues arrived, the reality of the evening reception turned out to be somewhat different. Within an hour, an age-related segregation had imposed itself on the augmented wedding party: contemporaries of the bride and groom monopolised the noisy bar and dance floor, while the older generations of both families took refuge in the chintzy comfort and tranquillity of the lounge of the old house, where they fortified themselves with large pots of tea and coffee.

Sarah initially attempted to mingle with the happy couple and their friends, but quickly realised she had neither the desire nor the ability to keep up with the endless rounds of drinks they all consumed. After enduring the increasingly febrile atmosphere for an hour, she admitted defeat and retreated to the lounge. The place offered a welcome haven of calm, and Sarah settled down in a quiet corner with her parents to tell them about the play.

The eleven-year age difference between Joan and her father meant they had lived quite separate lives while growing up, and her parents were fascinated by her account of Joan's most recent activities. Throughout their conversation Sarah made no mention of Toby, and after she had last year abruptly ended what her family had come to regard as a long-term relationship, they had offered only quiet support and not asked any questions about her personal life. Once she had finished her story, her father inquired if there were still tickets available, and Sarah promised to check when she returned to East Upbury. She thought if she managed to obtain tickets for them then they might even meet Toby, although she had no idea how she would introduce him.

As the long evening wore on, an elderly lady staggered over to join them from another group of refugees at a nearby table. She introduced herself as the bride's long-widowed grandmother and, delighted to have found a captive audience, uncorked a torrent of family anecdotes, mostly about the bride and how naughty she and her two sisters had been as young girls. With no immediate end to these stories in sight, Sarah eventually decided she needed to escape and, as an excuse to leave the security of the lounge, suggested a final round of drinks. Her father ignored a spousal frown of disapproval to accept her offer, and Sarah set off on the long trek back through the house.

As Sarah approached the bar the sound of the music increased massively in volume, and once she arrived there, she could finally recognise the song playing rather than merely feel the regular thump of its heavy bass line. With the room crowded with escapees from the dance floor queuing for drinks or cooling off after their exertions, Sarah realised it would be some time before she would be served.

She had just decided to give up and return to tranquillity of the lounge when Viola, exuding bonhomie and goodwill, materialised next to her. 'Sarah, how wonderful to find you here. I've been so busy all day that we've not had a chance to catch up at all.' Sarah realised Viola was still relishing every moment of her starring role and sensed danger.

Viola drained her glass and, with a swift gesture to the barman, indicated he should add another glass of prosecco to the large order she had just given him. 'We were glad you were able to come today. It meant so much to Sebby.'

Sarah had no contact with either of her cousins from one year to the next, but in view of the occasion she decided to be polite. 'I'd never miss a family wedding if I could. We have so few opportunities to get together now we're all so busy with our careers.'

Viola's smile filled with daggers: she had recently begun the most recent of what, over the years, had turned into a long list of jobs, none of which ever gave her the immediate recognition and reward she felt her talents deserved. 'I know. Life's always such a rush, but when Sebby met Flick I told him not to lose such a good catch and made sure he acted fast. Everyone loves the romance of their whirlwind courtship, but he only did it because I told him to get a ring on her finger damn quick.' She glanced down at the unadorned ring finger on her left hand. 'My chap's a good man, but we need to get to know each other a little better before there's any talk of wedding bells for us.'

'That's very wise of you. I know all too well the danger of committing yourself too quickly.'

A look of *faux* contrition filled Viola's face. 'Oh, Sarah I'm so sorry. I hadn't meant it like that at all. When the family heard your news last year, we all felt so wretched for you.'

'Thank you, but it's history now.'

'Of course, we originally had the two of you on the guest list, but once we knew what had happened Sebby wondered if we should invite you with a plus one or just you by yourself. In the end, they were a bit pushed for numbers, so I told him to go with you solo. I trust I didn't cause any issues for you.'

'No problem at all.'

'And I hope you didn't mind us putting you on a table with Cousin David. I'm not trying to match-make, but Flick assures me he's an eligible bachelor with an extremely successful career. She said he's mostly harmless, but you never know—today could be the start of something special for you both.'

Sarah laughed. 'It might be the start of something special for him, but definitely not with me. Throughout the meal, he only had eyes for the young waiter serving us.'

Viola's smile froze, and to cover her confusion she switched into interrogation mode. 'So, are you seeing anybody at the moment?'

Sarah paused for a moment to give maximum effect to her reply, as she knew Viola would file any shards of personal information she disclosed for use at some point in the future. 'Yes, I am. I've been seeing him for several months.'

Viola's smile turned glacial. 'That's great news.'

'But I wouldn't want to expose him to the whole family yet.'

'I quite understand. Some of us can be a bit of an acquired taste.' After the briefest of pauses, the interrogation resumed. 'What does he do?'

Sarah decided to continue feeding her cousin only the smallest titbits of information. 'Something corporate at the moment. But what he really wants to be is a writer, and that's his long-term ambition.'

'Interesting. Hopefully, we can all meet him sometime.'

'Perhaps you could invite us both to your wedding? It seems to be only weddings and funerals that bring the family together nowadays, and I like all my elderly relatives too much to sacrifice one of them for the sake of a family reunion.'

Viola fell silent, and Sarah realised she had struck a raw nerve: any timescales on her cousin's matrimonial aspirations were evidently far more elastic than Viola had intimated earlier. A loud cheer from the dance floor, as another classic wedding standard started up, interrupted their conversation.

Viola picked up her tray of drinks from the bar and initialled the receipt. 'I'm afraid we'll have to finish our chat later on: they're finally playing my song!'

'No problem. Enjoy the rest of your evening. Hopefully, we can catch up some more tomorrow morning before we all go our separate ways.'

Sarah watched her cousin push her way through the heaving throng of revellers, and as she returned to the lounge with her own tray of drinks, she decided to revise her plans once again: she would get up as early as possible and leave for East Upbury straight after breakfast.

The next morning, Sarah arrived in the dining room as the waiting staff were setting up the breakfast buffet. The reception had continued long after Sarah had gone to bed, so with peace reigning throughout the hotel she had the dining room to herself while she ate a swift meal. Once she had finished, she collected her case and went up to her parents' room to say goodbye.

As Sarah drove back towards East Upbury, she thought again about the events of the previous day. She had surprised herself by what she had admitted during her unexpected encounter with Viola: despite promising herself not to talk about her private life, she had not only mentioned Toby but also acknowledged, to Viola of all people, that he meant something to her. Then she thought again about Sebastian's whirlwind engagement, or at least the version she had heard from Viola—she knew her cousin too well to accept any information at face value unless corroborated by another more trustworthy source—and feared the worst for the future of his marriage.

At the beginning of the year, she had made a private resolution not to allow herself to rush into any new commitments, but her unexpected meeting with Toby at the theatre had initiated an entirely unexpected sequence of events that had taken her completely by surprise. She enjoyed her involvement in the East Upbury play and was delighted to have met Toby again. However, she wished the frantic pace of the production would slow down and allow her some time to work out what she really wanted to do.

Sarah arrived back in East Upbury before midday, but resisted her initial impulse to drive directly to Somerton Court as the rehearsal would still be underway. She decided instead it would be better to catch up with everyone once they had broken for lunch and then join them for the afternoon session. She therefore drove to Joan's house to unload the suitcase containing her clothes for her extended stay in East Upbury for the duration of the production. She knew Joan would be keen to hear all about the wedding although she had only met the groom and his family on a few formal occasions.

While Sarah unloaded her luggage Joan made a pot of coffee, and as they sat together in the lounge with their drinks, she turned to Sarah. 'Now tell me, how are my little brother and your dear mother?'

Sarah laughed. 'Dad and Mum are very well, and both send their love. I told them about the play, and they were absolutely fascinated by all my stories. I must have a good sales technique because if they can get tickets, they'd like to see the show.'

Joan's face fell. 'Oh, dear.'

'What's the matter? I thought you'd be pleased.'

'Well, I'm flattered, of course, but I'm also a bit tired. I didn't sleep too well last night.'

'Are you unwell?'

'No. Merely first night nerves, which hit me in the middle of the night and then kept me awake until dawn.' Joan gave her a weak smile. 'I began the play several years ago for a creative writing class one of my neighbours had started in the village. I thought a play would be easier than a novel as it had fewer words; little did I realise what a monster I'd created. The class folded within a year, but as I'd started the play I knew I had to finish it. Some of the class members pestered me to let them read the finished product and were very complimentary, so when a delegation from the Culture Committee approached me about performing it I could hardly refuse.' The worried frown returned to her face. 'But now the first night is just days away, and I don't know what I'll do if everyone thinks my play is rubbish.'

'I don't think you need to worry about the play. It's extremely good, believe me. All the cast are very excited about it.'

Joan squeezed her hand. 'Thank you. You're always so kind.'

'It's the truth. I've sat through enough rehearsals to see for myself what Maggie's done with it. There's a real buzz about the show.'

'All I wanted was to do justice to the story. Not only for the village, but for our own family as well. Your father and I have a great uncle who was killed at the Somme; he'd only recently married, and they never found his body.'

'I didn't know that.'

'One of the joys of my current life is that I finally have time to do what I've always wanted to do. I found it fascinating to explore the highways and byways of our family's history, but to find a direct link to the Somme after I'd written the play was an unexpected coincidence. Like so many other incidents in my life.'

'I think my encounters with Toby have been unexpected coincidences.'

Joan glanced at her curiously. 'If something is meant to be, then it will happen—whatever you do to try to stop it.'

'You sound like you're talking about my cousin's wedding. The story of the happy couple's whirlwind romance couldn't fail to charm everyone, and the bride was so slim you could see there were no shotguns involved. However, I later discovered the driving force behind everything was my cousin Viola, the bane of my early life: she'd have made sure the ceremony went ahead even if Sebastian had broken his leg on the way to the church and she had to push him down the aisle in a shopping trolley. The bride's parents had organised every aspect so well, but only realised they'd not booked a car for the bridesmaids when the bridal party arrived at the church. As someone almost said, "To forget one bridesmaid may be regarded as a misfortune, but to forget both looked like carelessness."'

Joan choked on her coffee and Sarah smiled at her. 'I'm glad I made you laugh.'

‘I feel better already. When we both have some time, I’d love to hear the full story of the wedding and find out what your parents have been up to since I saw them last.’

‘We could do it tonight if you like—once I get back from the rehearsal.’

‘That would be marvellous. I’ll arrange something simple for dinner in case you get delayed.’

Throughout the village numerous other people had their own specific concerns about the play. Irrespective of how well rehearsals have gone so far, as the dress rehearsal approaches the production enters a period of maximum crisis for all parties involved. The time to change what does not work is long past, and it is too early to have the unqualified feedback that only a live audience can provide. Compliments from friends and family who have sat through part of a rehearsal offer a degree of reassurance, but these can never eradicate the nagging doubts arriving unbidden in the early hours of the morning. From this point on, the level of commitment required from every person involved in the production rises exponentially: work, relationships, and whatever passes for normal life must all be put on hold until the final performance is over.

With Sarah away at the wedding, Toby had become the still point at the centre of the production maelstrom. However, Hetty, as ever, had proved herself an invaluable ally: whenever Toby suggested actors raise their urgent issues with her their intractable problems almost always melted away. Toby had been tired before the weekend started after another busy week of work, and during this time he saw little of Adam, who was fully occupied with the start of the company’s annual budget cycle. Toby therefore hoped he had enough energy to face all the crises that would inevitably arise over this final weekend of rehearsals: each production always brought its own unique demands, and he knew he could not anticipate everything he might have to face over the next few days.

A long list of unexpected issues arising during the rehearsal on Saturday meant Toby had no time to speak to Adam all day, although he saw him several times deep in conversation with Kate. Thus, he was not unduly surprised when a flustered Adam came to find him after lunch on Sunday demanding a confidential chat. Toby knew from painful experience that the only way to deal with Adam’s many concerns was to humour him, so he led the way into the empty barn and made a great show of checking they had the place to themselves.

Toby then waited for Adam to speak. However, Adam remained silent, so Toby realised he needed to take the initiative. 'What did you want to talk to me about?'

Adam glanced around conspiratorially, and Toby feared the worst until Adam finally revealed the reason behind his request for a chat. 'Josh told me he's gay.'

Toby breathed a sigh of relief: this was old news. 'I know. He told me last year. He only tells friends or people he trusts, so it's not for public consumption.'

Adam remained silent, and Toby realised he still had something on his mind. 'Did he say anything else?'

Adam's face fell further. 'He said he didn't fancy me, that I wasn't his type.'

Toby had no idea what Josh's type might be. However, shortly after Josh had come out to him, they had both been at a rowdy party and after too many drinks all round, he and Josh had shared an unexpectedly intimate kiss. He decided not to mention this to Adam. 'Isn't that good then? Otherwise, matters might have become complicated.' He paused and then realised he had to ask the obvious question. 'Unless you wanted matters to become complicated.'

Adam shook his head. 'That's not my scene: every single one of my innumerable failures has only ever been with a woman. What I want to know though is this: why does no one ever fancy me?'

Toby tried to reassure him, although he knew his answer risked stretching the truth way beyond its breaking point. 'That's definitely not the case this time. I think you have an excellent chance with Kate.'

His words appeared to make Adam marginally less miserable. 'Do you really think so?'

'I do. You need to let matters take their course while the show is on and then wait to see how everything plays out once it's over. I think next week will resolve matters one way or another for many people.'

As he finished speaking, Toby realised he had been talking about more than Adam's chances with Kate. He gave Adam a reassuring smile which Adam finally returned.

Without warning, Hetty materialised in the doorway of the barn, and as ever, she did not mince her words. 'Tobe, I need an urgent chat.' She looked meaningfully at Adam. '*Alone.*' Adam, needing no further prompting beyond Hetty's tone of voice, left without a word.

Toby had no idea what Hetty could want but felt if he could deal with all the events today had brought so far, then the performances themselves would be child's play.

Hetty came straight to the point. 'I suppose you've read the article in *The Journal*.'

'Yes. Everyone's trying to work out where the story came from. It's a real conundrum, as Maggie didn't even mention the bath to the journalist.'

'I know.'

'I'm keen to find out who else she spoke to. Everyone has their own theory, and people have talked about little else all weekend.'

'We don't need to find out who else she spoke to. I know that too.'

'So who's the guilty party? I have my suspicions, but I'd not risk any money on them.'

She looked firmly at him. 'It was me.'

Toby looked at her in astonishment: her name had not appeared anywhere on his list of likely suspects. 'You? Why?'

'I decided we needed to push our unique selling point, so I told the journalist about the bath scene. After that, I showed her which seats gave the best view.'

'And do you think it helped?'

'Definitely. She managed to blag a press ticket for our first night, so we might even get a review out of her as well.'

Toby looked at her with admiration. 'That's great news. But why did you need to tell me about it?'

'To show you that to succeed in life you sometimes have to do the unexpected.' She gave him a forceful look that made him take a step back. 'Don't forget: to get what you want you need to do something unexpected.'

Hetty left the barn without saying any more, while Toby attempted to work out what she had meant. Sarah's arrival for the start of the afternoon session broke his chain of thought. She seemed pleased to see him, but he only had time to let her know how the morning session had gone before Hetty returned to summon him for an urgent consultation with George and the technical team.

Immediately after this, the Morris Band needed him to show them where to set up on stage. As Toby listened to them tune-up, he realised the afternoon session would probably be a lively affair: the musicians had assembled at the Puppy and Duckling two hours ago for a public rehearsal which their leader explained had required several rounds of drinks to lubricate the performers for the long afternoon ahead. However, despite this, the rehearsal went far more smoothly than Toby had expected, although the numerous interruptions from the musicians as they checked and re-checked their cues kept him busy all afternoon.

Toby only had a chance to tell Sarah he had missed her as they returned the furniture to the barn after the rehearsal. She told him she had missed him too, and then she turned away and looked awkward. After a moment, Toby broke the silence. 'You haven't said anything about the wedding. How did it go?'

'The bride looked radiant, the groom was dashing, and most of the guests thought they made a wonderful couple.'

'That's good then.'

'Only if you don't know my dear cousin Sebastian. I give them three years at most.'

This response surprised Toby as it revealed a side of Sarah he had not seen before. 'Isn't that a little cynical?'

'No: realistic.'

'Ouch.'

'What else do you expect from a whirlwind relationship where neither party knows what the other is really like?'

Toby fell silent. He knew how little they knew each other, and desperately wanted to know as much about Sarah as he possibly could. He had hoped she felt the same way about him and had not anticipated the direction this conversation had taken. He decided to try another tack. 'If you have time after we've cleared up, would you like to head off and find somewhere to eat? I haven't had a proper meal all weekend and I'm starving.'

'Actually, I'm already booked for tonight. My aunt is cooking dinner, and I need to spend some time with her as she's suffering from first-night nerves.'

The disappointment in Toby's voice gave away his feelings. 'Do you have to?'

'After everything that's happened to me, she's made me so welcome here. If I can do this one thing for her, then it'll be a small repayment for all her kindnesses over the past few months.'

By now, Toby felt even further out of his depth. 'But what about us? We never have any time together when we're not both bound to the wheel of this play. I'd love to escape from Somerton Court with you, even if it's only for an hour.'

'I have to spend the time tonight with my aunt.'

‘Is that what you *want* to do?’

Sarah turned away again and glanced down at the floor. ‘It’s what I *have* to do. Once the play is over, we’ll both have all the time in the world.’

‘Once the play is ovcr you won’t have to come back here so much—or even at all.’

‘I know.’ A loud crash from the paddock outside made them both turn towards the open door of the barn, but no one appeared. ‘What I do once the play is over is for me to decide, but there’s still so much work on the play ahead for every single one of us—and always so little time to do it. Let’s not spoil things by rushing into something too fast.’

‘And once the play is over what shall *we* do?’

She looked directly at him. ‘What *you* do is up to you. But I still have to decide if I want to come back here again.’ She shook her head sadly and walked swiftly out of the barn.

Chapter 14
The Understudy

'When signing off on the budget for a new production, Guild accountants assumed a company would recruit an additional performer to take over a role if an actor became incapacitated. However, Duncan considered this to be a waste of good money; he always found a far better use for such sums, usually in his own personal coffers. In his experience, an incapacitated actor would always find a way to make it on to the stage unless the incapacitation was terminal.'

The Musician's Destiny

The dress rehearsal went well, although the event presented the actors with an unforeseen challenge as they undertook the long trek across the paddock from the barn to the stage in darkness for the first time. Nonetheless, George had not been in the least fazed by this, as he believed actors should always approach their first night with a healthy dose of adrenalin in their bloodstream.

Once public performances begin, actors face a very different set of issues to those they have encountered during rehearsals as they no longer have any opportunity to remedy a badly timed entrance, check a half-remembered line, or move a misplaced prop. Now the entire cast, rehearsal rivalries hopefully far behind them, must work together as a team to perform the play from start to finish followed, if all goes well, by wild and enthusiastic applause from an appreciative audience. However, in every production, irrespective of their ability, at some point the actors will have to deal with an unexpected issue. Thus, the director must also instil in every cast member sufficient confidence to recover from, or at least to find a workaround for, any issues they encounter so that, all being well, the incident remains invisible to the audience.

Despite his role as executive producer that granted him an automatic right of access to all areas, George decided to stay away from the backstage area during the initial scenes on the opening night. He knew the additional challenges a first public performance presented to both cast and stage crew, and did not want his unnecessary presence to cause them any problems. He therefore spent the first act standing at the rear of what turned out to be an appreciative audience, with everyone enjoying Peggy's tour de force performance as she marshalled the domestic staff of the big house to prepare for the family wedding. The act went well, with the cast suffering no noticeable mishaps, so George decided he might risk venturing backstage after the interval to watch part of the second act from there.

George's duties as executive producer kept him busy long after the interval, and he finally arrived in the wings with the second act well underway. He then took up an inconspicuous position close to Toby, diligently following the dialogue on stage in the prompt copy, and safely away from Hetty, standing close to the front edge of the wings from where she could watch the action on stage.

Without warning, Hetty turned and trotted over to speak to Toby in an urgent whisper. 'Chris's towel is in the wrong place. He can't reach it from the bath.'

Chris had been one of the most vociferous complainants over Maggie's edict that actors and stage crew should work as a team to move props and items of furniture, and George now saw Chris's towel lying a good three paces away from the bath in which he sat.

George turned to Hetty in confusion. 'What can he do?'

She surveyed the situation critically. 'Either Adam or Josh could pass it to him, but only if he asks them first.'

The practical nature of Hetty's response reduced George's sense of panic; despite the terror Hetty had instilled in him during their first encounter, he had become increasingly impressed with her abilities over the weeks of rehearsal. 'Let's hope he does so.'

Meanwhile, Toby continued to follow the dialogue in the prompt copy, although after several long evenings of extracurricular tuition with Adam to reassure him that he knew all his lines Toby now knew the scene almost as well as the actors. A sudden gasp from the audience made him look up. 'What's happened now?'

Hetty turned round. 'Chris just solved his own problem. He got out of the bath and picked up the towel himself.'

Toby laughed. 'What an exhibitionist.'

George was curious. 'Who could have moved it?'

Toby thought for a moment. 'Apart from the actors on stage, he's also upset the rest of the cast as well as most of the stage crew, so round up the usual suspects.'

Hetty had maintained a forensic level of scrutiny over both cast and crew from the first day of rehearsal and had her own theory. 'My guess is he did it himself to impress that journalist who's here tonight. She might even mention it in her review.'

The subsequent performances brought no further obvious mishaps, but after a string of long and exhausting evenings, both cast and crew felt a sense of relief as the weekend finally arrived. After such a tiring week, George decided he needed to prepare himself for the combined rigours of the final performance and the cast party that usually continued well into the early hours of Sunday morning. Therefore, on Saturday lunchtime, relaxing in a comfortable chair on the patio of Beech Cottage and with a glass of his favourite beer in his hand, he began to review his plans for the long evening ahead.

Before the performance began, George was due to host a drinks reception for the great and the good of East Upbury, in other words the Village Elders, the Culture Committee, and their partners. For his first production, he secured some useful local sponsorship to cover elements of his production costs, and in return provided the sponsors with free tickets and an invitation to a drinks reception before the performance. This led to a string of pointed questions from some of the more traditionally minded members of the Culture Committee, who felt such blatant commercialism did not fit well with their perception of village values.

However, a proposal from George for a similar reception for the Village Elders and the Culture Committee caused the immediate cessation of all such rumblings of dissent. The success of this event prompted George to hold another reception the following year, and thereafter it became a key fixture in the village's social calendar, with invitations much prized by those with aspirations to join the ranks of the great and the good in the local community.

George planned to use this evening's reception to build common ground with the historical faction of the Culture Committee. Then, assuming this went well, he would use this small majority to outvote the heritage faction when they came to select the play for next year's production. For this, he planned to propose a play combining History and Shakespeare and hoped his choice of *The Life of Henry the Fifth* would win their unqualified support. On the assumption that the assembled members of the Culture Committee enjoyed the evening's performance, he would press for the committee to make the decision at its meeting in early September.

The last night of any production is a strange affair. Many of those involved will have juggled their commitments to the play with their responsibilities to work and family all week, but the arrival of the weekend gives both cast and crew a chance to catch up on sleep so all can approach the final performance with enough energy left over to enjoy the party as well.

On Saturday morning, Toby slept late, and then filled the hours until he had to set off to Somerton Court with mundane tasks like shopping for food and washing his clothes. With the demands of both work and the production, there had been no time for him to undertake any such activities all week, and if he did not take immediate action to remedy the situation he would have nothing left to eat and no clean clothes for the approaching working week. However, both of these tasks failed to occupy him sufficiently to prevent him from wondering what might happen later on with Sarah.

Their commitments to the production had kept them both busy all week, so they had no opportunity for any private moments together to continue the discussion they had begun in the barn. He also felt increasingly guilty that, over the past few weeks, he had failed to spend any time on his novel. He had been pleased with the idea of introducing his hero to a potential girlfriend, but since then had been unable to work out how to develop their relationship any further, let alone how to bring it to any form of resolution.

When Toby arrived at Somerton Court to begin his preparations for the performance, the heat of the day had scarcely diminished. He and Hetty transported the boxes of props from the tack room in the stable yard to their backstage area, and once they had completed this task Hetty disappeared on a mysterious errand of her own. Toby then set about laying out all the props ready for the performance and had just arranged the contents of the final box when George, resplendent in a striped blazer and colourful bow tie, arrived for their usual pre-performance review.

While they worked through their checklist, Toby could hear the actors arriving and drifting over towards the barn to change into their costumes. Tonight, the atmosphere backstage felt far more relaxed, as for the earlier performances an overrunning meeting, heavy traffic, or even a delayed train had meant some of the cast had cut their arrival a little fine. On previous evenings, Toby had checked that all the cast had arrived well before the performance was due to begin, but tonight he had not included this very high on his list of priorities.

Once they reached the end of their checklist, George left Toby and went off to instruct the front-of-house manager to open the theatre to the audience before heading up to the big house to prepare for the imminent arrival of his guests. Then, as Toby continued with his preparations, he heard running footsteps coming down the steep steps of the auditorium towards the stage and someone else shouting his name from the opposite wings. Moments later Josh sprinted onto the stage and skidded to a halt in front of him, Adam ran across to join them from the opposite wings, and Hetty materialised through the gap in the hedge behind Toby.

Despite breathing heavily, Josh nonetheless managed to speak. 'Toby, we have a problem, a massive problem.'

Josh's hyperbole before a performance never ceased to amuse Toby; for him, even the slightest issue always assumed calamitous proportions. 'If Mr Big's escaped again, there's a packet of pony treats under the table to help us catch him, and I've got plenty of time to remove any unsolicited deposits he's left behind.' Since his arrival at Somerton Court, the pony had proved to be an accomplished escape artist, and Toby now kept a bucket and a pair of rubber gloves under the props table in order to clear up after him.

On previous evenings, Toby had never failed to calm Josh with a few well-chosen words, but tonight this would not be the case. Josh took another deep breath and finally outlined the essence of the problem. 'It's not Mr Big—it's Chris.'

This clarification did not unduly alarm Toby, as Chris had behaved like a prima donna before every other performance. Another issue with him should be no more difficult to resolve than clearing up after a free-range pony had escaped yet again from his temporary paddock. 'What's his problem tonight?'

Josh continued to pant heavily; despite his rigorous gym regime, he had not significantly improved his aerobic fitness. 'He's not here, and he can't get here. I've just picked up a message: he's had a double puncture, his car's undrivable, and he's still waiting for a recovery vehicle.'

This news made Toby laugh. The car had been a standing joke between the three of them ever since they had first seen it after the audition, and for some reason Fenrir took every opportunity to relieve himself against it whenever he came close. 'Oh, dear. Not his flashy, top-of-the-range, ever-so-expensive sports car...'

'The same.'

Toby could still not understand the reason for Josh's concern. 'But he doesn't live too far away. Can't someone collect him? A taxi would be even quicker.'

'He's not at home. He's stuck down at the coast with that journalist who was in on Monday night. The punctures happened on a country lane in the middle of nowhere, and he struggled to get a phone signal to call for help. He's only now managed to send me a message.'

Toby finally realised the full implication of Josh's concerns: the play began in under an hour, and they had no understudies. He remained silent for a moment as he tried to work out what to do before spitting out the first idea that came into his head. 'We'll have to delay the start.'

Adam analysed Toby's suggestion with his usual objectivity. 'He's more than an hour and a half away. Even if he managed to find a taxi right away, he'd do well to get here much before nine.'

Josh's panic finally infected Toby as well. 'Then we'll have to cancel the show.'

Adam continued his objective analysis. 'We can't cancel. We sold every ticket weeks ago, and there's even a queue for returns. There'd be a riot when we broke the news.'

Toby moved on to his second plan. 'Well, someone else can play his part.'

Josh shook his head. 'There isn't anybody.'

Toby clutched at a passing straw. 'What about George?'

Overcoming his residual panic for a moment, Josh managed to laugh. 'Are you serious? He's far too old.'

'Will would do it. He'd jump at the chance, and he's actually very good.'

'If he did the part, it would just create another problem, as we'd need to find someone to cover his part for Act One. But anyway, he doesn't know the Morris Dance, and without that, the whole final scene can't happen.'

A long pause ensued while they continued their search for an option that might be even remotely viable. Finally, Adam finally broke the silence with a fateful suggestion. 'Toby knows the Morris Dance.'

Toby immediately sensed a massive chasm open up in front of him. 'Forget it. I'm strictly backstage, and anyway, I don't know the rest of his moves.'

Josh stepped in to cut off any thoughts he might have entertained of a strategic retreat from the edge of the precipice on which he now found himself. 'You know them better than anyone else. You've sat through every rehearsal.'

Hetty had not moved from the gap in the hedge, where she both blocked a potential escape route for Toby and prevented anyone else from joining their crisis summit. But Toby had not even noticed her presence, as he had to use every ounce of his energy to deal with the combined assaults from Adam and Josh.

'I don't know the lines.'

Adam quickly blocked off this escape route. 'You know them better than anyone else. You've spent hours working on the script with me.'

Josh came to his support. 'And, under the circumstances, no one would mind if you used a script.'

Toby knew the edge of the precipice was crumbling inch by inch, but this did not mean he would fall without a fight to the death. 'I am not doing it.'

Until this moment Hetty had remained silent, but now she moved in to deliver the *coup de grace*. 'If you did the part, it would be the perfect way to impress Sarah.'

As he heard her words, the last piece of solid ground beneath Toby's feet dissolved into thin air. He knew he could not defy gravity by sheer force of will, and within seconds, there would be only one way forward—or rather down—for him. 'If I imagined for a moment that doing the part would make the slightest difference with Sarah, I'd say "yes" straightaway. I thought there was something between us, and I thought she did too. But she's hardly spoken to me all week, and I don't know what's going on. I can't stop thinking about her, and when I see her I get tongue-tied and feel awkward. Then, when I do say something, I sound even more of an idiot than usual.'

He paused while he considered his words, and the utter despondency that a moment ago had filled his face resolved itself into an expression that looked almost heroic. 'But if this is the final challenge I have to overcome, then so be it. I can't feel any worse than I do right now, so I'll have to face it—just like I've faced all the others.'

Josh turned to Adam in confusion. 'What the hell is he talking about?'

Adam had worked with Toby long enough to recognise what they had witnessed. 'Don't worry. He's gone into fantasy mode. He does the same at work when someone dumps a massive job with an urgent deadline on him. It's usually a good sign.'

Toby swallowed hard and looked at them each in turn. His eyes displayed a hunted look, but his face remained heroic. 'I will do the part. I don't know how it'll go, but I'll do it anyway. I won't do it to impress Sarah—or anyone else. I'll do it because I can't let the rest of the cast down. Then, once tonight is over, I might have some time to make sense of this lunatic world and finally work out what's happening with my life.'

Josh and Adam watched in silence, amazed by what they had witnessed, while Hetty grinned at them all from the gap in the hedge. Toby now began to examine the many challenges he had set himself, the most urgent being to find a replacement stage manager; however, he knew he could swiftly and easily resolve at least this one. He turned to Hetty, whose grin grew broader by the moment. 'I know it's a massive ask, but if I play Chris's part tonight would you be willing to take over as stage manager?'

Hetty paused for a moment to make it look as if she had to consider Toby's request. She already knew her answer, but she had additional demands. 'Do I get your headset too?'

'Yes, of course.'

'Done. Hand it over.'

Toby removed his headset and held it out to her. Hetty took the device reverently, picked up the prompt copy from the table, and then rushed off to break the news to the stage crew and the front-of-house team.

Josh watched her go and then whispered to Adam. 'We need to get over to the barn and spread the word among the cast before he realises what he's let himself in for and tries to wriggle out of it.'

Alone in the backstage area Toby collapsed back onto his chair, picked a spare copy of the script, and started to mark all of Chris's lines with a highlighter pen. As he turned the pages, the sheer number of words horrified him, but once he had completed the task he felt marginally better: the highlighted script should keep him anchored with the rest of the cast, and he hoped he could remember most of the moves from sitting through so many rehearsals. All he had to do now was to get through the performance itself; to appear on stage and speak all those lines in front of a sell-out audience would be the most terrifying ordeal he had ever faced.

An announcement over the tannoy jolted him back to reality. 'Hello, everyone. This is Hetty. Tobe will be otherwise engaged tonight, so as of now, I'm in charge of everything. This means if anyone does anything wrong they'll be answerable directly to me—and as most of you know I have a very long memory. I need you all to do whatever you can to help each other out because tonight we're all in this together.' There was a pause, and then the tannoy crackled into life again. 'And make sure you keep your seatbelts fastened as it's likely to be a bumpy ride.'

Chapter 15
The Final Performance

'In all of Duncan's productions, what took place behind the scenes was always far more interesting than the play itself. However, the Guild would never licence a story so full of drunkenness, lechery, and violence for public performance.'

The Musician's Destiny

Late afternoon turned into early evening and, as the first members of the audience arrived for the performance, the gardens and grounds of Somerton Court were full of the soft scents of summer. By now, the gentle breeze that had helped temper the heat of the afternoon had faded, and the still air carried the delicate tang of freshly mown grass, skeins of smoke from a distant bonfire, and the varied fragrances of the formal garden's herbaceous borders, for these few short weeks at the peak of their annual brilliance. These disparate elements helped enhance the general air of anticipated enjoyment, as those arriving, having heard so much about the production from friends and neighbours, now looked forward to seeing the performance for themselves. The villagers always considered the final performance of their annual production to be the best, and the audience had high hopes tonight would be the same.

The cast shared the same view, and many also felt if their performance tonight impressed the great and the good of the village, generously lubricated after the lavish drinks reception due to begin shortly in the big house, then such an achievement would stand as a true measure of their talents. With the production the culmination of weeks of hard work by so many people, the atmosphere backstage on the last night would always have been electric. However, when Josh and Adam broke the news that Chris had been unavoidably delayed, and as a result, Toby would be playing the role of David for the evening, the voltage went up by an order of magnitude and the resulting level of apprehension became almost palpable.

Once George had checked that the final preparations for the reception had been completed, he made his way towards the front entrance of Somerton Court from where he would greet his guests as they arrived. From here, he would escort them to the reception, where the trays of drinks and the plates of carefully labelled canapes, that, hopefully, met all dietary and allergy requirements, awaited them. He had just positioned himself where he could keep a close eye on the main gates, a smile of welcome ready on his face, when a sharp dig in the small of his back made him jump.

He turned round to see a compact bundle of energy with a determined look on her face standing in front of him. 'George, I need a few words with you right away.'

George knew to refuse a direct request from Hetty risked a potentially serious injury or even worse: the great and the good would have to wait for a few minutes. 'Of course. What's the matter?'

'You need to know that I've just taken over the running of the place. This means, as of right now, I'm in charge of everything that happens.'

For one glorious moment, George wondered if Hetty had somehow staged a coup in the village and overthrown the Culture Committee; based on some of the wilder rumours about her activities circulating around the neighbourhood she certainly had the potential to do this. However, on reflection, he knew if this had happened then she would not have told him, as no one ever witnessed what locals assumed were her operations. He banished his wishful thoughts and realised he needed to find out more. 'What on earth has happened?'

Hetty summarised the events of the last half hour in three succinct sentences. 'Chris is stranded miles away with a double puncture, so there's no way he can get here on time. Therefore, Tobe has agreed to stand in and read the part as he's the only one who knows the Morris Dance. As a result of all that, I'm running the show tonight.'

George recalled Toby's blunt refusal even to audition for the play and regarded Hetty with astonishment: her powers of persuasion were clearly far greater than his own. 'Despite this potentially monumental calamity that has befallen us, you seem to have the evening back under control already.' Hetty accepted his compliment with a knowing grin. 'I'm not asking you to disclose your methods, but if you're willing to share them I'd genuinely be interested to learn how you managed to persuade Toby to agree to all this?'

'It wasn't difficult. I used his weak spot.'

George wondered whether she had resorted to blackmail, and if so what dark secrets she had found out; he considered himself a good judge of character, and to him, Toby did not look like someone who harboured any dark secrets. 'Which is?'

'Not "which", "who".'

'What? "Who"?'

'Isn't it obvious? Sarah.'

George thought for a moment while he worked out how to respond. In any conversation with Hetty, he always chose his words with care. 'That's good then. Thank you.' He paused again while he marshalled his thoughts. 'Please let me know if there's anything I can do to alleviate this additional burden of responsibility you've so generously shouldered this evening.'

Hetty replied immediately. 'You need to tell Maggie everything that's happened right away, so she doesn't get just part of the story from someone else. Then you'll have to make an announcement about Tobe to the audience before the show begins. Everything else is under control.'

'Are you sure? It's a massive task for you to take on.'

'I know, but tonight will go well because I don't do failure.' She spoke with the certainty of someone who always got her own way.

'Me neither. I want our show to be a success too—for the sake of all those who've worked so hard on it. I'm certainly not doing it for our friends on the Culture Committee.'

'Good, so we're on the same side. But to complicate matters further I have another job on here tonight which I need to bring to a satisfactory conclusion.'

George decided to risk exploring this unexpected intimacy with Hetty a little further. 'Dare I ask what it is?'

Her expression remained unchanged, but the tone of her response delivered an unequivocal rebuttal. 'You can ask—but I won't tell you. If you don't know, then you can plead ignorance if there are any questions later. It's a personal assignment, and I've been working on it for a while.'

George had no idea what she meant and, all too aware of her reputation, did not dare press her further. However, before he could say anything else a loud burst of static followed by a few unintelligible words from Hetty's headset interrupted their conversation. The message obviously meant something to Hetty, as she muttered something into the microphone in response and then turned to George. 'Duty calls. I need to get backstage right away.'

'Of course. Keep me in the loop if you need any help.'

'Thank you, I will. With Tobe otherwise engaged, we could definitely do with some extra muscle backstage after the interval, but you'll need to be in costume. I'll speak to Miss Milton and see what her team can dig out for you.'

Without waiting for a reply, Hetty sped off up the drive and across the paddock towards the backstage area. A mass of actors, musicians, and members of the stage crew, all engaged in their final preparations for the performance, filled the paddock, but as she crossed the open space the throng parted, as if some unseen but powerful force preceded her. George watched until she disappeared through the beech hedge and then, as he turned back towards the main gates, he saw the first of his guests making their way up the gravelled drive towards him. With a broad smile of welcome on his face and his hands outstretched, he walked forward to greet them.

Toby knew most fantasy novels contain a scene in which the hero finally accepts he must leave the shelter of his village, relinquish his safe life there, and set out on his appointed quest in order to confront his ultimate destiny. As the start time for the performance grew ever closer, he found it increasingly difficult to resist a desire to leave this village and set out on his own quest—or indeed on anybody else's quest—as long as his journey took him far away from East Upbury as quickly as possible.

In the paddock behind the stage, the actors and musicians continued with their preparations for the imminent start of the performance, while excited murmurs of expectation floated in from the tiered rows of seats as the first members of the audience took their places. Neither of these helped reduce Toby's gnawing anxiety, so he decided he might feel a little better if he behaved like an actor. He therefore left his backstage sanctuary and, desperate to project a confidence he did not feel, walked briskly and resolutely across the paddock.

When he reached the barn, Toby found the place full of actors in various stages of undress as they changed into their costumes, while in the far corner members of the Morris Band tuned up their instruments. As Toby pushed his way through this heaving throng, a small elderly figure pounced on him.

Beneath several heavy costumes on wire hangers almost obscuring her tiny body, Toby recognised the diminutive figure of Miss Milton. Once she had hung the costumes on a nearby rail, she shook Toby's hand with enthusiasm. 'I'm so impressed with what you've stepped up to do tonight. It's truly courage of the highest order.'

'I couldn't let the side down, could I?'

Miss Milton nodded her approval. 'Good man. Now you need to try these on right away so I can see if they need any alteration.'

On the opposite side of the barn, Toby saw Sarah deep in conversation with Hetty, who had by now rounded up several of the stronger members of the front-of-house team to help backstage for the evening. Without warning Sarah looked up, turned her head towards him, and gave him a warm smile before resuming her discussion with Hetty and the new members of her team; they had a great deal to cover before the performance began, without any opportunity to rehearse the complex scene changes they would face. With his head full of so many conflicting thoughts, Toby could not even begin to work out what Sarah's expression might mean, as she had not smiled at him like that all week. However, for the moment merely the sight of her face made him feel much better, gave him a positive memory to cling to, and helped lessen, at least for a moment, the massive sense of panic still growing inside him.

Toby usually spent the time immediately before a performance cocooned in the quiet of the stage manager's area and, as a result, had no idea where to go to try on his costumes. After gazing blankly around the vast interior space of the barn, he finally spotted Josh and Adam, both dressed and ready, sitting on chairs in a quiet corner. He set off towards them through the rails of costumes, piles of chairs, and assorted tables, and as he neared his destination, he noticed Adam had positioned himself so he could observe Kate as she applied her make-up. Then, with some surprise, he realised Kate had set up her mirror so she could watch him in return. Their fascination appeared to be mutual, but Toby had far too many other pressing issues on his mind for him to consider this any further.

Whenever he used a public changing room Toby always experienced an irrational fear that everyone was watching him, and as he removed his shirt, the usual fear arrived on schedule. He endeavoured to reduce it to a manageable level by way of a judicious application of common sense. However, the fear immediately returned at full strength as he remembered that in less than two hours, he would be appearing without any clothes at all in front of the entire cast, the stage crew, and a sell-out audience. He tried to convince himself the bath scene represented the epic climax of his quest tonight, and as a true hero, he would face his destiny unflinchingly. However, the sight of the familiar faces surrounding him in the barn made it clear beyond any doubt he was not living in a fantasy novel. His only crumb of comfort came when he tried on the costumes: all the items fitted him well, so Miss Milton's team had no need to carry out any last-minute alterations.

Once in costume as a farm worker, Toby sought out a quiet space so he could use the last remaining minutes to focus on the script. However, this proved to be difficult as a regular stream of well-wishers, all insisting on congratulating him on his bravery, made it impossible for him to concentrate.

Throughout these interruptions, Toby continued to clutch his script closely to his chest in the vain hope the activity might, through some novel form of textual absorption, help him lodge the lines more firmly in his mind. He would of course have the script with him while on stage, but for the sake of the performance he felt he should try to rely on it as little as possible, especially in the bath scene where he would need both hands for his towel. Fortunately, the first act involved little dialogue for him, so he could at least become accustomed to being on stage without too much need to think about his lines as well.

Toby's intense focus on the script meant he failed to notice Josh, a solicitous look on his face, arrive to speak with him until a discreet cough attracted his attention. 'How's our unexpected hero feeling as he readies himself to go over the top?'

'More terrified than I've been in my entire life.'

'I'm not surprised. I think you're utterly mad to volunteer for this, but I've known you long enough to always expect the unexpected.'

'What happened backstage earlier on was most definitely unexpected—especially by me.'

Josh laughed. 'I'm glad to see you haven't lost your sense of humour. And in case you're wondering how you're going to get through tonight, I'm here to offer some help.'

'I think I'll need every scrap of help available, so thank you in advance for any survival strategies you can share.'

'You're most welcome, as ever. Most of your scenes are with Adam and me, and both of us know the script pretty well, so if you go wrong don't panic and we'll do our best to cover for you.'

‘Thanks. That sounds exactly like what people in my day job call teamwork.’

‘All for one and so forth.’ A slight grin appeared on Josh’s face. ‘And dare I mention the bath scene?’ He paused and raised a quizzical eyebrow. ‘The Coven want to know if you’ll be performing *au naturel*, and they asked me to find out.’ In order to protect Toby’s feelings, Josh had diluted the truth of his encounter with the Coven with diplomatic understatement: Louise, Helen, and Jane had been visibly shaken by the news of Chris’s absence as they played the majority of their scenes with him. However, when Josh then announced that Toby had taken over his role for the evening their shock had been replaced by loud guffaws of laughter, followed immediately by the inevitable question from Louise as to what Toby would wear in the bath.

‘I guess I got a bit carried away in the heat of the moment earlier on, and I committed to doing this before I’d thought it all through. Out of everything, I’ve managed to drop myself into, that particular scene is my worst-ever nightmare. But now the entire cast and crew know what I said, there’s no way I can back out. The fact I’ll shortly be appearing naked in front of a sell-out audience that includes half my team from work makes it even worse.’ A rueful smile appeared on his face. ‘At least, it’ll give the office something different to talk about next week.’

‘Let me give you some friendly advice: the anticipation is far worse than the reality. The first time I did the scene for real I was terrified, but now I feel liberated.’

Josh meant his words to be reassuring but they did not have this effect on Toby. ‘Don’t forget I’m only doing the scene once, so I’ll have to stay terrified.’

‘But you can “minimise” your exposure if you want to. There’s no need to dry yourself slowly in my big speech as Chris does. He was always a scene stealer, but all you need to do is wrap your towel around yourself and watch me act. After all, it is my best scene.’

‘Thanks for the guidance. The only shred of comfort I can find in this living nightmare is that the weather is still quite warm.’

A tannoy announcement from Hetty summoning the entire cast to an urgent meeting in the paddock brought their conversation to an end. Everyone in the barn immediately began to move towards the open doors, and they assembled outside far quicker than they had ever done when Toby had called such meetings in the past; they all knew Hetty’s reputation and were both keen to find out what she wanted and worried about what she would do to anyone who arrived late.

Hetty smiled broadly as the actors gathered around her. 'As you all know, we've had to make a few changes tonight because of the unfortunate absence of Chris. Firstly, I want to put on record that his punctures were nothing to do with me and that I have alibis for the whole of today to prove it.' She scanned the assembled faces and acknowledged the numerous mutterings and nods of assent. 'I'm in charge of everything tonight, and my first action is to declare a state of emergency with immediate effect. This means I can allocate any job to anyone and there will be no question about doing exactly what I ask right away. Have I made myself clear?' She scrutinised the crowd again, and this time there was silence. 'Good. I'd hate there to be any trouble in the village after tonight. Now listen carefully as I only have time to say this once.'

When George broke the news of the unexpected cast change to the assembled worthies at the drinks reception, he chose his words with care, as he knew he needed to put a positive spin on a catastrophe that could have ruined the entire evening. However, with his announcement finished, the widespread rumbles of murmured appreciation for his effective contingency planning made him realise he had achieved his objective.

He decided to regard this first small victory as a good omen for the success of the strategy he planned to execute over the course of the evening. Having already identified the key members of the Historical Wing of the Culture Committee, he planned to speak further with each of them during the interval. Once he had assessed their initial response to his proposal for next year's production, he would take formal soundings on the extent of their support when they reconvened for a *digestif* after the performance.

After George had escorted his guests to their reserved seats in the front row of the theatre, he decided to remain with them and watch the first act from what should be a safe vantage point; with Hetty's imposition of emergency powers, he knew the backstage area would definitely be perilous tonight. The act passed without incident, and Toby managed to acquit himself reasonably well; despite his obvious nerves he even managed to win a laugh with an unscheduled pratfall during the horseplay with Josh in the opening scene.

As George shepherded his guests back to the big house for interval drinks, he decided he should attempt to build bridges with the Heritage Wing of the Culture Committee. He therefore fell into step with an elderly matriarch, one of Frederick's most ardent lieutenants, who ran the local branch of the WI as her own personal fiefdom, and attempted to initiate a conversation. 'Despite the unexpected change of cast, the first act seemed to go down well with our audience. I hope you're enjoying our little show as well.'

'It's good to see so many locals on the stage but, as I said to dear Freddie just now, the story *is* a little predictable.'

'It's supposed to be. After all, we're commemorating a key event in village history that affected the lives of our predecessors a century ago.'

'I'm aware of all that. But if you want to portray a story from history, I can't see why you couldn't have chosen something a little more heart-warming. Our island story teems with so many uplifting stories that make us proud to be English. I don't see why you couldn't have chosen one of those instead so we could all celebrate an occasion that made us what we are today.'

'There are indeed many such stories, and of course, Shakespeare has already forged a path for us with his great Epic of England. But magnificent as all these plays are, none of them have a direct link to East Upbury at the time of the Great War—and that is of course what we are commemorating here tonight.'

The woman gazed blankly at him, and George decided he had reached the end of his olive branch. 'I wonder if you could excuse me, but as host my duties are never-ending, and I need to check that everyone's glasses remain full.'

George moved around the room with a wine bottle in each hand, and as he did so, he carefully sowed the seeds of his idea with the potential supporters identified earlier on. He hoped when the Culture Committee next met to make its decision each of these would subsequently blossom into a strong endorsement for his proposed production. Once he had completed his task, he hurried off to the barn to discover what costume Miss Milton and her team had found for him.

The second act was well underway by the time George, now resplendent in a somewhat unconvincing tweed suit and deer stalker, arrived backstage. Miss Milton had struggled to source anything properly authentic at such short notice, and observant locals might recall the costume's previous appearance in a mildly amusing sketch about Sherlock Holmes and the Hound of East Upbury, a highlight of the most recent Wassail.

Hetty sat on the stage manager's chair like a monarch on a throne, with the prompt copy open on the table in front of her. Perhaps to reflect her enhanced status, tonight she had selected a different costume for those brief moments when she ventured onto the stage to direct the stage crew as they moved props and furniture. For previous performances she had concealed herself under the shapeless dress and woollen shawl of a field worker, but after an urgent consultation with Miss Milton at the beginning of the evening, she had ascended several significant rungs of the socio-economic ladder and now wore a long dark skirt and tailored jacket, topped off by a small straw hat with artificial fruit around the brim.

She looked up as George approached her with an open question. 'How's everything going?'

'Under the circumstances, not at all bad. Tobe rewrote a few lines in his last scene, but not so much for anyone to notice.'

'That's excellent news. And if I may say you're wearing a striking outfit tonight.'

Hetty purred at the unexpected compliment. 'Thank you.'

'Now I'm here please let me know what you need me to do.'

'You've arrived bang on time. The next scene change is our big one; we need to get the bath on during the blackout and then top it up with warm water. The buckets are heavy, and Tobe always does that. Whatever else you do, make sure Tobe's towel doesn't wander like on the first night. I've issued a general warning that if anyone moves his towel by even an inch they'll suffer a slow and painful death, but with this lot you can never be too careful.'

George knew with Hetty in charge, no one would dare step out of line. 'All you have to do is tell me what you need, and it will happen forthwith.'

The arrival of Toby, Josh, and Adam brought their conversation to an end. Toby clutched a white towel around his waist with one hand and his copy of the script with the other; his face matched the colour of his towel.

Hetty gave him a reassuring smile. 'Good luck, Tobe. This is your big scene.'

'I know, and I'll be doing it without the safety net of a script.'

'I'll follow all your lines in the script, so if you need a prompt just snap your fingers.'

'Thank you for your dedication.'

'No problem. I'll check out what you looked like in the bath when I watch the recording later on.'

'Recording? No one mentioned anything about a recording.'

George hastened to explain. 'It's purely an artefact for the village archive. We always record the final performance of our summer productions for posterity. Most of the cast order copies to keep as a souvenir. If you want to remember tonight, let me know and I'll add your name to the list.'

Toby remained silent, and Josh glanced at the ghostly figure next to him who had somehow turned even paler. 'It's not too late to change your mind you know.'

'It is. My boxers are back in the barn.'

Adam tried to offer some reassurance. 'Don't worry about the team from work. They're only seeing a different side of you.'

'It's not my side that I'm worried about them seeing.'

Hetty jumped down from her chair and moved towards the stage. 'Okay, people. Stand by for the blackout—and get ready for the scene change. Let's get this bath on the stage. Go. Go. Go.'

As the stage plunged into darkness, she charged forward with the stage crew following close behind.

As Adam left the stage at the end of the scene, he realised he had enjoyed his experiences over the past few months more than anything else he could remember for a very long time. After this final performance, he knew there would be a large hole in his life; he would even miss performing the Morris Dance. The weekends he had spent in the company of Kate had been wonderful, but he had always known any hopes he might have cherished about her would, as ever, end in disappointment. However, he decided to be positive and thought if, at some future point, he managed to obtain a part in another play he could perhaps meet another woman more in his class, and then finally have a love life of his own to worry about.

When Joan wrote the play, she had paid little regard to the logistics of scene and costume changes, and the final scene, which culminated in the Morris Dance, followed soon after the bath scene. During the dress rehearsal, Adam had almost missed his cue when he returned to the barn across the dark of the paddock to change into his army uniform. As a result of this near catastrophe, he now left his costume in an octagonal summerhouse, built in the form of a classical temple, he had discovered in the formal gardens adjacent to the theatre. Away from the bright lights illuminating the action on the stage, the rest of the garden was in darkness, but moonlight picked out the mown lawn fringed with dense herbaceous borders leading to his destination.

The moon shone directly on to the white pillars fronting the portico of the summerhouse, and as Adam approached the building, a figure stepped out from between them. Kate had changed into her silver ball gown ready for the curtain call, and as she moved, the beads on the fabric glittered in the moonlight. Now Adam had no doubts that she was indeed a goddess.

Kate smiled when she saw Adam and walked down the shallow steps to meet him. 'Hetty said we all needed to help each other tonight, so I thought you might appreciate some support from me.'

Overcome by her unexpected presence, Adam initially failed to register the army uniform she held in her hands. When he finally noticed it, he could do no more than utter awkward monosyllables. 'Oh, thank you.'

He always found Kate's smile distracting, and he retreated back into silence as she explained the reason for her unexpected presence. 'It's good for me to have a specific job to do. Usually, all I do after the interval is sit round in the barn and wait for the show to end.'

Adam struggled hard to act normally as he recalled the unexpected events of the evening. 'Tonight has been a bit chaotic, but Toby's done well so far. It was quite a debut for him.'

'It was! Despite the lack of preparation, he's definitely the hero tonight.' She glanced carefully at Adam. 'Do you know this is the first time in weeks I've seen you without your folder of notes?'

'The play's almost over, so I don't need them anymore.'

Kate laughed, but a sudden outbreak of shouting from the stage made her stop and look back towards the bright lights shining out from the theatre. 'Don't you have a quick change about now?'

Adam tried to remember why he had come to the summerhouse. 'Oh, yes.'

'That's why I'm here to help you. What do you need first?'

Adam had to summon all his considerable intellect to continue the conversation. 'Boxer shorts and trousers, please.'

She removed them from the hanger and held them out to him, but he made no move to take them. She laughed. 'I think you'd find it easier if you gave me your towel.'

Adam looked at the smile on her face, took a deep breath, and handed her his towel. As he struggled into his clothes, he started to talk to himself. 'Louise always refused to believe me. But I knew I was being authentic—I always said I was being authentic. How could she have ever doubted I wasn't being authentic?'

He became aware of Kate's voice interrupting him. 'I never doubted you. I could tell from the first rehearsal that you were totally committed to this show.'

He would treasure this compliment forever. He wanted to savour the moment, but Kate knew the clock was ticking. 'What do you need next?'

Once again Adam had to think carefully in order to answer such a difficult question, but after another titanic struggle, he finally remembered the correct sequence. 'Shirt, please. Then socks and boots. And then my jacket and cap.'

'You've worked so hard right from day one. Don't forget your tie.'

Adam grimaced. 'I can never do this properly without a mirror. It always gets all knotted up.'

'Let me have a go. I played a schoolboy once and had to tie one of these every night. I think I can still remember how to do it. Come up here into the moonlight so I can see what I'm doing.'

Kate led him up onto the top step, and as she focussed on his tie, she gently placed both her hands on his chest. In all his dreams of a moment like this, Adam always appeared so self-assured, so very different from how he currently felt. He could still remember the simplicity of his conversation in his dream, so despite his inner turmoil he decided to try the same approach. 'Will you be staying for the party?'

She glanced up at him. 'I wouldn't miss it for the world. I only hope I don't get too pissed in case I do something outrageous and then regret it afterwards.'

She giggled at a recollection and smiled again; these actions caused Adam's distraction to return, and he lost the power of speech once more. Then, while clutching at every available straw, he remembered a line addressed to Maud by one of the junior officers during the ball scene. 'Then perhaps, Madam, you would honour me with a dance later on?'

Her face lit up. 'As long as it's a slow one.'

This line did not appear in the play, but it was music to Adam's ears. 'As slow as you want it to be.'

By now, he had run out of words again, so instead he leant forward and kissed her. A loud cheer from the stage made Kate step back. 'I hate to break this up now we've finally got started, but aren't you due back on stage on about now?'

'Shit. Shit. Shit. Shit. Shit.' Adam grabbed his cap, kissed Kate again, and then sprinted back past the dark shadows of the border towards the lights of the stage.

Kate watched him disappear through the archway back towards the theatre at speed. She hoped that, if matters now played out as expected, her current mission would reach a satisfactory conclusion before the evening ended, and she would then be free to enjoy herself.

As the final scene began, Hetty knew she had completed the major part of her work for the evening. The actors she had called to the stage earlier on now waited in the wings, and the rest of the cast were drifting over from the barn to be ready for the curtain call; she could now sit back and watch the final scene which took place on an empty stage. The minor key Morris tune playing quietly in the background added another layer to a powerful scene that for each of the previous performances had reduced several members of the audience to tears.

Now Louise, flanked by Helen and Jane, walked to the front of the stage. Louise remained in character to speak her own dialogue, while Helen and Jane took turns to address the audience directly.

'And so the men went off to join up. Once they'd completed their training and were ready to embark for France, they all returned home for one last time.'

'Then when the time came for them to leave, they formed up in the centre of the village, all ready to march off together.'

'But before David left he came over to Rose. Smiled. Saluted. Then he turned on his heel and went back to the others without once looking back.'

'They marched off down the road together. Rose stood and watched David as he went away. Down the long straight road and then around the corner.'

'I never saw him again, and they never even found his body. He was—is—one of the missing.'

'But, for the rest of her life, she never forgot him.'

'And every Whitsun, early in the morning, she would put on a white dress and walk by herself down to the village green. Where she had first seen him dancing so many years before.'

As Helen and Jane reached the end of their speeches, they left the stage together. The Morris tune now increased massively in volume, and Hetty saw Toby, Josh, and Adam begin their dance in the opposite wings. Maggie had struggled to decide what the three should wear, and had finally settled on full military uniforms instead of traditional Morris costumes. She felt this contributed to the air of unreality she wanted to give to the scene. Hetty watched as Adam and Josh finished the dance and marched off together into the wings. Toby now stood alone on the stage with Louise. The end of the play was fast approaching and Hetty had no more dialogue to follow; all that remained was one final piece of action.

The music reached a crescendo and ended as Toby reached the front of the stage directly opposite Louise; he had timed his movements to the second. A deep silence now spread out from the stage to engulf the entire audience as, for the first time, Toby seemed to acknowledge Louise. He looked towards her, smiled lazily, and then saluted. After that, he turned on his heel and marched briskly offstage without once looking back.

Louise watched him leave, exactly as she had done with Chris for the previous performances. As Toby disappeared into the wings, she stretched out a hand towards him, while in the other she held a handkerchief that she clutched to her mouth to stifle a silent sob. For a long moment, she stood motionless and alone in the centre of the stage; then she rushed offstage into the opposite wings.

The lights stayed bright on the empty stage, and the audience sat in total silence.

Chapter 16
The Aftermath

'It was easy for Duncan to convince an audience they had witnessed magic without ever resorting to wizardry of any kind: for him it was merely a matter of technique and stage craft. Despite years of close scrutiny by the Auditors, the Guild had never managed to find even the smallest shred of evidence that his company ever breached any of the Guild's myriad of laws against the use of sorcery.'

The Musician's Destiny

As he stood in the crowded wings, Toby became aware of the unexpected silence, but struggled to understand what it meant. Then he heard Kate's voice. 'What's happened to the audience? Don't they realise the show's over and we've all got a party to go to?'

She must have spoken to Josh, because Toby now heard him reply. 'I think our performance tonight must really have got to them.'

Then Toby heard Hetty's voice, and for the first time since he had met her, he detected a note of uncertainty in it. 'Why aren't the audience applauding? Does anyone know what's going on out there?'

Josh peered around the edge of the wings, from where he could glimpse the front row of the audience illuminated by the bright lights on the stage. 'They look as if they're in a state of shock. We must have cast a truly powerful spell tonight.'

This information did not help Hetty, who had by now recovered herself, and with every moment her frustration at the lack of expected reaction from the audience continued to grow; the performance was not supposed to end like this, so as stage manager, it fell to her to get the evening back on track. She switched on her headset and spoke to the front-of-house manager whose team, each armed with a powerful torch, had positioned themselves to guide the members of the audience out of the theatre through the darkness of the summer night. 'Fred, we have an unexpected situation on our hands. I need you to get your team into the back of the theatre to start some applause. The audience seems to have forgotten what they're supposed to do once the play is over.'

The silence continued for a few moments more, and then, finally, from behind the topmost tier of seats, Hetty heard a short burst of applause. This struggled on by itself for a few desperate seconds, before spreading out in all directions and growing in volume until it became a mighty roar. Amongst the applause, she also heard the occasional sound of cheering, and when she peered around the edge of the wings, she saw some members of the audience on their feet. Even the members of the Culture Committee and their partners, although all resolutely seated, joined in the applause with enthusiasm.

Hetty allowed the cast to enjoy the experience for a few more moments before gesturing magnificently to them all to return to the stage and take their bows. Maggie had insisted the actors rehearse a whole sequence of curtain calls, including a final reprise of the Morris Dance, but Toby had never taken any notice of these as by this point he had completed all his responsibilities as stage manager. However, flanked by Adam and Josh, he managed to be in the right place each time and even to get through to the end of the Morris Dance with no obvious mistakes.

With the last of the actors having left the stage and the applause from the audience dying away, the party could finally begin. During rehearsals, numerous relationships had begun to develop between various actors of all genders, and most of these would either blossom or wither within the next few critical hours. The cast party had a well-deserved reputation for licentiousness, and in previous years, numerous village relationships had been made or sundered over the weeks of the summer production.

Most residents living within earshot of Somerton Court were involved in the production in some capacity or other, and to those who were not, George always sent an invitation to the party together with a carefully selected bottle of wine. He regarded these gifts as a low-cost insurance policy against any complaints of noise or rowdy behaviour, as the festivities continued well into the early hours of Sunday morning and always culminated in a firework display as the *pièce de résistance*. In its budget for the summer production, the Culture Committee included a substantial sum to cover the cost of the party, and no committee member ever questioned the budget allocated for such a celebration.

While the actors looked forward to the party as a fitting reward for their efforts over the past few months, the stage crew still had a great deal of work to complete. As the audience continued to stream out of Somerton Court, Hetty instructed the volunteers she had co-opted into the stage crew for the evening to gather the props and the more portable items of furniture, and then return them all to the store in the Stable Yard before joining the party. Meanwhile, she had a personal mission of her own to fulfil, and she needed Sarah to help her.

Toby joined the slow tide of actors drifting back across the paddock towards the barn, and once he arrived there, time passed in a blur of activity; all around him cast members hugged and kissed each other, and many came over to hug and kiss him too. He had observed this behaviour from the outside after past productions, and tonight it felt strange to be on the receiving end of such attention himself, although on reflection no stranger than anything else he had experienced so far over the course of the long evening.

As stage manager, Toby always arrived late at cast parties, but tonight the party would take place in the grounds of Somerton Court, and he relished the novelty of watching it slowly develop around him. Although the actors had not yet changed out of their costumes, the barn had already begun to fill up with friends, family, and well-wishers who came to congratulate them on their outstanding performances. Many people had already opened bottles, there was a regular chinking of glasses, and with each minute the interior of the barn became more and more crowded.

A sudden flurry of activity near the large double doors caused those standing close to it to move aside to reveal a beaming George, who proceeded to lead a small party of Village Elders into the centre of the crowded space. George gestured for silence, and for a moment all activity and conversation ceased. Then the elderly Chairman of the Village Society, flanked by a grimly smiling and blazer-clad Frederick representing the Culture Committee, made a short speech congratulating the actors on such a splendid show, which he described as the best the village had ever produced and a worthy tribute to its history.

George, diplomatic as ever, smiled broadly throughout this unexpected slight to all his previous productions; he later told Toby that the Chairman made a variation of the same speech each year. Meanwhile, Toby had been delighted to hear the old man mention the history of the village rather than its heritage, and wondered if the Village Elders contained a sleeper cell of historians.

Once George had shepherded his party out of the barn and back towards the big house to re-join what he had called his post-production soiree, Toby decided he should get ready for the party. Adam had changed out of his uniform already, and Toby watched him disappear outside into the darkness of the paddock with Kate. Meanwhile, Josh, still in costume, had collapsed onto a chair in a corner. Toby could see no sign of Sarah anywhere in the barn, but assumed she would still be busy with Hetty and the other members of the stage crew back in the theatre; he knew how much work they needed to complete before they would be free to enjoy the festivities.

Toby looked around at the throng of actors and audience members crammed into the barn and, for a moment, wondered where he should go to change out of his costume before realising the absurdity of this idea: almost everyone present had seen him in the bath earlier on, so he had no need for any false modesty. He therefore unfastened the stiff buttons, and had just removed his tunic and trousers when Joan appeared beside him, a large glass of white wine in her hand and a broad smile on her face.

She wore a pale pastel summer dress, with a tartan fleece blanket wound around her shoulders, and carried a furled golf umbrella in her other hand; previous experience of chilly outdoor productions made her come prepared for every type of weather that a British summer could throw at her. She enveloped Toby in a hug and kissed him on both cheeks. 'Other people may have had their doubts, but as soon as George told me what had happened, I knew you would save the evening.'

This comment both surprised and pleased Toby. 'Did you?'

'Oh, yes. Much of the future is an open book to me.'

Toby wondered if she might be willing to offer any clues about his own immediate future, especially the next few hours of the party. He decided to probe the matter further and chose his words with care. 'Thank you. Now that the play is over, I hope we'll be able to get to know each other a little better.'

He hoped his response had been subtly ambiguous, but her sudden guffaw made him jump. 'Don't forget I watched you take a bath tonight, so I think I already know all of you quite well.'

His sudden awareness of his lack of appropriate clothing made it impossible for him to respond, and instead he blushed deeply. Joan regarded him enigmatically. 'But you'll get no spoilers about your future from me tonight. We'll have to save all discussions about that for another day.' She glanced wistfully around the room. 'Duty calls, so you'll have to excuse me. I need to head back up to the big house to support George and dear Maggie, although if I was by myself I'd much prefer to stay down here for your party. However, before I return to the fray, I'll drink a toast to celebrate your achievements tonight. You've made an old woman extremely proud.'

Josh had observed their exchanges from his chair, and as Joan sailed majestically out of the barn, he laughed. 'You seem extremely relaxed about talking to strange women in your boxers.'

Toby pulled on his trousers and quickly changed into his own shirt. 'She's always been strange—one of the strangest—and among her many talents she claims she can see the future. I wish I could! After what's happened to me so far tonight, the possibilities seem infinite, but right now, there's only one thing—or rather one person—that I want. Is that too much to ask?'

Josh frowned. 'I know who I want too. After my performances this week, I've shown the world I've nothing to hide on stage. Now it's time for the same to happen in real life.' He swallowed hard and looked directly at Toby. 'Stephen is coming to the party later on so people can meet him.'

Toby had never heard Josh mention that name before, but from his manner, this was undoubtedly an event of some significance. 'Congratulations.' He hoped he had said the right thing but felt he should find out more before committing himself further. 'Forgive my question, but who is he?'

Josh lowered his voice. 'He's been my partner for a while, but since last weekend, he's been upgraded to my fiancé. Most of my friends know about me, but not about him. Now it's time to let the world know about us both.' He glanced towards the distant table where Louise, Jane, and Helen were opening another bottle of wine. 'At least it will get them out of my hair for good.'

Until this moment, Toby had not appreciated Louise had extra-sensory powers, but somehow she sensed Josh had just mentioned the Coven. Without any prompting, she turned towards them, raised the glass of wine Helen had just poured for her in a silent toast, and blew them both a kiss.

Toby's grin froze. 'Do you know where Sarah is? I need to find her fast.'

'The last time I saw her, she was backstage with Hetty. The two of them were busy boxing up the last of the props.'

Elsewhere in the village, three figures and eight legs walked slowly away from Somerton Court. Hetty had attached a thick lead rope to Mr Big's head collar, and Sarah carried a large torch, which she used to illuminate the road ahead of them. When they finally reached Mr Big's home paddock, Hetty unlocked the gate and then turned to Sarah. 'So, are you going to see Tobe later on?'

'Probably. I assume he'll still be at the party.'

'Not probably. You *definitely* need to see him when we get back to Somerton Court.'

An uneasy silence reigned while Sarah refilled Mr Big's water bucket and Hetty released the little pony from the lead rope. Before they left, Hetty re-checked the fastening on the gate; the pony had a notorious reputation as an escapologist, and neighbours regularly pulled back their curtains to find an uninvited guest breakfasting in the centre of their immaculate lawns.

As they set off back towards Somerton Court, Sarah turned to Hetty. 'I heard everything Toby said about me backstage before the play started. I'd already planned to talk to him tonight, and I wanted to see him then, but you wouldn't let me through the hedge. Why did you stop me earlier on if you're so keen for me to see him now?'

'It wasn't the right time, and Tobe had more than enough on his plate with everything he still had to do. You needed to wait for him to get through to the end of the play and clear his head. But now it's all over, and he'll be ready for you. He finally knows what he wants.'

Sarah hoped she knew the answer, but nonetheless felt she had to ask the question. 'And what, precisely, is that?'

'Easy: you, more than anything else in the world. I could've told him weeks ago, and then I'd have saved a whole load of hassle for you, me, him, and just about everyone else as well. You wouldn't believe how hard I've had to work to make all this happen.'

Sarah glanced at the short figure as she strode purposefully along the road beside her. 'Do you control everything around here?'

'I wish! I currently have a few projects on locally, but there's still some way to go before I can expand operations outside of the village. And whatever anyone else says, those punctures were definitely nothing to do with me, although I try never to let a good crisis go to waste.'

Sarah gave an embarrassed laugh. 'So let me be frank with you. Earlier today I'd already decided that, with the play and all its demands finally over, I definitely want to see more of Toby.'

'Well, if you missed anything earlier on you can borrow my recording of the show.'

'I think I prefer the live version rather than the film. But where will I find him when we get back? With the barn full of people and crowds all over the paddock as well, I've no idea where he's likely to be.'

Hetty remained silent for a moment, a look of absolute seriousness on her face, as she reviewed the options. 'Tobe will probably want to be by himself and well away from all the noise of the party. So head towards the stage, as the whole area will be quiet and dark. My guess is he'll have hidden himself away while he wonders what's going to happen next.'

As they made their way back through the dark village streets towards the high brick pillars and iron gates leading back into Somerton Court, Sarah smiled to herself.

Chapter 17
The Cast Party

'It's midsummer's eve, a time of ancient magic when anything can happen.'
'No. It's time for events to happen exactly as they were planned—and my task is to make sure that they do.'

The Musician's Destiny

Those who have experienced the dubious pleasures of cast parties know such events consist of three distinct phases. To begin with, actors are buoyed up with the illusions about themselves and their precious talent they have worked so hard to cultivate over the weeks of rehearsal and nurture during performance. Thus, they arrive at the party in a mood of heady optimism, expect generous compliments about their performance from other actors, and are willing, for the most part, to offer more or less equivalent amounts of reciprocal praise in return. However, over the course of the evening an inevitable transition into the second phase takes place, as all those present gradually realise that a metaphorical final curtain has fallen on their current artistic venture, and on Monday morning real life and the world of work will return with a vengeance.

Inevitably, other agendas are also at work, and a significant number of actors view the party as an opportunity to resolve the amatory campaigns they have pursued so assiduously over the weeks of rehearsal. However, with the final performance over, the cold clear light of reality quickly exposes the lack of substance to such romantic illusions, and outside of the protective cocoon of the production most of these tender plants soon wither. Further let-downs also occur for those harbouring such illusions when a potential love object arrives at the party with a hitherto undisclosed partner in tow.

The combination of the two anticlimaxes then triggers the final phase of the party, as all those liberated from delusions of both talent and romance lubricate their return to reality with copious amounts of liquid refreshment. For each individual, their journey through the three separate phases progresses at its own unique speed, and only when all those present have reached the end of the final phase will the party truly be over.

For most of the cast parties Toby had attended, the buffet included variations on a standard menu: a selection of takeaway pizzas, several supermarket quiches, and a few pots of prepared salad still in their plastic pots. However, he knew this only from a forensic examination of the remnants left in the kitchen, as hungry actors had usually devoured most of the food long before he arrived. The catering for tonight's party would be somewhat different, as a gaggle of village ladies now staggered into the barn, weighed down with trays of the food they had prepared earlier in the kitchens of the big house. They proceeded to set out the dishes on the long tables in the centre of the barn: the pizzas and quiches were all home-made, and the varied selection of fresh salads was displayed in a range of picturesque pottery bowls.

This was only the first of several deliveries, and even before the ladies had returned to the big house to collect the next batch, the smell of the hot food permeating throughout the barn made Toby realise how hungry he felt. A nearby table covered in bottles and glasses already showed signs of significant depletion, as this had been the first port of call for many of the actors when they first returned to the barn after the curtain call.

With the first phase of the party now well underway, the air was thick with compliments. All over the barn, a steady stream of new arrivals commandeered the chairs and tables the cast had used when getting ready for the performance: husbands congratulated wives; parents gave encouragement to their prodigiously talented offspring; and boyfriends and girlfriends flattered each other outrageously. Maggie's objective when casting the play had been to depict the villagers of a century before, but those now filling the barn represented a true microcosm of the village as it existed today.

Toby had no idea what phase his own party had reached; his experiences over the past week, and particularly the events of the past few hours, had already eroded whatever illusions he might previously have held about his own future. In his current state of exhaustion, he no longer had any idea what might happen if Sarah arrived at the party later on. However, the return of Josh after handing over his costumes to Miss Milton's team brought his introspection to an end.

Toby looked up, and the frown on Josh's face surprised him: for the most part Josh enjoyed parties, sometimes too well. 'Cheer up. It may never happen.'

The frown did not disappear. 'But it will—and soon. I've just picked up a message from Stephen to let me know he's trying to find somewhere to park. Don't forget tonight is my coming out party.'

'Do you have to come out to everyone tonight? Can't you do the deed on an as-and-when-required basis?'

'Stephen told me I have to do it tonight. He says it'll do me good.'

'Why do you have to do what he says? Don't take this the wrong way, but it's not like you to listen to anyone.'

'In his case, I have to because I don't want to lose him.'

This uncharacteristic openness surprised Toby. 'Lucky you to have someone who wants you.'

'You do too.'

'I thought I did, but right now, I don't know where Sarah is, if she's staying for the party, or even if I'll ever see her again.'

'I think I might have some good news for you on that front. Hetty told Will she had to take Mr Big back to his home paddock as he's likely to panic when we have the fireworks, and she planned to rope Sarah in to help. Shortly after that, he saw the three of them disappearing down the drive together.'

'So she hasn't run away.'

'Hetty told him they'd be back within the hour—and if Hetty says so, they will be. She also told him to make sure there was some food left for her and to warn me not to wander off as she wants to dance with me later.'

'Hetty dancing! I'll believe that when I see it.'

'After what's happened so far, I think anything is possible tonight.'

'Is this a private party, or do you have room for three little ones?' A familiar voice made them jump, but before either of them could respond, Louise sat down at the table and carefully set down the two open bottles of wine she had brought with her. Helen followed close behind with a tray of glasses, and finally Jane staggered over, weighed down by the two extra chairs she had carried. With all three now dressed for the party, the clash of such vibrant primary colours in such close proximity was not a sight for sore eyes.

Once she had filled five of the glasses, Louise beamed at Toby and Josh. 'As we're all singletons, we thought we'd better band together to give each other some moral support in the face of so much coupledom. Unless you two want to be alone for some reason?'

The frown reappeared on Josh's face, and he remained silent as Toby jumped in to fill the breach. 'No, that's fine. We were only comparing notes about what happened tonight.'

Josh recovered himself a little and came to Toby's support. 'And I was congratulating Toby on his sterling debut performance—and also on his unexpected lack of inhibition. As everyone saw, I think he has the makings of a useful actor—provided he continues to work at it.'

Louise gave Toby a knowing look. 'We were all extremely impressed by what we saw of you—and we definitely saw everything.' She handed round the glasses. 'We performers need to stick together, so here's to you: a toast to Toby, the accidental actor.'

Toby took a large sip of wine; it felt good, and after everything that had happened, he definitely needed it. 'What I did tonight was entirely unexpected—and totally unplanned. Basically, it's the story of my life all over again.'

Louise replaced her glass on the table and glanced meaningfully at Helen and Jane. 'All we need now for a perfect evening is a quorum—thanks to our training as Girl Guides, we even have the sixth glass ready.'

Toby wondered what she meant. 'A what?'

'You know: boy, girl, boy, girl—for the seating plan.'

Helen sighed deeply. 'It's the story of my life: never enough men. Or to be more accurate, mostly no men.'

Jane sighed too, and then gazed wistfully towards the entrance to the barn where she caught sight of Adam deeply engrossed with Kate, both oblivious to the activity all around them. 'It was nice while it lasted with Adam, but tonight he appears to be otherwise engaged.'

Louise, ever the pragmatist, never dwelt on the past as she had far too many lost opportunities to make it easy for her to ignore them. 'And then there were two. What we need now is an understudy to replace Adam.'

Helen had been scanning the growing throng of partygoers who continued to crowd into the barn and waving to those she knew, but so far no one had made any move to join them. Then a figure caught her eye, and she gestured towards a new arrival standing uncertainly in the doorway as his eyes scanned the crowded interior of the barn. 'There's a chap over there by himself. He looks a bit lost.'

Jane was quickly alert. 'Who are you looking at?'

'The fair-haired chap in the chinos and the yellow polo shirt.'

Helen scrutinised the new arrival. 'I've never seen him before, but he's bound to be with someone—they always are.'

Jane suddenly looked happy. 'I can't see anyone else. I bet he's here by himself.'

At that moment, the new arrival, still looking around the crowded mass confronting him on every side, spotted the group and set off towards them with a broad grin on his face. 'Hi, Josh, sorry I'm late. I had to park miles away; there are cars all the way back to the main road and beyond.'

Josh smiled awkwardly. 'No problem. Glad you got here at last.'

All remained resolutely silent while Jane pulled out the empty chair between her and Louise.

As the new arrival sat down, Louise turned to Josh. 'So are you going to introduce us to your friend?'

'Sorry, of course: this is Stephen.' After Josh had run through everyone's names, a chorus of "hellos" and "nice to meet yous" followed, and once this was over, hands were shaken, and cheeks kissed.

'I'm sorry I couldn't make it for the show, but at least I'm here for the party.'

Louise switched on a charming smile. 'So let me fill you in on what you missed earlier on. A group of men from this village were killed in the First World War. Before that, these two got their kit off, a little treat for us ladies. As for what happens now, then who knows?'

Stephen laughed politely while Louise reached her point. 'And forgive my impertinence as we've only just met, but life is short and we're all adults here. Tell me, apart from you being Josh's friend, are you actually with anyone?'

Stephen glanced for a moment at Josh, who gave him an almost imperceptible nod. 'Indeed, I am.' He gestured at Josh. 'I'm with this guy. We've been together for a while now, and we're a lot more than friends. In fact, last weekend, he finally did me the honour of agreeing to make an honest man of me.'

This news silenced even Louise. She looked at Stephen and then back at Josh, who nodded solemnly before a broad grin filled his face; he had not anticipated breaking the news like this, but it appeared to have done the trick.

Helen and Jane were beyond speech too, so Toby broke the silence. 'Congratulations. This is brilliant news for you both. We definitely need another toast.' Toby took a large drink to cover the silence suddenly engulfing them all. Despite the warmth of the summer evening, the air around their table now felt distinctly chilly.

Josh glanced at the stricken faces of the Coven and knew he had to escape. 'Come on, Stephen, I need to introduce you to a few more of my friends before they all get too pissed to remember our news. Cheers, all.' He drained his glass, took Stephen's hand and led him away from the table.

Helen watched them disappear into the throng. 'I never managed to get the hang of maths in school. Can someone please explain to me how one plus one equals zero?'

Louise turned towards Toby. 'And then there was one. Now you have all three of us to yourself. Lucky you.'

Toby's brain worked fast as he tried to work out an escape strategy. He decided, for the moment at least, he should remain calm and not make any untoward moves. 'Lucky me, indeed. But, before I drink any more, I need to get myself some food; if I don't eat soon, I'll pass out. My unexpected adventures earlier on have left me absolutely ravenous.'

Louise gave him what she regarded as her seductive smile. 'You restore yourself with some sustenance, and we'll keep your seat warm while you're away.'

The food for the buffet now filled several large tables, but both these and the adjacent drinks tables were surrounded by a crush of hungry and thirsty partygoers. Toby squeezed into the crowd, and as he edged along the first table and helped himself to some bread and cheese, he congratulated himself on the successful completion of the initial phase of his escape plan. Then a tap on his shoulder almost made him drop his plate. Before he turned round, he braced himself to face whatever further challenges the evening still had in store for him, only to see George, exuding bonhomie, standing in front of him.

'Dear Toby, as a temporary refugee from the drinks reception from hell, I'm delighted to find you so I can share my good news. I reckon I now have a majority of the Culture Committee on board to support *Henry V* next year, so it should be all systems go. As a further protection, in case the heritage faction attempts to mount a last-minute rear-guard action, I plan to announce that I'm offering gender-neutral casting. What do you think?'

'That's excellent news, and an extremely commendable approach.' It amused Toby to discover George had begun his machinations for next year's production so soon, but after witnessing the behaviour of the Culture Committee over the past few months, he could understand George's sense of urgency.

'In order to excuse myself from the assembled hordes of the great and the good, I told them my duties as executive producer were never-ending, and I needed to check on an urgent matter; now I've found you I can tell them I have. I trust I can report that you have not been scarred for life by your unexpected travails this evening.'

'I'm fine—thank you. Absolutely shattered, but any reports of my imminent death would be a gross exaggeration.'

'Excellent. Whenever I have to fabricate a story, I always try to embed a kernel of truth within it, even if the kernel is homoeopathically small. So, many congratulations on your sterling performance tonight.'

Toby was unaccustomed to receiving so many compliments and had no idea how to respond. 'Thank you. It was the least I could do—I think.' He knew his words had made no sense, but before he could clarify what he wanted to say, he realised George could also help him. 'George, it's good to see you too. I need to ask you a favour in return: I want you to give what we're about to do a kernel of truth as well.'

George spread both arms wide, almost knocking a full plate of food from Miss Milton's nervous hand as she edged her way past them. 'Ask away. After your performance tonight, the entire village is forever in your debt.'

'It's not much. All I need you to do is keep me talking while you lead me out of the barn and across to the far side of the paddock.'

'Dare I ask why?'

'I urgently need somewhere to hide. The Coven have identified me as the sole eligible male of approximately the right age left in the cast, and even as we speak, they're setting their traps.'

George glanced back towards the table where the Coven had established themselves, and Helen immediately waved at him. Without delay, he put his arm around Toby's shoulder and suggested they continue their discussion in the open air.

Outside the claustrophobic atmosphere of the barn, they enjoyed the gentle warmth of the night air. A selection of classic pop tunes played over the tannoy, and in the corner of the paddock, several couples made ineffectual attempts to dance. Soon George and Toby found themselves in an open area full of small groups of partygoers eating, drinking, and chatting, each of their individual experiences of the party at their own unique stage.

George smiled and nodded to all those they passed as he led Toby towards the opposite side of the paddock, and soon they found themselves far beyond the reach of the bright lights shining out from the large doors of the barn. Then George stopped and turned to Toby, a puzzled expression on his face. 'I've never pretended to be able to keep up with all the extracurricular activities going on during rehearsals. However, when we met for dinner Chez Joan the other weekend, I received the strong impression you were "seeing" Sarah. What's happened to her?'

'What about her? I had the same impression as you, and I thought she did too. However, right now, I have no idea what's going on—or even where she is.'

'Don't worry! I'm sure matters will work out in time—as all such matters generally do. But what about Adam and Josh? In the unfortunate absence of our much-missed star actor, they both seem as eligible, that is unattached, as you are or rather—hopefully—are not.'

Toby took a deep breath and summarised the events of the evening. 'Adam is currently otherwise engaged with Kate. It was a complete surprise, but my mentoring actually worked out. I think you'll find them both hiding away in a dark corner somewhere.' He laughed. 'I wish I could mentor myself even half as well.'

'Good for him; she's a stunning woman. But what about Josh? He's always available, a perpetual butterfly.'

'Not anymore. Earlier on, he introduced the Coven to his boyfriend, who proceeded to compound their misery by announcing that he and Josh are now engaged. All three are in a state of deep shock, and when I managed to extricate myself, I left them drowning their sorrows in another bottle of wine. By now, they'll probably be well on to the next one.'

'Well, he kept that pretty quiet.' He turned around, scanned the paddock for a moment, and then gave Toby a conspiratorial wink. 'I think you'll find the coast is now clear. I need to return to my hosting duties indoors, and by the time I get back, I'll probably need to rescue Peggy from the clutches of one of our local bores. The great and the good have unslakeable thirsts, and as long as I replenish their glasses on a regular basis, they'll stay happy and promise me their support for next year. Will you be safe if I abandon you here?'

Toby looked cautiously back towards the distant barn. 'I think so.'

'Good man. Then I shall inform my guests that, having checked with our unexpected understudy, I can confirm he suffered no long-term damage from what he endured tonight. As a bonus point, I can also let them know the party is going well.'

'It's going extremely well—at least for some people.'

'Excellent, excellent. Once more into the breach and all that. I'll need plenty of actors for *Henry V*, so if you're up for a part next year, I'll let you know when we're auditioning.'

Toby watched George stroll back towards the distant lights of the big house. Far away from the barn, he felt safe as he knew the Coven were unlikely to stray too far from there for the rest of the evening. However, his sense of relief came to an abrupt end as a distinctly female hand slipped under his arm. He hoped the hand belonged to Sarah and feared it might after all belong to Louise, but to his surprise, he found it was attached to Joan.

Joan had a hunted look on her face. 'Did I make you jump? So sorry, but I need to engage you in conversation immediately about anything you like—the choice is yours. Only you can save me from being bored to death by that silly old man over there.' She gestured vaguely over her left shoulder but did not turn round. 'I left George's soiree to escape from him, but he's followed me all the way down here. Come on, we need to move quickly.'

Still clutching his arm, Joan dragged Toby at speed towards the thick hedge bounding the far side of the paddock. Toby had no idea which old man she meant but did not dare look back as he needed to keep both eyes firmly fixed on the ground to prevent himself from tripping on the uneven turf. As she led him towards the security offered by the dark shadow of the hedge, Joan explained the reason for their urgent flight. 'He's the treasurer of the Culture Committee, and he holds the purse strings for next year's show.'

She paused for a moment as she navigated them through a thick clump of dock leaves, and then continued with her monologue. 'Somehow, he thinks this gives him the right to fill me in on his extended family history since his grandfather set up his accountancy practice here in the 1930s. He actually wants me to write a play about them all. The family saga is clearly a fascinating subject for him and his relatives, but it's nothing I'd dare inflict on the rest of the world. I promised I'd be on my best behaviour tonight to support George and Maggie, but my commitment has a limit.'

This news of yet another attempt by the Culture Committee to dominate village life amused Toby. 'I'm at your service, as ever. I'll do whatever I can to protect you.'

'I knew you were a gentleman. After I met you at my little dinner party, I told Sarah not to let you go.'

This welcome news caused Toby to smile.

Joan looked around. 'But where is Sarah? I thought she'd be with you.'

'So did I. I haven't seen her since the play finished, and then I had to escape from the barn and take refuge out here to escape from the clutches of the Coven.'

A look of concern appeared on Joan's face, but she quickly rallied herself. 'Don't worry, she'll be back soon. Something similar happened the first time we met, but everything worked out for the best in the end. Many good men on both sides lost their lives in the fighting, and there was blood everywhere, but once the killing was over, it was fine. You and I are both survivors.'

'I wish.' Toby's hope for the evening had been for a great deal more than survival.

'Don't forget you still owe us both a dinner, and I intend to hold you to your promise and collect on my debt. Believe me, all will be resolved by then.'

'Will it?' This suggested to Toby that the outcome of the evening might be more than survival, but as ever, he struggled to glean any specific detail from Joan's statement.

Before she left, she gave his hopes one final boost. 'The game will always play out as planned, but sometimes an unexpected detour means that matters can take a little longer to reach their scheduled conclusion.' She steered him towards the gap in the hedge, where the shadows seemed even deeper. Then she turned and peered back towards the distant barn.

The solid stream of light pouring out through the double doors silhouetted all those on the grass in front of it. This group included three familiar figures, who had abandoned their table and now scanned the mass of partygoers spread out across the paddock. 'I see the members of the Coven have begun their hunt, so you'd better stay out of sight while I send them off on a wild goose chase. Earlier on, a little bird told me the Morris Band is full of eligible bachelors, so if I can engineer a rendezvous, they can all take their pick. Be brave! Sarah will find you soon, and then everything will work itself out.'

Joan turned and strode purposefully towards the distant lights of the barn. Meanwhile, Toby slipped further back into the darkness beyond the hedge.

Ahead of him, a patch of moonlight illuminated the grass, and as he approached the open space, he found himself at the side of the stage. By now, Hetty's team had returned all the portable items of furniture to the store in the stable yard, but a few solid pieces, too heavy to move easily in the dark, remained scattered around the stage.

Toby sat down on a solid bench and put his glass and plate on an adjacent table. On the other side of the hedge, he heard music, talk, and laughter in the paddock, but here on the stage, there was only silence. As he allowed himself to relax and enjoy the tranquillity, he remembered how hungry he felt and finally began to eat the bread and cheese he had carried all the way from the barn.

Back in the paddock, he heard the music increase in volume as more people joined in the dancing. Then the sound of footsteps and a rustling in the hedge at the side of the stage attracted his attention, and he froze. He had no desire to disappoint a couple in search of some privacy and had just decided he should cough to let them know they were not alone when Sarah emerged slowly into the moonlight.

As soon as she saw him sitting on the bench, her face lit up. 'I'm glad I've finally found you. I thought we had a date for tonight, but I hadn't expected it to start with a game of hide and seek.'

Toby gave her a tentative smile, still uncertain what this meant. 'We do have a date—if you want one. But I wasn't playing a game; I needed somewhere to hide, and Joan told me to wait here.'

'And Hetty told me I'd find you here once we got back from taking Mr Big home. His little legs are so short, and his paddock is right at the other end of the village, so our trip took forever.'

'So that's where you've been.'

'Hetty insisted that I help her, and I didn't dare refuse.'

'No one ever can. She always gets whatever she wants.'

'She's not let me out of her sight all evening. Sometimes, I felt she was guarding me.'

'I think she'd make an excellent warder. She's tiny, but she terrifies me.'

'Me too.'

Sarah laughed and then looked at Toby with curiosity. 'But who are you hiding from?'

'Once the play was over, matters became a little heavy in the barn. Josh introduced Louise and her pals to his boyfriend, and the Coven are now in deep mourning.'

Sarah was not impressed. 'I can't think why. It's hardly a surprise.'

'Isn't it? I thought it was supposed to be a secret. Oh, well.' This was not the conversation Toby had expected, but by now, he was used to this when talking to Sarah. 'I feel like I'm waking up from the craziest of dreams. Earlier tonight, I was in an open space just like this. There were people all around me, and I knew what some of them were going to say before they even opened their mouths. Then, at one point, I wasn't wearing any clothes.'

Sarah laughed again, a happy sound that made him feel good. 'It wasn't a dream. It was the play—and I saw it as well.'

He turned to her, a serious look on his face. 'What I did tonight was the most terrifying experience of my entire life.'

'What you did tonight was one of the bravest things I've ever seen.'

This sounded far more positive than he had expected, so he decided to build on it. 'I couldn't let the cast down, could I?'

'Of course, you couldn't. It was very commendable of you.'

'But that wasn't the real reason I did it.'

'Wasn't it?'

'It was all for you.'

'Me?'

'Because from the moment I first saw you at the theatre all those months ago, I haven't been able to get you out of my mind. After you disappeared, I spent weeks wondering if I'd ever see you again and beating myself up for everything I should have said and done. Then, when you walked into the production meeting, I couldn't believe my luck: for once I had a second chance to get things right although, currently, I'm not at all sure how things actually are.'

Sarah turned and gazed out at the tiers of empty seats standing in ghostly rows in the moonlight. 'I'm glad we're here by ourselves because we need to talk.'

This did not sound so good. In Toby's experience, when you were with a woman, and she said you needed to talk then that generally presaged bad news. But then he saw Sarah still had a smile on her face, and people did not generally give bad news when they looked like that. He decided from now on his best tactic would be to stick with the truth. 'For the first time in my life, I know exactly what I want, but currently I don't know if it's going to happen.'

The smile remained on Sarah's face, but now it was ambiguous. 'Once upon a time, I thought I knew what I wanted. But I was wrong.'

This made no sense to Toby. Was she talking about them? And if so, was this her way of letting him down? 'Is that what you wanted to say to me? "I made a decision when I came to your flat, but now I know I was wrong."'

She shook her head and looked away again. 'I was wrong about a decision I made two years ago. I came here to visit my aunt to get away from something that happened to me, to escape from someone who hurt me terribly—but that's all history now. My history. What's important is I couldn't get away from me.' She stopped and became cross with herself. 'Oh! Nothing's coming out right. I knew we had to talk tonight, and I'd wanted to be so matter of fact. I'd planned everything so carefully. But now everything's gone wrong, and I can't say it.'

This confused Toby even more. 'Why not?'

She turned back to him, a look of desperation on her face. 'Because of what happened tonight.' Then she started to giggle.

Toby decided his life might become more straightforward if he gave up trying to make sense of what was happening. 'You have to tell me, please. If I never hear anything ever again, I need to know exactly what you'd planned to say.'

By now, Sarah was laughing uncontrollably. 'I can't. I just can't.'

'Don't laugh. There's nothing to laugh at. What is there to laugh about?'

She turned back to him and put her hand on his arm. 'I'm laughing at myself. I'd planned to be so spontaneous. I'd been rehearsing it all afternoon.' She paused, but her hand remained on his arm. 'I was going to say, ever so calmly, now the play's over and we'll finally have some time to ourselves, that I very much wanted to see more of you. But, after your performance in the bath tonight, I don't think there's a single part of you that I haven't seen already.'

The words came unbidden into Toby's mind. 'You can't get what you want until you know what you want.'

Sarah looked confused. 'Is that profound or did you find it in a Christmas cracker?'

'It's what someone said to me, just before I met you for the first time.' He tried to explain further but could not find the words, so instead he leant forward and kissed her. Suddenly, the night sky above them filled with brilliant flashes of purple and yellow light, while loud explosions echoed around the empty theatre; out in the paddock, the firework display had begun. 'Welcome to a brave new world.'

After a long moment together, Sarah moved away and looked up at the fireworks filling the sky. 'Your timing was spot on. That was truly impressive.'

'It was nothing to do with me. I think we should put it down as just another one of our coincidences.'

Then Sarah kissed him. Toby enjoyed the moment very much, but after a moment, he stopped and turned away to gaze out into the darkness surrounding them on all sides.

Sarah looked at him anxiously. 'Is something wrong?'

'No. Everything is right. Everything has never been more right. I was just waiting for someone to interrupt us, to run through the props list, to arrange a dance rehearsal, or to do something—anything—now—right away—because it's urgent.'

Sarah laughed again. 'The play's over. You've done everything you had to—and more, so very much more. The question now is to decide what' next for us.'

'For me, it's time to move on. No more stage management.'

'No?'

'Would you dare ask Hetty to return my headset?'

'I see what you mean. What about on stage then?'

'Tonight was a one-off. Definitely a one-off. Either with or without clothes. There'll be more time now to do other important things like finishing my novel. My hero met an amazing woman—but then I ran out of ideas. However, after what's happened tonight, I can see what happens next: they set off on a quest together. I can work out whether they defeat a dragon, find the treasure, or whether he's the long-lost heir later on; almost every novel I read is a variation on one of those three plots. What matters though is that they are finally together.'

He walked forward towards the rows of empty seats. 'But, before I leave this stage—or indeed any stage—for the last time, there's something I need to do. It feels like a lifetime ago, but when we met again at the production meeting, I invited you to this party. And, whatever else I do or don't do, I always try to keep my promises. Come on, let's go back and watch the fireworks with the others.'

He took her hand and led her back through the hedge towards the music, talk, and laughter of the party.